AMERICAN Beauty

ALEX AND MAGNOLIA
BOOK TWO

ALSO BY GEORGIA CATES

A BEAUTY SERIES NOVEL

AMERICAN

Beauty

ALEX AND MAGNOLIA
BOOK TWO

GEORGIA CATES

Published by Georgia Cates Books, LLC

www.georgiacates.com

Editing Services provided by Lisa Aurello

Cover Design by Swoony Cover Designs | swoonycoverdesigns@gmail.com

Print ISBN: 978-1-948113-46-5

"I shall do one thing in this life—one thing certain—that is, love you, and long for you, and keep wanting you till I die."

—Thomas Hardy, Far from the Madding Crowd

Chapter 1

Magnolia Steel

THE WHEELS HIT THE TARMAC WITH A JOLT, AND MY STOMACH lurches—not from the landing but from the weight of reality settling in.

Home.

Charleston's city lights stretch beyond the runway, welcoming me back, yet nothing about this place is the same.

I reach for my phone, turn off airplane mode, and check the time in Sydney. It's the middle of the night. I'm sure Alex is deep asleep, wrapped in sheets that still smell like me.

My chest tightens because I already miss him so much.

I pull up our text thread, hovering over the keyboard. What should I say?

Hey, I just landed, and it already feels wrong without you?

Hope you're sleeping well. Meanwhile, I'm awake, wishing I was still in your arms?

No. Simple, but honest, is the better choice.

> Just landed in Charleston. I love you, big
> guy. I can't believe how much I already miss
> you. We'll talk later. Sweet dreams. 😴 🤍

I hit send. The message delivers instantly—and as expected—the *read* notification doesn't appear, no typing bubble. Only a nine-thousand-mile silence.

I exhale, tilting my head back against the seat. Two days ago, I was curled against his chest, memorizing the rise and fall of his breathing, swearing I'd never forget the way he felt beneath my fingertips. And now I'm here. Back in Charleston. Back to reality.

A voice crackles over the intercom, welcoming us to Charleston. Around me, passengers unbuckle their seat belts, stretching and collecting their belongings. The woman beside me lets out an exhausted sigh before reaching for the overhead bin.

Time to move.

I tuck my phone into my bag and push to my feet, bracing myself for whatever waits beyond the gate.

Baggage claim is a madhouse. People hover around the carousel like vultures, ready to pounce the moment their suitcase makes an appearance. I maneuver through the chaos, scanning the crowd for Violet.

And then I spot her.

Correction: I spot a six-foot inflatable T. rex waving its tiny, useless arms in my direction.

Oh, for the love of—

I stop mid-step, eyes widening as I take in the full spectacle. Violet stands proudly, her ridiculous dinosaur costume inflating and deflating slightly with every movement. In one of her clawed tiny hands, she holds a massive sign that reads the following:

CUSTOMS CHECK: DECLARE YOUR REGRETS AND BAD DECISIONS HERE.

Unrefined laughter, impossible to contain, bursts from my chest. People around me gawk, some chuckling. Others pull out their phones because my best friend has made herself an airport attraction.

God, I missed that menace in mascara.

"Violet," I call, shaking my head.

She gasps as if she didn't see me coming and throws her little T. rex arms in the air, running at me.

Well... as much as one can run in a giant inflatable dinosaur suit.

"Oh my God, Mags!" Her voice is muffled by the costume. "Is that you? Have you come to declare your regrets and bad decisions?"

I plant a hand on my hip. "You do realize this is embarrassing, right?"

"Duh." She wiggles her tiny dino claws. "I knew you'd be sad, so I'm distracting you with my utter lack of shame."

And there it is. The reason behind the absurdity. She knew I'd barely be holding it together.

That's Violet. She's never been *the hug you while you cry* type. No, she's the *dress up as a prehistoric creature in a crowded airport to make you laugh* type.

Emotion knots in my throat, but I swallow it down and go to her, wrapping my arms around the big dumb dinosaur that is my best friend.

"God, I missed you, you damn freak."

Violet makes a sniffing sound. "I missed you too, Mags. And I hope you know that no other arrival at this airport tonight is getting this level of fanfare."

"I would be concerned if they were."

She pulls back, placing her clawed hands on my shoulders like she's about to drop some wisdom. "Now, I'll help you grab your bags, but first, I must ask—do you have anything to declare?" She gestures to her sign.

I swallow past the lump in my throat. "Only... sadness. It was hard to leave him."

Violet nods. "I know. That's why I'm going to shower you with unconditional love and endless entertainment."

I smirk. "Starting with a dinosaur suit?"

"Obviously." She gestures grandly. "Now, let's grab your luggage and get out of here before someone asks me to take a picture with their kid."

Violet stops mid-waddle, her inflatable tail nearly taking out a passing traveler. She spins to face me, her dinosaur head bobbing. "Wait a second. Where are the others?"

"Oh yeah. We missed our connection in L.A., so the airline had to split us up. They're on a different flight."

Honestly? Splitting up from them was a huge relief. A mercy actually. Pretending to be fine during the first leg of the flight was exhausting. I plastered a fake smile on my face, forcing myself to chat about meaningless things when all I wanted to do was sit in silence and ache.

"Good. You should marinate in your feelings. But not for too long because I need you emotionally stable enough to spill every detail about Mr. Bazillionaire."

I sigh, following her. God help me.

We step outside into the humid Charleston air, the automatic doors whooshing shut behind us. The moment we hit the sidewalk, people driving by honk their horns.

Violet lifts her short dino arms and waves at them like she's a damn celebrity on a parade float.

"Thank you, thank you!" she calls out. "I'm here all week!"

A guy leans out of his car window, grinning. "Love the costume, sweetheart!"

Violet gasps, clutching her non-existent dino pearls. "I'm not wearing a costume, sir."

I snort, shaking my head. "You are ridiculous."

"Yes... *ridiculously* on point."

We dart through the pedestrian crossing, collecting stares, honks, and one very enthusiastic marriage proposal.

"Whew. Being a national treasure is exhausting."

"Take off the suit, Violet. I've missed your face."

She sighs like I've asked her to give up oxygen. "Fine. It was fun while it lasted."

With several grunts and some truly questionable maneuvering, she fights her way out of the monstrosity, tossing it into the backseat.

She swings her keys around her finger, grinning. "Ready to blow this popsicle stand?"

I laugh as I climb in. "Let's go, you fucking spectacle."

Violet pulls out of the airport parking lot, weaving through traffic with the confidence of someone who thinks speed limits are merely suggestions.

"So, tell me. How did things go with the others?"

I glance out the window, watching Charleston blur past in a familiar haze of warm streetlights and Spanish moss. "Well, you're not gonna believe this one—Sophie and Elijah are a thing."

She gives me that what-kind-of-fresh-hell-is-this stare. "Could you repeat that with less clown and more logic?"

I brace for impact because Violet lives for drama.

"Elijah and Sophie—together."

Her jaw drops. "Like... *together* together?"

I nod. "Yup."

She gasps so hard I'm mildly concerned she might pass out. "And you casually drop this bombshell now? Like it's some fun fact and not a damn breaking news alert?"

"Forgive me but Elijah and Sophie's relationship hasn't been at the top of my concern list."

"Last I heard, Elijah was still sniffing around you."

"Stop it... that puts a disgusting image in my mind. But the answer is yes, he still does when Sophie isn't looking."

"So, let me get this straight. He's hooking up with Sophie but still trying to get with you?"

"Yup."

She lets out a low, disgusted noise. "God. Elijah gives me the ick."

"So much ick." A shiver rolls through me as I think about him.

She beats the steering wheel with her palm, accidentally honking the horn. "Men are so fucking exhausting. Except Mr. Bazillionaire, of course."

Alex is exhausting as well but in the best possible way.

"Speaking of Mr. Bazillionaire... when do I get the soul-baring, blush-worthy details, hmm?"

I release a slow breath, shifting in my seat. "Yeah... it's a long story."

"Lucky for you, I'm a big fan of long stories. And caffeine. Which is why" —she flips on the blinker and whips the car into a sharp right, sending me crashing against the door— "we're taking a little detour."

"Where are we going?"

She grins. "To your favorite bakery. We're getting coffee and macarons... and you're telling me everything about Sydney and Mr. Bazillionaire."

I'm bone tired, struggling to hold myself together. But I need this. The talking. The catching up. The feeling of being understood.

The moment we step into the bakery, the warm scent of vanilla and espresso wraps around me like a hug. It's the kind of place that belongs in a Hallmark movie—pastel walls, twinkling fairy lights, display cases filled with delicate French pastries that look almost too pretty to eat. Almost.

Violet beelines for the counter, ordering our favorite cappuccinos and an assortment of macarons like she's feeding an army. "We're celebrating your return. And" —she shoots me a pointed look— "distracting you from your heartache."

I force a smile, but my chest tightens.

We settle into a quiet corner with our steaming cups, a tower of pastel macarons stacked between us. I should feel better. This is my happy place. I'm with my best friend. I have sugar and caffeine. But instead, my throat tightens, and my vision blurs.

Of course, Violet notices. "Oh, Mags."

I shake my head, blinking against the sting. "I'm fine."

"You are not fine." She reaches across the table, her hand resting over mine. "What happened?"

Emotion rises, thick and sharp. "I left him, Vi." My voice cracks. "I got on a plane and left him, and I swear to God, it was like ripping out my heart."

Her face softens, and for once, she doesn't crack a joke. "Tell me everything."

I exhale, fingers tracing the rim of my cup. "We agreed it wasn't a goodbye. We left it open-ended—*see you later* instead of *this is over*. But with so much distance, it still seems like goodbye."

"That's because you love him and want to be with him."

I nod, pressing my lips together.

She squeezes my hand. "Okay, first, you didn't leave him. You came home. There's a difference."

I give her a doubtful look.

"It wasn't possible for you to stay in Australia forever. You have a life here. You couldn't drop everything and stay because of some good dick."

"It is some *really good* dick. But more than that, it's love."

Violet's smile softens. "That's even more reason it isn't over."

I release a shaky breath. "I don't know how this works, Vi."

She pops the rest of a macaron into her mouth. "You'll figure it out one step at a time. And let's be real—you and Mr. Bazillionaire? This is only the beginning."

I want to believe her. God, I *need* to believe her. But for now, all I can do is try to breathe through the ache in my chest and take it one moment at a time.

I tear off a piece of macaron, rolling it between my fingers before popping it into my mouth. The sweetness melts on my tongue, but it does nothing to ease the tightness in my chest.

Violet studies me over the rim of her coffee cup. "Has Alex changed his mind about marriage?"

"His search for a wife is on pause. For now."

Violet hums, considering that. "I mean, that's kind of huge for Mr. Commitment-or-bust."

"Yeah. But that's not even my biggest concern."

She cocks her head. "What is?"

I swirl my cappuccino. "Being with Alex long-term means moving to Australia." I whisper it, as though saying it too loud might make it real. "It means giving up everything here—my job, my home... *you*." My voice wobbles on that last word.

Violet's face falls but only for a second. She straightens, pointing an accusatory finger at me. "Oh hell no, Mags. You do not get to lump me in with things you'd be leaving behind. I'm not a Charleston-based best friend. I'm a lifetime best friend. You could be on Mars, and I'd still be texting you memes and demanding you spill the tea. You don't lose me because you change your zip code. That's not how this works."

Warmth spreads through my chest, loosening something I had clenched tight.

"Nothing—not distance, not time zones, not even some bazillionaire rugby god with great dick—is ever going to end this friendship." She gestures between us. "You and me? This is forever."

Tears sting my eyes, but I blink them back, managing a smile.

She smirks. "Might as well get used to it now. You're stuck with me."

"Thank you for always being there for me." I reach across the table, squeezing her hand. "I love you, Vi."

"Damn right you do."

Her voice is light, teasing... but when I look up, her eyes are shining, a little too glassy under the warm cafe lights. She blinks rapidly—like she can will them away—and looks down at her coffee.

And just like that, I see past the jokes, past the bravado.

I take a slow breath, staring down at the delicate shell of a half-eaten macaron. "I love him, Vi. I love him so much. And leaving him tore me apart."

Violet is silent for a moment. She watches me, her eyes softer now, her expression unreadable. Then she leans back, crossing her arms over her chest. "So what does that mean? For the future?"

A long breath escapes my lips. "I don't know. I have a lot to think about."

Violet hums, tilting her head. "Hmm."

I raise an eyebrow. "What?"

She smirks. "Oh nothing. Only mentally planning your wedding, that's all."

I roll my eyes. "That's quite the leap."

She shrugs. "Not really. You're in love with a man who will absolutely put a ring on it. A huge one. Wait and see."

Her words settle somewhere deep in my chest. Because despite everything—the distance, the uncertainty, the choices I still have to make—I don't know if she's right.

The drive to my apartment is quiet, a stark contrast to the nonstop chatter at the cafe. Violet hums along to the radio, tapping her fingers against the steering wheel, but she doesn't push for more conversation. She knows me too well. Knows I need a moment to sit with my thoughts.

Sunrise paints the city in gold as we drive through familiar streets, but nothing feels the same. Maybe I'm the one who's changed.

By the time we pull up to my building, exhaustion drapes over me like a weighted blanket. Violet grabs a couple of my bags without waiting for me to argue and walks me to the door. She sets them down inside, giving the place a quick glance like she's checking that it's still standing.

"I'm not gonna hover," she says, pulling me into a hug and squeezing tighter than usual. "You're wiped. You need sleep, not me breathing down your neck. Text me if you need anything."

I nod, forcing a small smile. "I will."

But as soon as I step inside, the facade cracks.

The door clicks shut behind me, sealing me inside the quiet stillness of my apartment. It's exactly the way I left it—neatly arranged furniture, the stale scent of the old building clinging to the air.

I cross the room and strike a match, lighting the vanilla candle I always keep on the coffee table. Watching the flame flicker to life feels like staking a small claim—like reminding this place that I'm back.

But I'm not the same.

I'm different.

My suitcase sits by the door, a tangible reminder that I was somewhere else not so long ago. That I was with him. Wrapped up in his arms, in his life, in a world that now seems impossibly far away.

I kick out of my shoes, making my way deeper inside, but the space is almost foreign. Like I don't quite belong here anymore.

Because a piece of my heart remains in Sydney.

Part of me is his.

I sit on the edge of my bed, staring at nothing, my thoughts tangled in all the ways I've changed since the last time I was in this room. How I used to think I had everything figured out. How I once believed that love was something I could choose to walk away from if I had to.

But I was wrong.

I love Alex Sebring. Endlessly.

He's still in every breath I take, and I don't think that will ever change.

Chapter 2

Alex Sebring

THE HOUSE FEELS HOLLOW WITHOUT HER. TOO STILL. Too quiet. Three months of waking up to her beside me, of her laughter echoing through these rooms, of her presence filling every space. And now there's just silence. Just absence. Just me.

I went through the motions today—woke up, showered, made coffee. But everything felt off. The sheets still smell like her, but she's not here to tangle herself up in them. Her coffee mug sits beside mine in the cabinet, but she's not here to fill it. My playlist shuffles to the songs she loves, and instead of catching her singing under her breath in my kitchen, I just stand there, staring at the space where she should be.

Her name flashes on my phone, and a heavy ache settles somewhere behind my sternum—but in the best way. I press accept, and the second her face fills the screen, the world tilts back into place.

God, she's beautiful.

Soft lighting glows behind her, casting a halo around her hair. And one word comes to mind: mine.

"Hey, favorite. How's my American Beauty?"

Her lips curve into a lazy smile. "*American Beauty*? That's a new one."

"It's fitting."

She hums, considering. "I'll allow it."

I smirk, settling deeper into the couch. "Jet lag kicking your ass yet?"

"You have no idea. It's like my body doesn't know what time zone it's in."

"You slept on the plane, yeah?"

A dry laugh. "Barely. The guy sitting next to me snored so loud the entire cabin vibrated. I thought about suffocating him with my travel pillow. But I figured murder would only delay dinner."

"Sounds like the Magnolia I know."

She grins, shrugging. "Yeah, well. You do know me pretty well."

I chuckle, but the sound fades as I take her in. The way her shoulders relax just seeing me. The way my body eases at the sight of her. Three months together, and now we're reduced to *this*. A phone screen. A whole damn ocean between us.

I hate it.

She sighs, shifting until her cheek rests against her pillow. "Being home is weird."

"Yeah?"

"Everything is familiar but strange. Like I know this is my space, but after three months away, it almost doesn't feel like mine anymore."

I nod, understanding exactly what she means. "I get it. My house doesn't feel the same without you in it."

"It was surprising to come back to that. But what wasn't a surprise? Violet putting on a full-blown welcome-home spectacle at the airport."

I laugh. "Sounds about right from what you've told me about her."

"Oh, but wait for it. You haven't heard the best part yet. She was waiting for me at baggage claim wearing a giant inflatable dinosaur costume, holding a sign that said, and I quote, 'Customs check: declare your regrets and bad decisions here.'"

Regrets. Bad decisions. It's a joke, but the words stick.

I wonder if she has any about me. Or about us.

Does she second-guess those nights tangled up in my sheets or the way she let herself soften in my arms or the way we blurred the line between casual and something else?

I wonder if she regrets walking away.

"She had the whole airport staring at us, and people were honking as we walked to the car. The whole thing was just so Violet."

"Did she ask about us?"

She smirks. "Of course. She grilled me about you—about us—the entire drive home. Even took me to my favorite cafe to continue the interrogation."

"Already judging me from afar?"

"Absolutely. She has to make sure you're staying in line."

"Tell her I'm on my best behavior."

Magnolia presses her lips together, the amusement still there. "She's convinced you are because she assumes you're well-trained by now."

"*Well-trained.*" I shake my head, grinning. "Your best mate sounds exhausting."

"Violet can be a lot."

I watch her for a second, cataloging the exhaustion in her eyes. The slight tension in her jaw. "Are you sleeping okay?"

She exhales, rolling onto her back, the phone tilting with her. "No. The bed is too big without you in it."

My throat tightens. "Tell me about it."

She turns on her side, studying me. "How about you?"

A humorless chuckle escapes me. "The bed doesn't feel right. I keep reaching for you in the middle of the night, only to find that you're not there. And the sheets... I know I have to change them, but I don't think I can. They still smell like you. Like vanilla and something else I can't quite put my finger on."

Her lips part, but she says nothing. She doesn't have to.

"The house is too damn quiet, lovie. I miss your voice filling up the space. Miss your weird music blasting while you do your makeup. Miss hearing you hum off-key when you think I'm not paying attention."

She exhales sharply, blinking fast, but not fast enough. I see it—the way her lashes dampen, the way she tilts her head as if she can somehow will the tears away.

My heart aches. "I miss the sound of your laughter bouncing off these walls."

She swallows, her fingers toying with the necklace I gave her. "Alex—"

"I can't help it, favorite. Nothing has been right since you left."

"I know."

A heavy quiet settles between us, thick with everything we're not saying. The weight of distance. The ache of something unfinished.

My chest tightens, the sting of tears pushing up hard and fast. I have to change the subject—fast—or I'm going to break down right here on the phone with her.

I clear my throat and force a lighter tone. "Did Robin and Charlene check on you?"

She scoffs, glancing away. "I texted Robin to let her know I was back. She gave my message a thumbs-up but still hasn't actually responded."

Not surprising. It just cements what I already knew about her.

Her eyes flick back to mine, the frustration softening. "Violet, on the other hand, has texted me no less than twenty times today."

Of course she has.

Violet is relentless, protective, *there*—all the things Magnolia's family should be but isn't. I've never met her, but I know enough to be grateful for her. Because when Magnolia walked into that empty apartment, when the stillness hit her harder than she'd admit, it wasn't her mother checking in. It wasn't her grandmother making sure she was okay.

It was Violet. Always Violet.

And as much as I wish I were the one there for her, I can't be.

I grip my phone tighter, wishing I could reach through the screen. "Fuck, I wish I could hold you."

Her face softens, her words barely above a whisper. "I know. Being away from each other is awful, isn't it?"

"Dreadful."

A silence lingers, stretching across miles and time zones, thick with the weight of absence. Neither of us says it outright, but we feel it. The wrongness of this. We're looking at each other through pixels and static, but it's not enough. It never will be.

Magnolia exhales, shifting against her pillow. "Tell me about your day."

"Tinā and my sisters came by this morning. They made me breakfast. Leilani and Sefina hovered like I was some kind of tragic figure in a romance novel."

Her laughter is loud and unfiltered. "To be fair, that *is* the vibe you're giving off right now."

I groan. "Glad you're enjoying my misery."

"Make no mistake. I'm sharing in the misery."

"I know, babe."

She grins, but it softens as she studies me. "Your family loves you so much. They want you to feel better, and that makes me happy––to know that someone is taking care of you."

I nod. "Yeah, that's one thing I can always count on with my family."

Speaking of things that make us happy... I reach to the side, fingers grazing the worn leather journal beside me, lifting it just enough for her to see.

Her gaze flickers, and I catch the moment she notices—the subtle shift in her expression, the way her breath hitches ever so slightly.

I glance down at the journal she left for me. The one I've barely been able to bring myself to open.

"My journal."

I nod, thumbing the edge of the leather. "I know you probably expected me to have read it cover to cover by now, but I want to take my time with it. I'm a slow reader, and I plan to savor it one page at a time."

She doesn't speak right away. Just blinks down at the journal, like she's fighting something she doesn't know how to say.

"I wouldn't have given it to you if I didn't trust you with all of me."

The force of her words wrecks me in the quietest way.

"It means everything that you trusted me with this." My fingers tighten around the worn edges, grounding myself in what it represents. "I know what this is, Magnolia. I know what it means. You've given me a part of yourself, and I don't take that lightly."

Her throat moves as she swallows, blinking once, twice. And her mouth curves into something small but real. "I don't expect you to fly through it."

I shake my head. "I'm going to take my time with every word."

"So basically, you're telling me that you'll savor my journal like an aged whiskey?"

A slow grin tugs at my lips. "I think that's fair to say."

Magnolia shifts, tilting the phone slightly as she settles against her pillows. The glow of her bedside lamp casts a soft halo around her like an angel.

My angel.

She exhales, fingers drifting to the pendent around her neck, toying with it. "I haven't taken it off. I see it in the mirror, and it makes me think of you."

A knot tightens low in my gut. "Good. That's the point."

She runs her fingers along the chain again. "It's weird, you know?" She hesitates, then sighs. "Being apart after spending every single day together. I mean, I knew it would be hard, but—" She trails off, shaking her head. "I didn't expect it to feel like this."

Neither did I. "I know what you mean."

"I keep noticing little things. Like, I got in my car earlier, and one of your favorite songs was playing on the radio. I just sat there for a second, staring at the display screen like an idiot."

"Which song?"

"Guess."

It can only be one of two genres. "Country or R&B?"

"Country."

I tilt my head, considering. "Something by Chris Stapleton?"

She shakes her head. "Guess again."

"Luke Combs?"

"Nope." A mischievous smile plays at her mouth as she leans in slightly, like she's letting me in on a secret. "I'll give you a clue. We danced to it one night at your house. Out on the back patio—right after we finished dinner."

Oh yeah. That one.

She tilts her head, watching me through the screen. "Don't remember? Need to peek in my journal and see what I wrote about it?"

I huff a quiet laugh. "I remember, favorite. It was 'Dance with You' by Brett Young."

Her expression softens. "You do remember."

I meet her gaze, steady. "Of course I remember. How could I ever forget?"

She watches me for a moment, then shifts, curling deeper into her blankets. "I've been wearing your hoodie since I got home."

A slow, heavy ache blooms in my chest. "You have?"

Her smile is small, almost vulnerable. "Yeah."

She traces the fabric with slow, absent strokes and lifts it to her nose, closing her eyes for half a second as she breathes it in. "I sprayed it with your cologne before I left. It still smells like you."

My grip on the phone tightens. "I like the idea of you pulling it on and still smelling me."

Her breath catches slightly, her fingers tightening around the hoodie. "I don't think I can bring myself to wash it."

A silence falls between us, not heavy, but full.

I shift, forcing a smile, doing my best to stay steady for her. Because that's what she needs. But underneath, the worry gnaws at me. As much as I believe in us, some small, hollow place inside me wonders what's going to happen to our relationship. How long before the distance starts pulling at the seams we've barely stitched together?

The fear creeps up before I can stop it. The fear of distance. Of loneliness sneaking back in through cracks we worked so hard to seal shut.

And then, like she can hear the thought scraping through my chest, she looks up.

"Are we going to be okay?" she asks.

I meet her gaze without flinching. Steady. Certain.

"Of course we are."

For the first time tonight, she smiles. *Truly* smiles. "We haven't talked about when we'll see each other again."

"Soon, babe."

"Soon isn't a date, Sebring."

"Then tell me when I can come." All she has to do is say the word.

"I used all my vacation time for the trip to Samoa, so I can't take off again for a while." The disappointment in her voice hits hard.

Not seeing her every day already feels unnatural. Knowing there's no set date for when I'll hold her again? It's brutal.

She lifts my sweatshirt to her nose again, breathing in like she's trying to hold on to something slipping through her fingers. Her gaze flicks between the screen and some far-off place in her mind. "I hate this part. I wish we had a date set. Something to count down to."

So do I. The uncertainty of when I'll see her again is the worst part, gnawing at the edges of my calm. "I'll look at my work calendar, and we'll plan something. We'll figure it out."

Her face crumples for half a second—barely there, but enough to wreck me. Like my words found the rawest, softest part of her and pressed right against it.

"Okay," she says, her voice catching on the word. She nods, blinking fast like she's trying to stay strong for both of us.

Her lashes flutter, lips parting just slightly. I see it—the way my words settle inside her. The way they stitch something back together. The way they make her feel this—*feel me*—even from thousands of miles away.

"You and me," she says.

"You and me," I parrot.

A beat passes. Then another. And even though I can't touch her, I swear I feel her.

We're in this together. We're solid. And that's all that matters.

The conversation slows, settling into something quieter, heavier. Neither of us wants to say it, but it's late for her. And she's exhausted. I see it in her slow blinks, in the way her voice softens into something barely there.

"You're exhausted, babe." She frowns, like she wants to argue, but I don't let her. "I don't want to let you go, but you need your rest."

She sighs, the sound soft and reluctant. "Yeah. I've got to go back to work tomorrow."

I hate the reminder. That she's slipping back into her old life. That tomorrow will be the start of a new normal—one where I'm not beside her.

I shift onto my side, my voice quieter now. "Get some sleep."

She gives me a sleepy, heart-tugging smile. "Goodnight, big guy. I love you."

"I love you too, favorite. Sweet dreams."

Her lips curve, soft and tired. "Goodnight, big guy. I love you."

I smile even though the sun's high overhead on my side of the world, hot against the windows.

"I love you too, favorite. Sleep sweet."

A whisper of breath. A blink. Then—darkness.

She's ending her night, and I'm barely halfway through my day. Time for meetings and obligations and pretending I'm fine. But part of me is there with her across oceans and time zones.

Chapter 3

Magnolia Steel

THE GLASS DOORS OF SOUL SYNC GLIDE OPEN, AND I STEP inside, my heels tapping out a quick, impatient rhythm against the freshly waxed floor. The office is exactly the same—bright, modern, and buzzing with quiet energy—but something is different.

It's me.

I should feel excited to be back at Soul Sync. I should be ready to dive into work, to pick up where I left off before Sydney. But I sense a disconnection that wasn't there before, a strange heaviness in my chest that I can't quite shake.

Familiar faces greet me as I make my way to my office. Smiles, nods, welcome backs. I return them all, but it seems like I'm moving through a fog, present but not fully here.

When I push open my office door, I stop short. A welcome-back banner decorates the space, and bright pink, yellow, and orange balloons hover near the ceiling, perfectly matching the bouquet on my desk. Someone did an excellent job coordinating.

I set my bag down and reach for the card nestled among the blooms.

Welcome back, Mags! Work has been straight-ass dull without you. It was up to me to liven up the place. You're welcome.

— Violet

A small smile tugs at my lips. Of course, this was her doing.

"Wow, Sophie. Look at this."

I glance up as Whitney and Sophie step into my office, both surveying the decorations with amused expressions.

"No balloons for us," Whitney says, crossing her arms. "Not even a sad little streamer."

Sophie releases an exaggerated sigh. "I am so underappreciated."

Violet breezes in, her signature confidence filling the room before she even speaks. "Because neither of you have a friend as spectacular as me."

Violet's always been thoughtful, but I never expected anything like this. Maybe part of her has always tried to make me feel special because she knows I don't have family who would.

I blink back the sting in my eyes and manage a smile. "You didn't have to do all this, Vi."

She shrugs, grinning like it was the most obvious thing in the world. "Of course I did. Do you know how boring this place has been without you? I had to show you how glad I am that you're back."

I gesture toward the extravagant bouquet. "The flowers are stunning."

"You deserve flowers." Violet smirks. "And since you have no man to send them to you, I've taken it upon myself. It's a tough job, but someone's gotta do it."

Settle down, Violet. Let's not get carried away.

The banter and laughter fade as Violet and the others return to their desks, and I sink into my chair. The decorations, the jokes, the flowers—they're a pleasant distraction. But the moment I'm alone, that lingering heaviness creeps in again. But I don't have time to dwell on it.

Gabby calls out, "Team, conference room in five."

I push to my feet, and it's business as usual. By the time I step into the conference room, everyone's already settling in. Gabby stands at the head of the table. "Overall, the expansion was a success. The new team adjusted well and maintained a strong match rate. The transition was smoother than expected. But with fewer matches overall, even a single failure had a significant impact on our success rate—more than we would've liked. It's unusual, but I believe with time and refinement, Soul Sync Australia's success rate will improve."

My face is expressionless, but a knot pulls tight in my stomach. That failed match she's referring to takes up a lot of space in my mind.

Somehow, Celeste manipulated the system—slithered her way back into Alex's life, into our lives—and we still don't know how she did it. We still don't know who leaked his emails. Still don't know how she twisted the truth until it broke.

She threatened me. Forced Alex to pay her off just to keep quiet.

But even now—even with money in her pocket and distance between us—I don't believe for a second that she's truly gone. People like her don't vanish. They hide. They wait.

And some sick, instinctive part of me keeps looking over my shoulder, wondering when she'll surface again.

"Whitney, Sophie—thoughts on the new team?" Gabby asks.

Whitney speaks up first. "The Australian team is eager and well-trained, but they lack the intuitive flow we have here. They rely too much on metrics instead of reading the clients."

Sophie adds, "Agreed. They follow the formula well, but the best matches come from knowing when to bend the formula."

Gabby nods, taking that in. "And your thoughts? Can they handle it without you?"

Sophie glances at Whitney, cueing her for input. "They have

potential, but they may still need more guidance. Without us there, it'll take time to reach the standard we uphold."

"We'll see how things go without you there. If they don't improve, another trip to Sydney might be necessary."

My heart leaps as soon as the words leave Gabby's mouth.

"I'd be happy to return if needed." I probably jump in a little too fast, but there's no way I'm letting Macy play the martyr and volunteer herself first.

Gabby gives me an appreciative nod. "Noted, Magnolia. Thank you for always being a team player."

I look forward, refusing to even glance Macy's way. I don't care to see the irritation written all over her face.

The meeting wraps up, and my mind races. I shouldn't get my hopes up, but I can't help it. My mind is spinning.

A return to Sydney. It's not guaranteed, but Gabby put it on the table, and that's enough to set my pulse racing.

I barely make it to my office before Violet is on my heels. "You were practically vibrating in that meeting. Should I pack your bags for you?"

I try for nonchalance, but the excitement bubbling under my skin betrays me. "It's only a possibility."

And I can't wait to tell Alex.

Violet sits in the chair across from my desk, crossing her legs. "You're grinning like you've won the lottery."

She's not wrong. My face is cramping.

I settle into my chair, unable to fight the thrill pulsing through me. "I didn't think there would be a reason to go back. But if Soul Sync Australia needs help—hey, who am I to deprive them of my design skills?"

"Right," Violet drawls. "Because that's what *team players* do. You big suck-up."

A giddy, almost weightless feeling rises in my chest, impossible to suppress.

Violet's face softens, her usual sass giving way to something more touching. "Listen, I'm happy for you. Truly. If this is what you want, I hope it happens."

Something about the way she says it makes my heart sad. "But?"

Violet sighs. "But... I'll miss you. That's all."

The words hit me harder than I expect. I glance at her, taking in the sincerity beneath her usual playful tone. Violet is my person. My constant. And I know she wants me to be happy, but returning would mean leaving her again.

"I'm not gone yet. It's only a maybe. Nothing's set in stone." But even as I say the words, my mind is already drifting to Alex and what it would mean to be with him again.

I can already see it—walking into his house, into his arms. Falling asleep with the steady beat of his heart under my cheek instead of through a screen. Waking up to him, not an empty pillow. Life felt fuller with him in it in ways I hadn't even realized I was starving for. God, I miss him. I miss us.

Violet snaps her fingers in front of my face. "Earth to Magnolia."

"Sorry, Vi."

"You might be mentally booking a one-way ticket to Sydney, but some of us still have jobs to do." She stands, adjusting her skirt. "Try not to spend the day doodling 'Mrs. Magnolia Sebring' in the margins of your notes, okay?"

I let out a laugh, shaking my head. "Thanks for the advice, but I'm not in seventh grade."

"You're in love, Mags. And he's made you think about things you used to be scared to even imagine." She blows me a kiss and struts out, leaving me with the thoughts in my head.

I'm still half-lost in thought when Elijah appears at the door, leaning against the frame, arms crossed. "You volunteering to go back to Australia was the least surprising thing I've heard all day."

He steps inside—uninvited—dropping into the chair across from me. His expression shifts, more serious now. "You really want to do another three months in that place?"

I shrug like it's no big deal, even though there's nothing I want more. "If they need me, why not?"

"Because I can't bear to go back, and I was hoping you felt the same way."

I study him for a moment. "You should stay in Charleston. Be with Sophie. Work on things."

He lets out a short laugh, shaking his head. "There's nothing to work on. What happened in Australia wasn't a relationship. We were having a little fun, making the most of an unpleasant situation."

This guy's a discount fuckboy with delusions of grandeur. Bad combination. "Elijah—"

He lifts a brow. "What is it, Mags?"

There's probably no way to say this that'll actually get through his thick skull, but I have to try. "You need to talk to Sophie about that. Because I don't believe she sees it the same way you do. I think her perspective is quite different."

Before he can respond, movement in the doorway catches my eye.

Sophie.

She stands frozen for half a second, then turns sharply, disappearing down the hall before either of us can say a word.

Shit.

"Go talk to her."

For a moment, he sits there, jaw tight, running a hand over his face. Finally, he pushes to his feet and leaves.

I watch him go, a knot forming in my stomach. This is going to be a mess. But it's not mine to clean up.

Chapter 4

Alex Sebring

THE PHONE SITS HEAVY IN MY HAND, TAUNTING ME WITH ITS silence. Tension coils in my chest, my leg bouncing like I've got energy to burn. It's been less than a week since she left—still too long without seeing her, without touching her, without breathing her in.

Time zones and schedules have turned our communication into a game of patience, and I fucking hate it. Magnolia should be here, in my bed, curled up against me where she belongs. But all I have is this damn screen and the ache of missing her.

I stare at my phone like I can make it ring by sheer force of will.

My worry is unnecessary. She's going to call—she always does when she says she will—but that doesn't stop the restless energy thrumming under my skin. My leg bounces, fingers drumming against my thigh as I glance at the screen again. Still nothing.

As the edges of my patience fray, my screen lights up. Magnolia Steel—FaceTime. Incoming. Join.

My pulse kicks up as I swipe to answer. And then she's there—bright-eyed, smiling, looking more beautiful than ever.

"Hey, favorite."

"Hey, big guy."

My favorite. My girl. My American beauty.

She's still in her work clothes, perched on her couch, one leg tucked under her, hair spilling over one shoulder. The soft lighting casts a golden glow on her skin, making her look like she belongs in a painting you can't stop staring at.

"Still missing me?"

She rolls her eyes but grins. "Not even a little. I'm over the whole thing."

I smirk. "You're a terrible liar."

She pretends to think about it. "It's possible I miss you a little."

There's something different about her tonight. Her energy is lighter, her smile lingering. I know her too well not to notice. "All right, what's got you all chirpy?"

Her smile widens, and there's something in her eyes—excitement, anticipation. It's infectious, the kind of expression that makes happiness rush through me.

"I have the best news ever." She fights a smile by biting her bottom lip. "Okay... *maybe* the best news ever."

"You're killing me, babe. Let's hear it."

She takes a breath, dragging it out, and I'm certain she's doing it on purpose—making me wait.

"There's a chance Soul Sync might send me back to Australia to help with the new team."

Everything inside me jolts awake. I sit up straighter, my pulse kicking up, a rush of adrenaline sharp and immediate.

"That's amazing!" The words leave me fast, unfiltered, because fuck, it is amazing. The idea of her being here, of closing the distance, of having her in my space again sets my whole body buzzing.

She's supposed to be here with me.

"I'm trying not to get too excited since nothing is certain. But it's a possibility right now."

"Possibilities have a way of turning into reality, especially when you want something bad enough."

She smiles—that easy, tilt-your-world kind of smile that never fails to wreck me. "And you want this bad enough?"

I don't hesitate. "More than the air I breathe."

There's a special kind of spark in her eyes. "I'm excited... *really* excited. But I don't want to get my hopes up too soon."

"Sure, that's understandable."

I believe it deeper than blood and bone that this is where Magnolia is supposed to be. And I won't let her go again. I made the mistake of letting her slip through my fingers once. I told myself I was doing the right thing, that I was giving her space to figure things out, to decide for herself if we were worth fighting for.

But fuck that. I already know the answer.

And when she comes back, she's not leaving again.

She stretches, and the movement draws my attention to the soft curve of her neck, the way her blouse shifts and hugs her perfect tits.

"So," she says, tilting her head. "What have you been up to without me there occupying your every free minute?"

I'm a bloody sorry sap missing her like it's a full-time job. Every hour, every minute, hell—every bloody second she's not here feels off-kilter. I'm not fine. I'm wrecked. But no way I'm handing her all that mush on a silver platter. Not yet.

"Wouldn't you like to know?"

She narrows her eyes. "Yes, I would like to know. That's why I asked."

"Nothing interesting—working, venting my frustration in the gym. Mostly missing you."

Those full, pouty lips of hers press together like she's trying not to smile. "You miss me, huh?"

I hold her gaze. "Every damn second. But you know what I can't stop thinking about?"

She reaches up and thumbs the diamond pendant resting against her collarbone. "Tell me."

I let the moment stretch, my voice dropping lower. "Your touch. The feel of you."

Her breath catches a little, enough to make my cock twitch in response.

And that teasing smirk returns, slower this time. "Yeah? Is that so?"

She shifts, her body language changing, softening, her playfulness turning into something warmer. Darker.

"Hold on a second."

She disappears from view, and the screen goes dark. I thumb the screen of my phone, wondering if we lost connection. "Babe, are you still there?"

Her voice calls out from somewhere off-camera. "Hold on. Be patient."

My pulse kicks up, anticipation tightening in my chest.

Patient? Not a fucking chance.

A second later, soft, sultry music hums through the speakers. Low. Slow. Hypnotic. I recognize it straight away. "Glory Box" by Portishead. One of her favorites. One of my favorites now as well—because of her.

The screen shifts, and when she steps back into view, my entire body goes tight.

She props her phone up at the perfect angle, giving me a full view. She moves with the music, slow and deliberate, like she has all the time in the world.

Fuck. I love where this is going.

I grab the landline phone off my desk with one hand and hit the call button for Courtney. She picks up on the first ring.

"Hold all my calls. And I'm not to be disturbed for any reason. Not until I say otherwise."

A pause... because I never make demands like that.

"Of course, Mr. Sebring."

I hang up and shove out of my chair, crossing the room in only a few strides. The door locks with a loud, satisfying click that feels a hell of a lot like throwing away the last bit of self-control I have.

I sink back into my chair, the phone gripped tight in my palm, every muscle in my body coiled so tight it's a miracle I'm still breathing.

"Sounds like someone doesn't want to be disturbed."

"You better fucking believe it."

My American beauty begins with her hair, reaching up to unpin it, letting the chestnut strands tumble down over her shoulders. My grip tightens on the phone, my breath coming slower now, heavier.

She moves to the buttons on her shirt, undoing them one by one—so painfully slow it feels like she's trying to kill me.

The fabric slips down her shoulders, revealing the delicate lace of her bra and golden glow of her skin, still tanned by the Samoan sun.

My cock twitches, my free hand already moving to rub the hard length through my trousers.

Her hands trail down the front of her body, slow and teasing, fingers flirting with the waistband of her skirt. Eyes locked on the camera—on me—like she knows good and damn well what she's doing.

A slow, deliberate shimmy sends the skirt whispering down her hips, puddling at her feet. Lace and bare skin are all that's left.

Fucking stunning. Ethereal. A dream I can't touch—no matter how badly I want to.

Her fingers skate up her stomach, then higher, cupping her tits as she bites her bottom lip and moves her hips to the rhythm of the music.

I groan, my hand sliding into my pants, wrapping around my thick, aching length.

This is physical torture but the best kind.

Magnolia's fingers trail down her stomach, slow and deliberate, her eyes locked on mine. She reaches behind her back, unfastening her bra, letting the straps slide down her arms before tossing it aside. My throat goes dry, my grip on the phone tightening as she bares herself to me.

Fuck.

Her thumbs hook into the lace of her panties, dragging them

down her hips past her thighs, letting them fall in a heap on the floor before she climbs onto the bed.

She leans back against the pillows, one knee bent, her skin glowing in the soft light.

I can barely breathe.

"I've missed you," she says, her fingers trailing lower, teasing.

"Show me," I say, my voice rough, needy.

She doesn't look away as she spreads her legs, her hand slipping between them. She exhales a soft, breathy sigh as her fingers stroke over herself, her body arching into her own touch.

"I miss the way you feel inside me. The way you fill me up and stretch me."

A guttural groan rips from my throat. I lower my zipper enough to free myself, my hand grips my thick length, matching her slow, torturous rhythm.

The sound of her soft moans through the speaker sends a sharp pulse of need straight through me.

"You have no idea what I'd do to you right now." My strokes tighten as I picture her beneath me, my hands gripping her, my mouth kissing and sucking on her skin.

"Tell me." Her breath hitches as her fingers move in a circular motion. "I want to hear you say it."

My grip tightens. "I'd have you pinned to the bed, powerless, your arms stretched over your head holding the headboard."

Her eyelids flutter. "And what else?"

"I'd kiss my way down your body, taking my time." My strokes slow, matching the lazy tease of her fingers. "But you wouldn't be patient, would you?"

She shakes her head, catching her bottom lip between her teeth, a soft, desperate sound slipping from her throat—a sound that tells me no without saying the word.

"You'd be desperate. Already soaking for me. Already begging."

A breathy moan slips from her lips. "That's right."

I groan, my restraint unraveling. "I'd slide my fingers inside you first, stretch you, feel how tight you are. And then when you were nice and slick, I'd push my cock into you—slow and deep—until you were shaking underneath me."

She gasps, her back arching, her fingers working in slow, deliberate strokes.

"And then you know what, favorite? I'd wreck your perfect, tight little pussy. And when I came, I'd fill you with every drop of cum and then watch it drip out of you like a stream."

Her whimper is sharp, breathless, and fuck, I can't hold back any longer as her movements become more desperate. My body is right there with her, coiled tight, the tension unbearable.

The moment stretches between us, pulsing and electric, until neither of us can hold back.

She gasps my name as she shatters. I follow with a deep, ragged groan tearing from my chest as I fall over the edge with her.

Silence lingers, thick and sated, nothing but our heavy breathing filling the space between us.

I let out a breathless laugh, glancing down at the mess on my stomach. Fuck. It's been a long time since I acted like this. Not since I was a stupid, hormone-drunk teenager.

The silence between us is thick with satisfaction. Our breathing slows, the lingering heat ebbing into something softer.

Magnolia exhales a contented sigh, her lips curling into a lazy smile. "That was..." she trails off, shaking her head like she doesn't have the words.

I chuckle, still catching my breath. "Yeah. It was."

She laughs. "Damn, you have a filthy mouth. I love it. I needed that."

I smirk as I look back at the screen. "I needed it too, babe."

She shifts against her pillows. I brace my elbows on the desk, holding the phone tighter, like that could somehow bridge the thousands of miles between us.

She tugs the blanket higher, fingers curling into the fabric. "I can't wait until I can touch you again."

I swallow hard, my voice coming out rough. "Me either, babe."

She sighs, eyes flickering over my face. "I hate this."

"It's the worst."

I watch as she tucks her chin, curling deeper into the warmth of her bed, her breathing slowing like she's drifting. But she fights it, blinking hard, refusing to let sleep steal these last few minutes from us.

"You're exhausted. Go to sleep."

"Not yet. I... I don't want our call to be over yet."

It hits me low and hard, this need to have her with me.

"Nothing's over. This is temporary."

Her eyelids flutter, a drowsy smile tugging at her lips. "Say it again."

"This is only temporary. Soon, you'll be here, and I'm never letting you leave again."

Her sigh is so soft, I almost don't hear it. "Mmm. I like that plan."

I watch her a little longer, waiting for the moment her breath evens out, for the telltale shift of sleep pulling her under.

It's only after that I whisper, "Goodnight, favorite."

Her response is barely audible. "Goodnight, big guy."

The screen goes dark, and the hollow, gnawing weight of missing her is still there, sitting heavy in my chest.

Soon isn't soon enough.

Chapter 5

Alex Sebring

THE SUN HANGS HIGH OVER THE GOLF COURSE, CASTING A golden sheen across the fairways. The air is crisp, carrying the faint scent of just-cut grass and the distant hum of cicadas. It's a picture-perfect day—one that should be relaxing, easy.

But I'm not relaxed. Not even a little.

Magnolia has been gone for two weeks. Fourteen days of waking up alone, of reaching for her in the middle of the night only to find cool sheets. Of pretending like everything is fine when it sure as hell isn't.

I grip the wheel of the golf cart, steering us toward the next hole. Alexander Sebring—my father and the man who taught me golf, rugby, yachting, and just about everything else worth knowing in life —sits beside me.

"Overthinking the next hole?" Amusement threads his voice. "Might need to eagle this one if you plan on catching up."

I roll my shoulders, exhaling. "I'm still warming up, old man."

He chuckles under his breath. "That's what you said two holes ago."

I don't bother responding because he's right. I'm off my game today, and we both understand the reason.

Before I can reach for my club, a voice—sweet, flirtatious—cuts through the quiet.

"Drink for you, Mr. Sebring?"

I glance up to find a cart girl standing beside us, a bright smile plastered across her face. She's young, pretty, blond—the type I used to go for without a second thought. Another cart girl lingers beside her, two sets of eyes watching me like I'm the most interesting thing on the course.

She shifts her weight, batting her lashes. "Would you prefer I pick a beverage for you? Perhaps a cold beer?"

I offer a polite smile, already reaching into my pocket. "Don't need anything right now, thanks."

I pull out a bill and hand it to her, nodding toward their cart. "For your trouble."

The blonde's smile falters a fraction before she covers it with another sugary grin and takes the money. Her friend tries to salvage the moment, tucking a stray piece of hair behind her ear. "We'll be around if you change your mind."

I offer a polite smile. "No need but appreciate it."

They linger for a beat, like they're waiting for me to change my mind. When I don't, the blonde gives a small nod. The two of them leave, their conversation hushed as they saunter back to their cart.

My father smirks, leaning against his club. "The ladies have always loved you and your brothers."

I smirk, tossing my glove into the cart. "What can I say? We take after our dad."

He lets out a low chuckle. "Flattery won't help you win this round, boy."

I shake my head, grabbing a bottle of water from the cooler. "I'm not interested in chasing women anymore. Or in being chased."

"You're not the man you were before you met her—and that's not a bad thing."

"Magnolia's the only woman who has my interest."

"Funny how fast life shifts when the right woman shows up."

He's right—this is a change for me. There was a time when I would've taken the bait from the cart girls, let them giggle and flirt, perhaps even walked away with a number scribbled on a napkin. But now? My mind is on one woman... a woman who's not within my reach.

I take a long drink, letting the cold water settle the restless energy running through me.

"Your turn," Dad says, gesturing to the tee box.

I breathe in, rolling my shoulders back, but even as I step up to take my swing, my thoughts drift somewhere else thousands of miles away.

The driver connects with a sharp crack, but the ball slices hard to the right, vanishing into the rough.

Fuck.

It's hard to restrain a groan as I shove my club back into the bag.

My father smirks, amusement flickering in his eyes. "Solid technique... if you were aiming for the trees."

I bite back a response as we climb into the cart. This isn't like me; I play better than this.

I steer the cart toward the next hole, rolling to a stop near the tee box. My father climbs out first, taking his time selecting his club, stretching his shoulders before stepping up to the ball. He's methodical, patient—a golfer who plays smart rather than flashy. And today, he's playing well.

He lines up his shot, his posture relaxed. With one smooth swing, he sends the ball soaring down the fairway, landing on the short grass.

"Nice one."

He smirks, setting his club back in the bag. "Try to keep up, son."

I grab my driver, planting my feet on the tee. I should be able to crush this. Golf has never been my best sport, but I'm an athlete with precision, control, focus. Those are my strengths.

I exhale, drawing the club back in one smooth motion, and swing.

The sound of contact is solid, but the second I look up, I can see it's wrong. The ball slices hard to the right, veering off into the rough, where it disappears into the trees.

Fuck. Me.

My father chuckles, shaking his head. "What's this? My son, the legendary athlete, getting outplayed by his old man?"

I grip my driver tighter, forcing a smirk. "You wish."

He laughs as we climb back into the cart, and I can sense his eyes on me, assessing.

"You're off today. Your mind's somewhere else."

I steer the cart one-handed, the wheel loose under my palm as the tires crunch over the path. He's not wrong. My mind's not on the next hole or my scorecard. It's nine thousand miles away, curled up in a bed in Charleston, wearing my hoodie.

"How's Magnolia?" Somehow it feels like he's not just asking about her. He's asking about me too.

I grip the wheel tighter. "She's good."

It's not a lie. Magnolia is missing me, but she's back at work, settling into life at home again. While I'm a fucking mess without her. And my father, perceptive as ever, doesn't miss it.

He leans back in his seat, looking out over the course. "How are you holding up since she left?"

I look straight ahead. "Not my best if I'm being honest."

That's a bloody understatement.

Magnolia's absence sits on my chest like a weight that won't shift. I check my phone more times than I can count, hoping to find her name lighting up the screen. I still wake up expecting her to be next to me, only to find the sheets cold and untouched.

But saying all of that out loud to my dad? That's not me.

"There's no way she could stay in Sydney?"

"She has a life in the States—a job, responsibilities, friends who love her. I never expected her to give that up for a bloke she knew for three months."

Dad nods, adjusting his glove. "That's fair. But where does that leave you?"

The question is tough. "It leaves me... missing her like crazy."

He studies me for a moment and nods like he understands. And maybe he does.

Dad prepares his shot, his grip steady, his movements unhurried. He swings, sending the ball rolling onto the green before turning to me.

"She's there, you're here. What does this mean for the two of you?"

I grip my club a little tighter. "We're going to keep seeing where things go. But I'd be lying if I said the distance wasn't brutal."

"I don't imagine it's easy."

"We talk all the time. FaceTime, calls, texts." A smirk tugs at my lips. "Some of those FaceTime calls have been *eventful*."

Dad arches a brow. "Eventful, eh?"

I shake my head. "I'm going to leave it at that."

He chuckles. "Probably best."

We walk, the conversation stretching between us. And I throw him something I know he won't expect. "There's a chance she could return."

Dad stops mid-step. "Is that so?"

I glance over at him, my grip firming around my putter. "Her employer might send her back to Sydney."

The slow grin that spreads across his face is nothing short of victorious. "Now that's the best thing I've heard all day." His reaction is immediate—like it's already decided, like Magnolia's return is inevitable. And God, I hope it is.

"It's not set in stone. Just a possibility."

"Sounds like a damn good possibility. Your mum will be thrilled."

One thing is certain. If she comes back to me, I sure as hell won't let her go again.

"You love this girl." His statement is so direct, so matter-of-fact, it almost knocks the wind out of me.

My fingers tighten around the grip of my club as the truth comes out. "Yeah, I do. A lot."

Dad's face doesn't change, doesn't show a hint of surprise. Instead, he smiles—a knowing, satisfied kind of smile. "Your mother and I saw that from the start. Magnolia loves you for you. That's rare when you have money and fame."

He doesn't know the half of my love for Magnolia or the way she rewrote the map of my heart. Not the way her laughter stitched itself into my life. He's never seen the nights I lie awake, yearning for her in the dark. Never felt the hollow ache her absence has left behind.

She was mine before I even knew how to say it. She's still mine now, even across the distance.

Dad reaches into his bag and pulls out a putter, handing it to me. "Here. Let's see if you can at least clean up your short game."

He isn't only talking about golf.

He props his weight on his club, casual as you please, but his words hit harder than a fist. "The real question is what are you going to do about the woman you love being so far away?"

The weight of this conversation just shifted.

He steps aside, watching as I line up my shot. The green stretches before me, the hole just a few feet away, but my father's voice keeps me from focusing.

"Your mother almost slipped through my fingers."

I glance up, surprised. I've never heard that story. "How?"

He crosses his arms, looking toward the horizon like he's seeing something long past. "Before we were married, Malie returned to Samoa. She had her life there, her family. I had mine here. We both thought we were making the right choices, choosing the lives we'd built before each other. Being apart from her were the worst months of my life."

I understand that all too well. "What did you do?"

He smiles, like the answer should be obvious. "I got on a plane and went to Samoa."

"Just like that?"

"It wasn't *just like that*. Nothing about it was easy. There were a hundred reasons to stay put. But there was one damn good reason to go. Sometimes, you have to move the pieces around—hell, flip the whole damn board if you need to, to protect what's yours. You have to know what's worth the fight."

His words sink in. My dad's not just giving me advice. This is a challenge.

He claps a hand on my shoulder. "Do what you must for love, Alex. It's the only thing that matters."

I study the endless stretch of green before me and settle into my stance. The weight in my chest hasn't lessened, but something inside me has shifted. I understand what I need to do.

I draw my club back, steady and controlled. When I swing, everything clicks into place. The ball launches clean and smooth, cutting through the air in a perfect arc before landing dead center on the fairway.

Dad watches the shot and releases a low whistle. "That's more like it."

I exhale, gripping the club a little tighter.

It's time to clean up my short game and work toward a future where Magnolia and I are not separated by an ocean.

Chapter 6

Alex Sebring

UNREAD EMAILS HAVE PILED UP LIKE AN AVALANCHE, BURYING my inbox in a mess I have no patience to dig through. My personal assistant should handle this—sorting the urgent from the useless, deleting the spam, and spoon-feeding me what matters.

But I don't have a PA anymore.

Not since I fired her.

Even with the heavier workload, I don't regret it for a second. She leaked my Soul Sync involvement to Celeste—I'm sure of it. She lied to my face, swore she didn't, but I'm not stupid. And I know damn well I didn't match with Celeste. Someone helped rig it, and she was part of it. No doubt.

Until I figure out who else I can trust, I'm keeping my circle small and tight.

Which is why I did something I might regret.

A sudden thud startles me from my thoughts. A large tote bag lands on my desk, followed by the unmistakable sound of my sister's voice. "All right, golden boy. Let's do this. And when do I get a raise?"

"Jesus, Leilani."

She grins, unbothered, and plants herself in the chair across from me, kicking her feet up onto my desk like she owns the place. "Relax, big brother. I already know the answer. '*Start by not pissing me off.*' Or '*Never.*'"

Damn. She does a decent job of impersonating me.

"That sound about right?"

I stare at her for a long beat. "This was a terrible idea."

She gasps, clutching her chest like I've wounded her heart. "Wow. That hurts, Alex. But it's too late now. You hired me."

I did. Because I need someone I can trust, and right now, family is the only option.

"You realize this is an actual job, right? Not an excuse for you to sit around, annoy the shit out of me, and play on your phone all day."

Leilani scoffs. "Please. I can annoy you *and* be productive. I'm a multi-tasker."

"God help me."

She flashes a wide grin. "Oh, come on. It'll be fun. You and me, taking on the corporate world together. Just two Sebring siblings, making dreams come true. Changing lives."

I level her with a stare. "Your job is to read my work emails."

She shrugs. "Same thing."

Am I sure I can put up with this every day?

Leilani stretches her arms over her head. "So. Where do I start?"

I gesture to the computer. "My inbox—start there. Flag anything that's important, delete the junk, and don't—I repeat, *don't*—mess with my calendar. I don't need you moving things around without telling me."

Leilani mock salutes. "Yes, sir."

She slides into the chair behind the desk, cracking her knuckles like she's about to perform surgery. "So what you're telling me is that I'll be doing your job but on a much lower pay scale."

I meet her gaze with dry patience. "No. You're filtering out the bullshit emails that are a waste of my time."

She tilts her head. "Like I said—doing your job."

I grab a pen off my desk and launch it at her. She dodges it with ease, laughing. "You're so damn grumpy since Magnolia left."

She clicks through emails, humming under her breath. "All right, let's see what we've got. Spam, spam, someone wants to sell you a new, bigger yacht." She pauses, eyebrows lifting. "Hmm... this one sounds kind of legit about expanding your social media presence."

"Delete it." I don't want to be in the spotlight any more than I have to be.

She clicks on one, and snickers. "Ooooh, here's one about performance enhancement pills. Stronger, longer, harder. Bro, you need pills for that?" She bursts out laughing. "It's no wonder Magnolia booked a one-way ticket out of here."

I groan, dragging a hand down my face. "Shut up, Lei."

She wipes a fake tear. "This is already the best job I've ever had."

I shake my head, cursing myself. This was a mistake.

A knock sounds at the door, and before I can tell Leilani to behave, it opens.

Courtney steps inside, a folder tucked under one arm, her expression as composed as ever. She's been with Sebring Hotels longer than I have—first working for my father and now for me as I step into his role. If anyone knows the ins and outs of this business, it's her.

"Good morning, Mr. Sebring." She nods toward Leilani. "I see you're introducing your sister to the business."

Leilani spins in her chair, flashing a grin. "My brother needs someone he can trust. So here I am."

Courtney smirks, seeming unimpressed. "Lucky him."

"Right?" Leilani leans back, propping her feet up on the desk again. "We're already making substantial progress on these emails... and I'm expanding his knowledge of prescription enhancement options."

Courtney blinks at her and turns to me. "Prescription enhancement?"

I sigh, rubbing my temples. "Regret is a slow burn."

Courtney hands me the folder. "Quarterly reports. Your father wants a review before the next board meeting. Also, you have a call with the Brisbane architect at three."

I nod, flipping through the pages, not reading one damn word. "Thanks for this."

She lingers for half a second, her gaze flicking to Leilani. "Let's do our best to keep things running smoothly for Alex."

Leilani smiles, but it drips sarcasm. "I am the picture of efficiency."

"Mm-hmm," she says beneath her breath and exits the office, leaving me with the menace my mother calls her surprise blessing from God.

Leilani cuts her eyes my way as soon as the door shuts behind Courtney. "Dad has always bragged about how fantastic she is, but to be frank, I don't like her."

I shoot her a look. "Dad isn't wrong. She is fantastic. She's been running this office longer than you've been alive."

Leilani smirks. "Plenty of time to perfect the art of villainy. I'm telling you, bro—she sets off my Spidey senses."

"Please behave, Lei."

She doesn't smirk this time. Doesn't joke. Simply holds my gaze. "Fine. Ignore a Malietoa woman's gut feeling at your own risk. But be ready. Because I'm gonna back my car into the garage at your house and unload a whole bunch of *I told you so* when you figure out that I'm right."

My phone buzzes on my desk, Magnolia's name flashing across the screen. Before I can grab it, Leilani snatches it up, grinning like someone gave her a winning lottery ticket.

"Leilani, don't—"

Too late. She answers, dropping her voice into something low and sultry.

"Sebring Hotels. CEO unavailable. This is his incredibly beautiful, highly competent, underpaid personal assistant speaking."

There's a pause as Leilani listens to whatever Magnolia is saying.

Leilani cackles. "Kidding. This is Leilani, Alex's favorite sibling—obviously."

I glare at her. "Give me the damn phone, pest."

She twists away, keeping it out of reach. "Hey Alex, it's Magnolia—the woman you're obsessed with, the woman who has turned you into a lovesick puppy."

I lunge for the phone, but she dodges me again. "He's very busy at the moment. Brooding. Missing you. Staring at your photograph. Writing lousy poetry about you."

"Haha. You're hilarious. Now give me my damn phone."

I manage to snatch it from Leilani's grasp and press it to my ear. "Please ignore her."

Magnolia laughs. "I don't think Leilani is one to be ignored."

My sister smirks, looking far too pleased with herself. Without doubt, hiring her is a mistake.

I point to the door. "Out."

Leilani blinks at me, all fake innocence. "What? I'm just getting comfortable."

"Out," I repeat, leveling her with a glare.

She sighs, rising from her chair like it's the greatest hardship of her life. "Fine, fine. I'll leave you two lovebirds alone to chat." She turns toward the door but pauses long enough to call out, "Magnolia, if he chooses to discuss his prescription enhancement options with you, please know that I support whatever decision he makes."

"Get the fuck out, Leilani!"

"Fine. I'll go grab a coffee so you don't make me throw up with how in love you are."

I press the phone back to my ear. "Sorry about her."

Magnolia's soft laughter carries through the line, melting the tension coiled inside me. "Don't be. She's hilarious."

"That's debatable."

"So... prescription enhancement options, huh? What's up with that?"

"Just my sister ragging on me about some erectile dysfunction spam emails."

She laughs. "Oh, you one hundred percent don't need that."

"Damn straight."

Like hell I ever would. Not with her. Magnolia turns me on beyond reason—always has, from the moment I laid eyes on her. It's the way she moves, the way she teases, the way she looks at me like she knows what she's doing to me. She doesn't have to try. One word from her, and it's like flipping a switch—every nerve wired straight to her.

"What are your plans for tonight?"

"Dinner and drinks with Violet. A new sushi bar opened downtown. We figured we'd check it out."

I wish like hell I could be there—sliding into a booth beside her, stealing bites off her plate, kissing the soy sauce off the corner of her mouth.

Instead, I'm imagining every bastard in that bar looking at what's mine. "Wish I was there."

"I do too."

I smile, even as something tightens in my gut. "Have an old-fashioned for me."

"I'll have two. One for you, one for me."

"Don't let Violet talk you into trouble."

"She wouldn't dare. Besides, I'm trouble enough on my own."

And damn if she isn't.

The thought of her out there—radiant and laughing—makes a part of me want to lock her away and keep every smile for myself. But the smarter part of me knows her light isn't mine to dim.

I clear my throat, shifting gears because if I stay on that thought, I'll end up booking a damn flight tonight.

"Any word yet about being sent back to Sydney?"

"Nothing yet. I don't expect to hear anything for a little while. Gabby wants to see what Team Australia does without us."

It's a job trying to keep my frustration in check. "Sorry. I'm anxious."

"I know. Same."

I get up and walk to the window, staring out over the harbor, the sky stretching wide and endless. "I don't think I can wait for you to come back."

Her voice turns playful. "Umm... Alex. Are you breaking up with me?"

"Never, lovie. I'm saying maybe I should come to you sooner rather than later."

I brace for her to tell me it's a bad idea—that it's too soon, too complicated—that it'll only make things harder when we have to part again.

But she says, "Yes, Alex. Please come. Nothing would make me happier."

Relief punches through me, knocking loose some of the ache lodged in my chest since the moment she left. "You don't know how much I needed to hear that."

"I think I sort of do." Her voice is so certain.

I glance at my work calendar, my head spinning through everything I need to clear. "How soon do you want me there?"

"As soon as you can get here." She doesn't hesitate. "I miss you too much to pretend otherwise."

"I could be free in two weeks. Three at the latest. I need to tie up a few loose ends here."

"Two weeks..." A small, shaky laugh crackles through the phone. "It's soon, but it feels like forever. Will you be able to stay long?"

"I'll stay as long as I can."

"I'll take whatever time you can give me."

The weight between us shifts—no longer heavy with sadness but humming with something new. Anticipation.

"So... word on the street is you hired a new assistant?"

What a fuckup on my part. "Yeah. Worst bloody mistake I ever made."

"What does Leilani do for you?"

Aside from annoying the fuck out of me? "She's my personal assistant. And I'm already regretting it."

Magnolia laughs, the sound so sweet it cuts straight through me. "I think she'll be the perfect personal assistant. She can keep you in line."

"Well, we'll see about that."

Before she can respond, there's a knock at her door. "That'll be Vi. Hold on."

I hear the door creak open, followed by Violet's voice carrying through the phone. "What up, bitch? I've aged five years waiting for you."

Magnolia laughs. "Sorry, I was just talking to Alex. I'm putting you on speaker."

"Ohhh," Violet drawls. "The boyfriend."

The boyfriend. I don't hate being called that.

"Violet, are you going to keep my girl out of trouble tonight?"

"I damn sure hope not. I'm taking her out for sushi and cocktails. Hopefully a little dancing if I can talk her into it. She's been moping around missing your ass, and to be honest, it's killing my vibe. A little trouble would be fun."

"Show her a good time—but not too good, yeah? I'd like my girlfriend returned in one piece."

"*Girlfriend*, huh? About damn time you started claiming her."

Oh, I've claimed her in a proper manner. Trust me. "You two behave. Mostly."

"We'll try," Magnolia says, her voice warm with laughter.

"Love you, favorite."

"Love you too, big guy."

I set the phone down, a stupid grin tugging at my mouth. She's halfway across the world, but it doesn't matter. I don't need proximity to know she's mine.

Chapter 7

Magnolia Steel

THE LAST HALF HOUR OF WORK BEFORE QUITTING TIME ALWAYS seems like a crawl, but not today. I'm buzzing with so much energy I can barely sit still.

I've just left a meeting with Gabby, Sophie, and Whitney—one that confirmed what we'd all been sensing. The Aussie team is struggling.

Soul Sync Australia had a rough week. Matches fell apart. Feedback was brutal. And Gabby, never one to let a problem fester, decided that we're not sitting on this. She's sending part of our core team back to Sydney to stabilize things before the situation gets any worse.

Back to Sydney.

Back to Alex.

The thought alone makes my heart stutter. I can barely focus, already counting the minutes until I can call and tell him. We'll soon be on the same side of the world again—and this time, nothing is pulling me away.

Shoving back from my desk, I grab my phone as I hurry toward

Violet's office. She looks up as I push the door open without knocking, raising a brow at my not-so-subtle entrance.

"Well, well. To what do I owe the pleasure of Hurricane Magnolia blowing through my door?"

I drop into the chair across from her, unable to sit still. "Gabby's going to send us back to Sydney. Australia is floundering."

Realization dawns across her face, her lips parting. "No way."

"Yes."

She lets out a breath, leaning back in her chair. "Wow, Mags. That's—" She shakes her head, forcing a smile. "That's great. I mean, it sucks for me because I'll have to live without you again, but—"

"You'll survive," I say, snapping a rubber band at her arm, wearing a wicked grin.

"Oww." She picks up the rubber band from her lap and tosses it back into the holder like she's filing it away for future revenge.

We sit in the moment, the excitement buzzing between us. Violet is less than thrilled about my return to Sydney, but she understands it. She knows how much this means to me.

I pull out my phone, my fingers already flying over the keyboard to message Alex.

> I have good news! Call me the minute you get this text.

I hit send, my stomach flipping with anticipation. Violet watches me with a smug little smile. "You told me first, right? I'm your emotional-support best friend. There's a hierarchy here and I'm on top."

I laugh. "Straight up. You're the first to know."

She leans back in her chair, satisfied. "Good. Because if you'd told your boyfriend first, I would require flowers, chocolates, and an apology written in calligraphy."

I roll my eyes. "God, you're so dramatic."

She shrugs. "What can I say? I have standards."

I glance down at my phone. The message delivered, but no response yet.

Violet's grin falters. "Chill Mags."

"I'm sure he's busy with work." I set the phone on my lap, trying to ignore the knot of impatience tightening in my stomach.

He'll text me back soon. And when he does, he's going to be ecstatic to hear the news.

We're going to be together again. And this time, it's going to be perfect.

The sun has long since set by the time I step into my apartment, kicking off my heels and tossing my bag onto the couch. The golden glow of the city paints the room, but I'm too distracted to care.

I've been checking my phone every few minutes for the past hour, waiting for Alex's response. This is unusual for him. He's always quick to respond—especially when I tell him to call me. But tonight? Nothing. Not a single text.

It's... odd. And disappointing.

I stare at the message still sitting there with that quiet, mocking delivered status, more annoying than reassuring. A flicker of unease nudges at my chest, but I push it aside. I'm sure he's tied up with work, or family, or perhaps something came up with the new hotel they're building. There are a dozen reasonable explanations.

Sighing, I set my phone on the counter and head for the kitchen cabinet. If I'm going to sit here spiraling like a lovesick fool, I might as well do it with a glass of wine in hand. I pour a generous amount of pinot noir, the glug-glug of it filling the quiet with a strange comfort. I take a slow sip, savoring the way it warms my throat, then lean back against the counter, trying to stay calm.

It's fine. He'll text any minute now.

And a minute later, he does.

Shit, what took so long?

This relationship isn't working for me.

Tell me about it, big guy. It's not working for me either.

I need to be with him. Not an ocean apart. Not sharing goodnight texts instead of good-night kisses. I need to be near him. With him inside me. Every night.

My fingers fly across the keyboard, typing out my response, telling him I want him to call me as soon as possible because I have something wonderful to tell him. But before I can hit send, another message from Alex comes through.

> I've had time to think about this, and I've made some decisions. I need a woman in my bed every night. My sex drive can't handle the distance between us. If I don't end this relationship now, I'll end up cheating on you, and I don't want to hurt you in that way.

Wait. What?

A sharp pain slams into my chest, like I've been sucker-punched. I blink, forcing myself to keep reading.

No, this can't be right.

> I need a woman who's wife material. And that isn't you.

My breath shudders, the room tilting around me.

> Don't call or text me again. That would only make this worse. This relationship is over.

The wine glass slips from my grasp and shatters on the floor, mimicking the way my heart has cracked into pieces. Red wine seeps into the cream rug, a slow, brutal bloom, no different from how my heart feels—broken and bleeding out.

My hands tremble, the simple act of breathing turning into a losing battle against panic.

This can't be real.

I reread the text, my vision blurring, desperate to find something

—anything—that makes it make sense. But the words don't change. The meaning doesn't shift.

A cold, ugly panic rises in my throat. My fingers move on autopilot, hitting the call button.

The line rings once. Then—straight to voicemail.

My pulse stutters. That's not right.

I try again. Voicemail.

Again. Voicemail.

Again.

A strangled sound claws its way up my throat. No. No, no, no. This isn't happening. Alex wouldn't do this. He wouldn't end things like this.

A violent twist rips through my stomach as panic takes hold, my breathing shallow and erratic. There has to be an explanation. There has to be. Nothing about this is right.

I yank open my laptop and type with shaking hands. *What does it mean when calls go straight to voicemail?*

The screen fills with answers I don't want: one ring, voicemail, blocked.

Blocked?

The word echoes like a gunshot.

A sharp, splintering pain cracks through my ribs, radiating outward like wildfire. Alex blocked me. He ended things and cut me off. Erased me.

I choke on a sob, pressing a hand to my mouth as the weight of it crushes me. Only an hour ago, I was planning my return to Sydney. Planning a future with him.

And now? He ended it without even knowing I was on my way back to him.

Nausea churns in my gut. I barely make it to the bathroom before my stomach wretches, heaving up stomach contents but also everything I am, everything I feel.

I don't remember how I end up on the bathroom floor. One moment, I'm staring at my laptop screen, the word *blocked* searing into my brain like a flashing neon sign, and the next, I'm crumpled on my knees with my body folded in on itself as if that might protect me from the pain.

This can't be happening. It can't be real.

I squeeze my eyes shut and try to drag in a breath, but nothing about it helps. The panic keeps pressing into me—tight around my ribs, sharp against my lungs. My hands tremble as I fumble for my phone again.

There's nothing. No warning. No shift. No buildup I missed.

Just days of thread after thread—*I miss you. I love you. I can't wait to hold you again.* His voice in written form, a digital echo of promises and plans. Of forever.

And then—*this.*

It's over.

Don't call or text me again.

The words sit there, taunting me.

Cold. Final.

This doesn't sound like the man who looked at me like I hung the moon. The man who said he wanted everything with me. This isn't him. It can't be.

I call him again. Voicemail.

Again. Voicemail.

Again. Again.

Still voicemail.

A broken sob tears from my throat, and I drop my head to my knees, phone still clutched in my shaking hand. Desperation claws at my chest as I open my messages again and type.

> Alex. Please tell me this is a mistake. Please call me. Please.

I hit send. Nothing. Not even a delivered status.

I try again. Nothing—like it's going into space.

Blocked.

The word slams against my skull, pounding out the only truth that matters now.

Alex Sebring

The man I love.

The man who told me I was his favorite.

The man who called me his American beauty.

The man who kissed me like he never wanted to stop.

Dumped me by text.

And blocked me.

My heart doesn't just ache—it shatters. Piece by piece, crack by jagged crack, until all that's left is a hollow shell and the unbearable weight of disbelief.

I press my fists to my temples, trying to hold myself together, but it's too late. Everything is breaking. I open my mouth to scream, but nothing comes out. Just the broken sound of air slipping past the knot in my throat.

No. This can't be how it ends. He doesn't even know I'm coming back. He ended us without even knowing that I'm on my way to him.

The cruelty of it stings sharper than anything I've ever known. No one—*no one*—has ever hurt me like this. Not even Robin.

I reach for my phone again, but my fingers slip, and it tumbles to the hardwood with a sharp clack. I stare at it for a beat, chest heaving, then lunge for it and hit the first name my brain can conjure through the fog.

It rings once. Twice.

Violet picks up, her voice bright and loud. "Well? What did lover boy say? Should I start writing my maid-of-honor speech now?"

Her words slice straight through me—and it's my undoing. I crumple to pieces. The sobs come fast and brutal, loud and gasping and broken.

"Magnolia!? What's wrong?"

My attempts to speak are nothing more than uncontrolled sobbing.

"I'm coming, Mags. Give me fifteen minutes, and I'll be there."

The call ends, but I stay right there on the floor, phone in hand, pain choking every breath. I rock back against the wall, curling into myself like I can block it all out.

Fifteen minutes stretch like hours. When the door bursts open, Violet comes in like a storm—ready to fight, to fix, to do whatever is needed. But when she sees me, her whole body softens.

She drops to her knees beside me. "Magnolia—"

"Vi." It's all I can say before the next wave crashes over me, and I fall into her arms.

She holds me like she's trying to squeeze the pieces back together. Her fingers stroke my hair, and I cling to her like I'm drowning.

"I don't understand what happened."

She rocks me like a mother holding her child. "It's okay. We'll figure this out."

But how do you figure out someone vanishing from your life in a single text?

I reach for my phone with unsteady hands and give it to her. I can't look again or say the words.

She reads for a moment and her whole body stiffens. "What. The. Fuck."

I bury my face in my hands, and sobs begin anew. "It makes no sense."

"I agree. It doesn't." Her voice is furious, sharp. "This isn't him. It can't be. Someone has his phone and they're punking you. But it's not funny."

No one has his phone.

No one is punking me.

I tell her everything—that my texts won't deliver, my calls go straight to voicemail. And when I voice my suspicion about him blocking me, she looks like she's ready to launch into orbit.

"This is wrong. So fucking wrong."

"I don't know what to do."

Violet takes my shoulders and locks eyes with me. "Yes, you do. You're calling his office right now."

I hesitate, my fingers curling into fists at my sides. I've never been the type to push myself onto anyone. It's survival—my way of protecting the parts of me that no one else bothered to. If I don't ask, if I don't reach, then I don't have to face the cold sting of rejection. I know this about myself. It's carved into my bones.

And calling him after this? After being blocked?

No.

Love is a loaded gun. Hope causes you to hand it over, placing it in his hands. His rejection is what pulls the trigger. And heartbreak is the bullet that never misses.

"I can't, Vi—"

"Fuck yes, you can. You deserve answers. He owes you that much."

My hands are shaking as I open my phone and scroll through my contacts. I don't want to do this. *Fuck*, I don't want to do this.

I land on the number for Alex's office and hesitate for a long moment before pressing the number.

The phone rings once. Twice.

"Thank you for calling Sebring Hotels Corporate Headquarters. This is Courtney. How may I help you today?" Her voice is calm. Familiar. Controlled.

The opposite of me right now.

I straighten, pressing the phone tighter to my ear. "Hi, Courtney? It's Magnolia. Can you please put me through to Alex?"

There's a pause, long enough to set every one of my nerves on edge. Her voice shifts to something colder, clipped, distant. "Mr. Sebring isn't taking your calls."

My stomach plummets. "I just need to speak with him for a moment."

"I'm sorry." She says the words, but there's no empathy in her voice. "Mr. Sebring has made it very clear. He doesn't want to talk to you."

The ground tilts beneath me, sending my world sideways.

"He was quite specific with his directions, Miss Steel. No calls. No messages. *No* exceptions." Each of her words is cold as ice.

I'm frozen in place, phone still pressed to my ear, when Violet lunges forward and takes it from me. "Listen up, Courtney." Her voice is sharp as a blade. "You put his ass on the phone right this fucking minute."

"I'm afraid that won't be possible."

Violet snaps. "Bull... shit...Courtney."

"I'm only following his instructions."

Violet takes a breath, ready to tear Courtney a new asshole, but the call ends before she can get a word in.

"Fuck you, Courtney!" Violet screams at my phone and then throws it on the couch like it's burned her. "What a bitch."

Violet mutters a string of curses under her breath, so tangled and furious, it sounds like she might be speaking in tongues.

"That motherfucker."

I'm quiet because I'm at a loss for words.

Alex broke my heart and threw up a wall between us so I couldn't reach out to him.

This isn't just heartbreak. It's erasure. He's deleted me from his life.

The silence that follows is endless, like the world has gone still just to watch me fall apart. I sit there, numb, staring at nothing as Violet paces in tight, angry circles in front of me, her hands clenched at her sides like she's holding back from throwing something—or flying to Sydney to wring someone's neck.

Every breath hurts. Every second drags across the raw edges of my heart. I don't know how to process any of it. Not the breakup text. Not the calls going straight to voicemail. And especially not Courtney's voice, calm and detached, telling me that Alex doesn't want to hear from me ever again.

I gave him everything.

My love.

My trust.

My body.

My future.

I wasn't ready to say yes to forever, but I loved him enough to try. I wanted to. And he turned me away like I was disposable.

Something sharp and ugly twists in my chest, and it breaks through the fog—rage, heartbreak, shame. All of it hits me at once like a scream that never makes it out.

Violet pauses mid-step. "Mags?"

I look up at her, hollow but steady. "If he's done with me, *I'm* done with him."

Her brows draw together. "What are you doing?"

I unlock my phone and scroll to his contact, the name ***Alex Sebring*** burning on the screen like a brand I can't scrub off. My thumb hovers for only a second before I press Block Caller. The confirmation to block contact pops up.

Final. Absolute.

I confirm.

Violet gasps. "Are you sure you want to do that?"

"Abso-fucking-lutely."

I set the phone down, like the act of not throwing it is the only thing keeping me from unraveling. "He told me not to call. Not to text. So I won't."

"He's not thinking straight. You know this isn't him."

"It doesn't matter. He cut off communication. That's all I need to know."

She crouches in front of me, searching my face like she's trying to see if there's anything left behind my eyes. But there's not. Not right now. I'm empty. Gutted.

This is a breakup, but it's also more.

Abandonment. Being forgotten.

My life story.

The girl I used to be—the one who wanted to be wanted, who clung to love even when it was slipping through her fingers—doesn't exist anymore.

I can't be her again. I won't. It hurts too much.

So I swallow the scream lodged in my throat, sit up a little straighter, and force the tears back down.

He doesn't want my love? Fine. He won't have it again. Even if it kills me to let him go.

Violet says nothing. She just sits beside me and slips her hand into mine. And together, we sit in the quiet wreckage of what I thought was my forever.

Love has done me dirty.

Chapter 8

Alex Sebring

THE ONLY THING WORSE THAN DRIVING TO A JOB I HATE IS driving to a job I hate without the love of my life in the passenger seat beside me.

"Love" by Kyle McKearney hums low through the speakers. It's one of those songs that carries her in every note. Not because she played it. Not because it's her favorite. She doesn't even listen to this kind of music. But every time I hear this song, I see her. Feel her. Like the lyrics were written by a man who knows exactly what it's like to love someone the way I love Magnolia.

I pull into the Sebring Hotels corporate lot with the energy of a bloke stepping onto the rugby field with no heart left for the game. No adrenaline. No grit. Just going through the motions, when the only thing I want is to be on a different field entirely—one where she's waiting on the sidelines, cheering me on.

The sleek glass facade of the building reflects the morning sun like it's doing something impressive, but all it does is remind me how cold everything is without her sweet Southern twang in my ear.

I tried calling her when I got up and again on my way to work.

No answer. It's afternoon for her, so she's probably tied up with work. That's what I tell myself when my call goes to voicemail.

She's probably elbow-deep in pillows, fabric swatches, and furniture layouts. Solving on-set chaos like it's nothing—that's Magnolia. Focused. Brilliant. Turning blank spaces into something beautiful.

Her voice has become my favorite part of the morning. She says my voice does the same for her—even when it's already afternoon where she is. So when my call didn't go through, I left her a voice message.

Wish I could start every day hearing your voice. Fuck, I miss you. Love you, favorite.

Maybe she'll listen to it on her break, and it'll make her smile.

I enter the building, nodding to the lobby receptionist before heading upstairs. In my office, I drop my bag by the desk and shrug out of my jacket. The space is modern—polished hardwood, steel accents, and the faint scent of espresso drifting from the break room down the hall. I used to feel like an impostor in this world. Some days, I still do. But lately, the weight of it hasn't felt quite so suffocating.

Because love has a way of softening sharp edges.

A soft knock breaks through my thoughts. Courtney steps in, polished as always, a folder in hand. "Morning. Here's your rundown for the day—meeting with Wyndham-Hawthorne Strategy Group at eleven, an investor call at two, and your mother called twice. She said it wasn't urgent, which means it probably is."

She doesn't hand me a written agenda, just a verbal rundown like she's done since I took the reins my father held for so long.

Perhaps she thinks I'm not cut out for this job. If so, she's right. I'll never fill my father's shoes. His are too polished. Too tight. And to be frank, too small for my size fourteen feet.

"Thanks."

I pull out my phone again, thumb hovering over the screen. Still nothing from Magnolia. I place it on my desk and open my email.

Instant regret.

The inbox is a disaster. My jaw tics as I scroll through subject lines. Why do so many damn people feel the need to email me? Half of this shit could've been handled without looping me in.

Leilani's been out sick the past couple of days. I hate to say it, but I miss her loud mouth and relentless sarcasm. Without her, I'm drowning in this inbox, and it's clear how much I need her help to stay afloat.

I'm knee-deep in emails, scrolling through corporate jargon designed to confuse me. The unread count at the top of the screen climbs every time I blink, like it's mocking me. I flag one for later, delete another, but it's like bailing water from a sinking ship with a thimble. I'm falling behind. Like always.

I lean back in my chair with a groan, ready to give up for the third time this morning—when a soft baby coo drifts in from the hallway, followed by the lilt of a familiar voice and a quiet laugh.

My fingers freeze on the trackpad. I push away from the desk, curiosity piqued, and step into the hall.

Hallie—our sharpest marketing exec who is currently on maternity leave—stands by Courtney's desk with a baby carrier slung on one hip and a smirk on her face that says she's enjoying the chaos she's brought into the office.

"Well, look at you, Sebring. You've got that buried-under-spreadsheets-and-bad-coffee-look down to an art."

"That's because I am buried. If one more email starts with *per my last email,* I might combust."

She laughs, looking down as the baby lets out a soft gurgle. "Thought I'd bring Ruby in for a visit. She's been dying to see where the magic happens."

I raise a brow at the pink bundle nestled in the carrier. "Is this the little boss?"

"The one and only," she says, all pride. "Figured it was time she met the people who'll be funding her future tuition and expensive daycare."

I chuckle, stepping closer. "You sure she's ready for corporate life?"

"She's already better at delegation than half the team."

I nod toward the baby with a smirk. "How's Dean adjusting to dad-life?"

"He's learning how to do nappies without gagging, so that's a win." Her eyes crinkle with affection. "He's smitten. He carries her around like she's made of glass and won't put her down unless I make him."

I chuckle, glancing down at the baby, who's blinking up at the ceiling lights. "And you? Are you surviving the newborn chaos?"

"Barely. But I put on real clothes today, so that's a victory." She lifts Ruby out of the carrier and holds her out to me. "Want to hold her? She's in a good mood. No blowouts this morning."

My phone buzzes in my hand, and instinct kicks in—I check it, heart stuttering for a second, hoping it's Magnolia. But it's not. Just a calendar reminder. Disappointment prickles under my skin as I set the phone on the corner of Courtney's desk.

"Oh why not? I could use a win today."

Hallie places Ruby into my arms, and everything stills. Her tiny body curls against me, warm and weightless, and something tugs deep inside—a sharp, quiet ache. I won't let myself think about what it would be like to hold a baby with Magnolia's hazel eyes.

Hallie watches me for a beat, grinning. "Damn, Alex. You look good holding a baby."

I huff a quiet laugh. "Don't let my mother hear you say that. She'll start knitting booties and planning a christening."

"Malie may know something you don't," she says, winking.

I shake my head, still looking at the baby. She's so tiny and perfect, yet she possesses the power to make me melt inside.

Ruby makes a soft, sleepy sound as I cradle her, and a ridiculous warmth blooms in my chest.

I tell myself not to go there—not to let my brain fill in the blanks.

But the second Ruby shifts in my arms, soft and weightless, my thoughts drift anyway—Magnolia with a baby balanced on her hip, smiling at me like she's in love with the life we've created together.

I want nothing more than a life with that woman.

Hallie eases Ruby from my arms with practiced care, her smile softening as the baby nestles back against her chest. "Better take her back before she gets too cozy. Dean might get jealous if he finds out his daughter spent the morning snuggled up in another man's arms."

I chuckle, stepping aside as she slings the diaper bag over her shoulder. "Tell him I promise not to steal his girl."

Hallie disappears down the hall after a cheerful goodbye. I head back into my office, closing the door behind me. I sink into my chair, glancing at the monitor like it's my enemy.

Today's forty-seven unread emails stare back at me like a wall that I don't have the tools—or the patience—to climb. I scroll through a few subject lines, already feeling the beginnings of a headache pulse behind my eyes.

I hate this part of the job. Words blur together. Sentences tangle. Numbers shift out of order. It's not new—I've dealt with it my whole life—but that doesn't make it any less frustrating. The only thing worse than reading this shit is trying to understand it before I've had three coffees.

I click on the text-to-speech software I've started relying on more lately. The calm British voice kicks in, and I settle in, listening as it reads a vendor proposal aloud. The voice butchers a few words and I wince.

"...quarterly revenue margins reflect a strong anal uptick..."

I groan. "Nope. We are not doing strong anal upticks this quarter but thanks."

If Magnolia were here, she'd be cracking up right now—snorting into her coffee, already reaching for her phone to record me muttering curses at a confused robot.

I shake it off, push the chair back, and stand, trying to relieve the tension in my neck. But it's not simple tension. It's the heaviness that lingers when the one person who makes this bearable is so far away.

I glance at my desk hoping for a new message or missed call, but my phone's not there. I pat my pockets and scan my desk again.

"Courtney?" I call out, already heading for the door.

She has my phone in hand. "You left it on my desk."

I take it, nodding. "Thanks."

I close the door behind me and glance down at the screen, thumbing it unlocked.

Finally! Magnolia messaged me.

> I have good news! Call me the minute you get this text. 😘 💚

A slow smile pulls at the corner of my mouth. My chest eases, the tension I've been carrying since this morning loosening a little. She has good news. I bet she got confirmation on returning to Sydney.

Her next text is a long paragraph. I already know I'm not in the right headspace to wrestle through reading that many words on my own, so I tap the text-to-speech option, letting the robotic voice read it out for me.

But what I hear next steals the air from my lungs.

"Alex, I've had time to think things over, and I realize this long-distance thing isn't working. I've known for a while, but I didn't have the guts to tell you. I've met someone here in Charleston, and he makes me happy. He doesn't want commitment, and that's what I need right now. I want to be with him. This relationship is over. I wish you the best in finding the wife you want, but it isn't me. Don't contact me. This is over."

Silence falls.

My heart misses a beat. Then another.

I blink at the screen, my mind refusing to process what I just heard.

What?

I listen to the message again like I'll find a different meaning the second time around. But it doesn't change. It's still there. Cold. Final. Brutal.

My pulse hammers in my ears.

I scroll back up and read the first text again.

> I have good news! Call me the minute you
> get this text. 😔 🩶

Then this. What the hell kind of good news ends in that?

My breath stutters, my lungs forgetting how to function. A cold sweat breaks along my back, beading at my temples as my fingers twitch around the phone.

No. No, this isn't right.

Magnolia wouldn't do this. Not like this. Not after everything. Not without a call. Not through a bloody text.

But the message is still there, staring back at me, mocking everything I thought I knew.

My stomach twists, a sharp, gutting ache I can't ignore. My hands go numb. I sit frozen, eyes locked on the words, willing them to disappear. Willing this to be a joke. A mistake. Something.

Anything but what it looks like.

Because if it's not... if this is real... I've just lost the woman I love.

And I never even saw it coming.

The last line of her message hits like a gut punch. *Don't contact me. This is over.*

I'm still staring at the screen when the soft knock comes. I don't answer, but the door opens anyway.

"Alex? Quick question about the Oakridge Group contract."

I don't look up at Courtney. My brain can't process contracts or logistics or anything that doesn't involve figuring out how the hell Magnolia just slipped through my fingers.

"Not now." My voice comes out flat. Sharper: "Close the door on your way out."

Out of the corner of my eye, I catch the briefest flicker of her gaze dropping to my phone. She backs out without another word, the door clicking shut behind her.

I scroll back to the top of the screen, staring at the thread again.

> I have good news! Call me the minute you
> get this text. 🐥 🖤

And then, right below it, that cold, calculated exit. She sent the second text thirty minutes after the first—smiling, then stabbing. What the hell happened in between?

It doesn't track.

Her first message must've come through while I was visiting with Hallie and Ruby. I didn't see it. I didn't respond. Then I left my damn phone sitting on Courtney's desk like a careless idiot.

I press her name with shaking hands. The dial tone never even kicks in. Just a cold, sterile voice telling me she's unavailable.

Straight to voicemail.

I try again. And again.

Still nothing.

She blocked me?

Magnolia—my girl, my future, my fucking heart—blocked me like I'm some stranger she's trying to forget.

Only last night, we were on FaceTime before bed. She was curled up under her favorite throw, hair messy, eyes soft with sleep. We talked about how much we missed each other—how hard the distance was, how much we couldn't wait to close it. Just like always. She told me to dream about her. I said I already was.

I swipe back to our thread, fingers numb, and scroll. Just this morning, I left her a voice message—my usual good morning, I love you, can't wait to talk later. And now this?

This can't be happening.

But it is. And it steals the air right out of my lungs.

My vision blurs. I stumble toward the private bathroom tucked inside my office, the walls closing in with every step. My hand wraps around the handle before I shove the door open and close it behind me, the soft click of the lock sounding deafening in the silence.

I lurch toward the sink, gripping the edges so tight my knuckles go white. My reflection stares back at me—haunted eyes, pale skin, chest rising and falling like I've run a bloody marathon. I don't recognize myself.

I turn on the tap and splash cold water over my face, but it doesn't help. Nothing helps. The pressure in my chest keeps building, a hot, aching weight that settles behind my ribs like a ticking bomb.

And then I crack.

I double over with a sound I didn't even know I could make—half-growl, half-sob—as my knees hit the cold tile. I fold forward, elbows braced against my thighs, fingers tugging at my hair.

What the fuck just happened?

I've met someone here in Charleston, and he makes me happy. He doesn't want commitment, and that's what I need right now. I want to be with him.

It doesn't add up. None of it does.

My heart slams against my chest, loud and frantic. My stomach lurches. I barely make it to the toilet before I'm sick.

I stay there, hunched and shaking, long after the nausea fades. The silence wraps around me like a straitjacket, pressing in, stealing what little breath I have left.

I am not okay.

I don't think I've ever been this kind of not okay before.

When I crawl back to my feet, I rinse out my mouth and lean against the counter, water dripping from my chin.

I make it back into the office somehow, each step heavier than the last. I drop into my chair, hands trembling as I lift my phone again.

Her contact photo blinks back at me—Magnolia in that straw hat from the day we spent at Bondi, windblown and laughing, cheeks flushed with sun and happiness.

My thumb hovers over the screen, like it might bring her back. Like I can hold on to her just a little longer.

But she's gone.

And I don't know how to breathe without her.

Chapter 9

Magnolia Steel

VIOLET STAYED THE NIGHT. SHE MADE ME DRINK TOO MUCH wine, ordered greasy takeout we barely touched, and didn't let me cry alone. I woke up to the sound of her snoring on my couch, with her makeup smudged and her arm draped over her eyes as though she's shielding herself from the weight of my heartbreak.

Or a hangover.

But she was there. She stayed. And somehow, that matters more than anything else.

But now?

Now I'm driving to work with a head full of fog and a heart ripped in two.

The drive is a blur—stoplights and street signs bleeding together in streaks of red and green. My hands clutch the steering wheel with a desperation, knuckles stiff with nails biting into my palms as if I grip hard enough, I can hold the pieces of myself together.

I should've called in sick. Taken the day. Hell, maybe the week. But I couldn't spend another second in that apartment, surrounded by silence and the echo of a future I'd started building around a man who doesn't want me.

I didn't even mean enough for him to end things via FaceTime. He only considered me worthy of a few distant lines on a screen— clinical, detached, as if I never mattered at all.

The words loop in my head on repeat. I've never hated a sentence so much in my life. I've never hurt like this.

I pull into the Soul Sync parking lot. The engine hums beneath me, and the morning sun blares against the windshield like some smug bastard, too bright, too cheerful. I release a shaky breath and drag trembling fingers through my hair.

I glance into the rearview mirror. My eyes are swollen, my smile is a lie, but it's all I have left to give.

You're fine.

You look like hell, but you're fine.

You have to be.

Squaring my shoulders, I reach for the door handle. Time to walk into work and pretend my world didn't just fall apart.

People smile and greet me as I pass, but their voices sound distant, like echoes from another world. The usual morning buzz— phones ringing, keyboards clacking, casual laughter—blurs against the pounding in my ears. Every step toward my office drags heavier than the last. By the time I close the door behind me, the walls feel too tight, the air too thin, and exhaustion seeps deep into my bones.

I sink into my chair, dropping my bag onto the floor beside me, and stare at my desk. It's covered in neat stacks of design proposals and client portfolios—proof that life moves on, with or without me.

A soft knock interrupts my downward spiral, and I glance up as Violet slips inside, holding a cup from my favorite coffee shop. Her expression is gentle, her eyes full of kind understanding only your closest friend can offer.

"Morning," she says, placing the cup on my desk. "I figured you could use this."

The familiar scent of caramel and espresso drifts up, but instead of comfort, it only makes my stomach roll. "Thanks, Vi, but I'm not sure I can keep anything down."

She sits in the chair across from me. "I'm sorry, Mags."

A fresh wave of pain crashes over me, and I blink, fighting back the tears threatening to spill. "I can't talk about him anymore."

Before she can respond, my office door opens with a quiet click, and Elijah steps inside like he belongs here. His gaze sweeps over me, slow and assessing.

"You look... tired." He steps closer, too close, as if he's testing how much I'll tolerate today. "Rough morning?"

Violet straightens in her seat, throwing him a warning glance, but Elijah doesn't acknowledge her.

I sit up straighter. "It hasn't been a great morning."

He moves around my desk and perches on the edge. "I worry about you, Mags. You push yourself too hard. You always do."

I clench my jaw, my patience wearing thin. "I'm fine."

Disappointment flashes across his face. "I'm trying to look out for you. I hate seeing you this way."

Violet clears her throat, her tone sharper than usual. "She said she's fine, Elijah."

"Sure." He pushes off my desk and stands. "I'll be around if you need anything. You know where to find me."

Violet gets up and shuts the door he left open. "Forget Elijah. Forget everything else for now. Let yourself feel this. You don't have to be strong all the time."

I nod, staring down at the untouched cup on my desk. "Thanks, Vi. For always being here."

She reaches for my hand and squeezes. "Always. And I mean that. If you need to fall apart, I'll be right here to help you put yourself back together."

"It may come to that."

"I've got a broom, duct tape and Gorilla Glue ready to go."

"You're the best, Vi."

"I know."

She leaves, and I let my head fall into my hands, wondering how much longer I can hold myself together before I break apart.

The morning drags on in a blur of unanswered emails and half-finished sketches, my brain refusing to focus on anything but the text burning a hole in my phone screen.

Don't call or text me again. That would only make this worse. This relationship is over.

I've read it so many times I can see the words even when I close my eyes, looping through my mind like a broken record I can't turn off.

I stare down at the mood board glowing on my tablet, the layout of fabrics, color swatches, and furniture samples blurring together into an uninspired mess. I've rearranged them at least a dozen times, but nothing clicks. Every combination is wrong—disjointed and lifeless.

My work, the thing that has always grounded me, is foreign today. Like I'm grasping at something that just isn't there. I set the tablet aside, rubbing at the ache forming between my brows.

A shaky breath escapes me, and I blink hard against the sting in my eyes.

I don't understand. I just don't. We were fine. Weren't we?

I squeeze my phone so tightly it's a wonder it doesn't crack.

What did I do wrong?

The logical part of my brain tells me that obsessing over this won't fix anything. But logic and heartbreak don't go hand in hand.

I flip my phone over on the desk, pushing it away as though that will somehow stop me from reaching for it again. I need to focus, to work, to do something productive.

Instead, I sit there, staring at nothing, my heart aching in ways I don't even have words for.

Gabby's voice cuts through the hum of my thoughts, making me jump. "Magnolia, can you step into my office for a moment?"

My stomach twists. This is it—Gabby's going to tell me I'm heading back to Sydney. And I should be thrilled. It's what I wanted. What *we* wanted. But now? Now I don't know what to feel. How can I go back to the city where he is and not see him? And worse... what if

I do see him? What would I say? What would I do? My heart's still in pieces, and the idea of pretending I'm fine in the same city as Alex Sebring seems impossible. But how do I decline after being so adamant about going without telling Gabby why? I'm not sure which version of this will break me more.

I force a nod and push myself up from my desk, hands trembling. The walk to Gabby's office seems longer than usual, my heels clicking against the tile floor in a steady rhythm.

She's already seated when I step inside, her expression unreadable as she gestures for me to close the door. I do, my pulse drumming in my ears.

Gabby folds her hands atop her desk. "Take a seat."

I lower myself into the chair across from her, every muscle in my body coiled tight.

She exhales, a beat of hesitation before she slides her tablet across the desk. "I received an email this morning. A complaint."

The words hit me like a slap. I blink, my mouth suddenly dry. "A complaint? Is someone unhappy with their suite? I can fix whatever it is."

Gabby shakes her head. "It's not about your work, Magnolia."

Something in her tone makes my heart stop.

She straightens, and her expression sends an icy chill racing down my spine. "It's about you. Someone reported you for fraternizing with a Soul Sync client."

The world tilts under me. Blood drains from my face so fast I become lightheaded. My lips part, but nothing comes out.

Fraternizing. The word is a grenade, ready to blow my entire career to pieces. Because I did far more than fraternize.

I fell in love.

My mind spins, latching on to every worst-case scenario imaginable. What has Gabby been told?

I swallow hard, forcing my voice to stay steady. "What does the complaint say?"

Gabby taps the screen of her tablet, her eyes scanning the text before meeting mine. "It states that you engaged in an inappropriate personal relationship with a Soul Sync client while you were in Sydney."

Shit.

The air leaves my lungs in a sharp exhale. My fingers tighten around the armrests of the chair, nails digging in.

"You're quiet. Is there anything you want to say before I go any further?"

My stomach twists into knots, dread curling in my chest. "What am I being accused of?"

Gabby's eyes search mine for a moment before she taps her tablet, pulling up the email. Her expression hardens as she reads.

"To Whom It May Concern. I am writing to report a serious violation of Soul Sync's policies regarding client relations. Magnolia Steel, during her assignment in Sydney, engaged in an inappropriate romantic and sexual relationship with a client—Alex Sebring. This behavior compromised the integrity of Soul Sync's services and created a severe conflict of interest, undermining the professionalism expected from your staff. It is in the best interest of Soul Sync that this breach of trust is addressed to protect the company's reputation and uphold the standards you pride yourselves on. Respectfully. A Concerned Party."

My entire body goes numb, the words slamming into me with a force that leaves me breathless.

She knows.

She knows everything.

My hands grip the armrests, the room tilting as I struggle to form a coherent thought.

Gabby lowers the tablet, her expression unreadable. "Magnolia?"

There's no point in denying it. Lying would only make this worse.

I force myself to meet her gaze, my voice barely steady. "It's true. All of it."

Gabby's expression hardens. "Tell me what happened. I need to hear the facts from you."

I take a slow, steady breath, my fingers twisting in my lap. "I never meant for it to happen. Alex—Mr. Sebring—he asked to speak with me in his dating suite. He wanted to practice his conversation before his date."

Gabby arches a brow. "That's not part of our services."

A sad smile tugs at my lips. "True, but it seemed harmless at the time."

I square my shoulders, wanting to defend myself. "You asked us to take on new roles, Gabby. You wanted us to be flexible, to put our clients at ease. I thought I was doing my job by fulfilling his request."

"Helping a client be comfortable and dating him are two different things."

"I wasn't dating him... at least not at first. I was helping him as he requested. And then he asked me to meet outside the suites. I didn't think it would turn into anything."

"He asked you to meet up?"

Well, I supposed that's not exactly how it happened. "He told me where he was going to be that night."

"And you took it upon yourself to go?"

It sounds so much worst when she puts it like that. "I perceived it as an invitation."

Her lips press together in a thin line, disappointment flickering across her face. "It sounds like you pursued him."

I don't have a legitimate argument for that.

Gabby sighs, setting her tablet down on the desk with a soft thud. "Do you have any idea what kind of mess this has created for Soul Sync? This isn't just about you and him." Her tone is sharp, but beneath it, I hear something worse—disappointment.

I already understand where this is going, but I stay quiet, bracing myself.

"There's a client who paid for a match that she didn't receive." She levels me with a pointed stare. "You realize that, right? This isn't just about your personal choices. It's about how they affect the business and clients."

Alex paid Celeste off with an obscene amount of money to stay quiet. So how is this blowing back on me?

"I never meant for any of this to happen. I didn't think—"

"No, Magnolia. You didn't think at all." She tosses the printed complaint onto my desk, the paper skidding to a stop in front of me. "We aren't certain if the person who sent this complaint will make it public."

Gabby leans back in her chair, the disappointment etched into every line of her face. "I never expected this from you. You were one of my best employees."

Were. The past tense slices through me like a blade, sharp and unforgiving.

I think I'm in serious trouble. "I put the company in a difficult position, and I'm so sorry."

Gabby sighs, rubbing her temple. "You broke the code of conduct and put the company's reputation at risk."

I stare down at my hands, unease coiling in my gut—not for what I did, but for how it all ended.

Alex isn't just any client. He is the man I fell in love with before I realized it was happening. The man I risked everything for.

I meet Gabby's eyes, bracing for whatever comes next. "It's over."

Gabby's expression softens for just a moment before the steel returns. "That doesn't change the fact that you violated company policy, and now we're dealing with the fallout."

I nod, swallowing hard. "I'm so sorry."

Gabby exhales a long breath, folding her hands on the desk. "I have no choice. Your employment with Soul Sync is terminated, effective immediately."

The words hit like a physical blow, knocking the air from my lungs.

"What?" My voice comes out small, shaky, like I can't quite believe what I'm hearing.

Gabby's expression softens, but her tone remains firm. "I'm sorry, but there's no way around this."

Another shock. Another piece of my life slipping through my fingers. The walls close in, and my chest tightens with panic. My job —over. Alex—gone. Everything I built, everything I thought I could count on, crumbling in front of me.

"There has to be another way. Reprimand me, Gabby, but please don't fire me."

"There's no coming back from this." Gabby shakes her head, her lips pressing into a thin line. "Security will escort you out now."

Security. Like I'm a criminal. The ultimate humiliation.

I nod even though I'm falling apart right here in this chair. "My things?"

"We'll box them up and send them to you."

I blink, my vision blurring. Just like that. Over six years with this company and I'm walking out of here with nothing. Not even my dignity.

The walk back to my office feels like a walk of shame. Security follows close behind, their presence a reminder that this is real—I'm being escorted out of the building like I'm a danger.

I grab my purse from my desk, my fingers trembling as I clutch it to my chest.

This isn't happening. It can't be happening.

But it is.

Stepping into the hallway, I catch sight of Violet emerging from her office. Her gaze finds me and flicks to the two security guards trailing at my heels. Her eyes widen, confusion flashing across her face. "Magnolia? What's going on?"

I shake my head. "Not now." My voice barely holds together. "We'll talk later."

Her brows knit, panic flickering in her eyes. "Later? No, we'll talk now. Why are they—"

They're watching. All of them. And they know Violet and I are best friends. If they suspect she was aware of my relationship with a client and didn't report it, she could be next.

"Please," I say, cutting her off. "Just go back to work."

Violet's mouth opens, but no words come out. She looks at me like she's searching for some explanation that will make this make sense. But there isn't one. Not one I can give her, not here.

Movement in my peripheral vision catches my attention—coworkers gathering to see what's happening, their curious stares slicing through me like a thousand tiny cuts. I can hear the whispers already. They don't even try to hide them.

She's being escorted out.

Wonder what she did.

Didn't see that coming.

She's always been Gabby's pet.

Shame burns through me, hotter than the grief that's been eating me alive. I lift my chin, refusing to let them see me break. Not here. Not now.

But inside, I'm crumbling. My entire life—my job, my relationship, my future—has fallen apart in a few days, and the one person I want to turn to isn't an option anymore.

Tears prick my eyes, but I force them down. I'll cry later. Right now, I have to make it out of this building with whatever shred of dignity I have left.

The security guard clears his throat. "Miss Steel."

I nod, swallowing hard, and let them lead me away, leaving everything behind.

Chapter 10

Alex Sebring

I can't breathe without her.

Chapter 11

Magnolia Steel

I'm not even sure what day it is anymore.

Chapter 12

Alex Sebring

THE HOUSE IS DARK. STILL. THE KIND OF CALM THAT suffocates, a quiet that makes you question if you're the only broken person in a world that stopped spinning.

I tried going to sleep earlier, but Magnolia's side of the bed still smells like her—cherry blossoms and vanilla.

I love it.

But I also fucking hate it.

I couldn't stand being in the bedroom anymore so I'm here on the couch, feet propped on the coffee table, head leaned back against the cushions. The TV and lights are off. Hours have passed since I moved.

My phone rests on my stomach, the screen black. I tap it once, thumb hesitating, but I open the music app.

She used to play music in my house all the time. Said it helped clear her head because silence made her overthink—and she was already too good at that without help.

I could never recall the song titles, but I remember the sound... and the way her bare feet padded across my floors. The way her voice hummed along under her breath when she wasn't singing off-key.

I remember how I felt when she was here, how the music softened the edges of the world. And softened my edges as well.

My phone is still logged into her account. I never signed out because I couldn't bring myself to. It made us too... *over*. Like closing the last door between us.

I scroll, finding her favorite playlist. The one I listened to countless times because she played the thing nonstop.

I'm about to tap it, needing to hear something familiar, when another playlist jumps out at me. My heart stumbles.

Missing Big Guy. Created one week ago—a full fortnight after she told me she met someone else, was moving on, and I should do the same.

I stare at the list, blinking hard, as though I could be imagining things. But there it is in her account—a whole list of songs dedicated to the playlist *Missing Big Guy.*

I hit play. The first few notes of song one drift through the room, soft and slow. It's too much... and still not enough.

I close my eyes, let it wrap around me. Her playlist. Her pain. Because if this is about me, she's not okay either.

I'm not sure what this means. But it isn't random.

And there's one person who might help me make sense of it.

She's always had a sixth sense about people—especially Magnolia. She recognized the shift between us before we understood what was happening. If anyone can hear past the noise and help me find the truth buried in this music, it's Laurelyn.

Before I can talk myself out of it, I grab my keys. I don't bother changing clothes or fixing my hair. I just drive, the weight of the music still sitting in my chest like an anchor.

By the time I reach the McLachlan house, the sun is dipping low behind the trees, casting the vineyard in a rich amber glow. I spot Jack stepping off the ATV, his boots thick with dirt, khaki work pants creased and stained from a long day tending his grapes. His button-down hangs loose, sleeves rolled to his elbows, dust smudging the fabric. He yanks off his wide-brimmed hat, revealing hair flattened and crimped from sweat.

He wipes a hand down his shirt before clocking me. "This is an unexpected surprise. Everything all right?"

I nod even though it's a lie. "Yeah. I've come to see Laurelyn. I have questions for her."

His laid-back tone shifts into something quieter. "You okay, mate?"

"Nothing's wrong. I just I need her take on something. Woman stuff, I guess you'd say."

"You mean *Magnolia stuff.*" There's no judgment. Just understanding.

"Am I that easy to read?"

He jerks his head toward the side of the house. "You've come to the right place. L's working in the studio."

I follow him around back, gravel crunching beneath our feet.

The McLachlan studio glows in the soft afternoon light—floor-to-ceiling windows spilling sunshine across a baby grand, instruments lining the walls like sacred artifacts. Laurelyn sits at the piano, her fingers dancing through something delicate and slow. She looks up at the sound of the door and smiles. "Hey you. I'm glad to see you crawled out of your hermit hole."

I lift a hand in a half-hearted wave. "Only because I need a favor. You're going to laugh at me about this, both of you, probably Jack more than you."

Her brow quirks, amused but curious. "Color me intrigued."

Jack goes to the fridge of the kitchenette and grabs two beers. He cracks one open and holds out the second.

"Thanks."

He nods and drops onto the leather sectional, one arm slung over the back, taking a big chug of beer.

I cross the room and hand Laurelyn my phone. "I'm pretty sure this qualifies me as a lovesick teenage girl."

Laurelyn studies my phone. "What am I looking at?"

"Magnolia's music collection. I'm still logged into her account."

Her eyes skim the lists. "*Missing Big Guy?*"

"She created it a week ago. Two weeks after the breakup text."

"I assume you're big guy?"

"Yeah, that's what she always called me."

A pair of creases forms between Laurelyn's eyes. "This isn't the playlist of a woman who's moved on."

My stomach knots. "You're sure?"

She glances up at me like I've asked if the sky was blue. "This is heartbreak in the form of music. She's grieving and missing someone she didn't want to lose."

Jack shifts forward on the sectional, setting his beer on the coffee table with a quiet thunk. "But you said she blocked you, right?"

"Yeah. She sent me a message saying she'd met someone new, and we were done. Didn't want commitment. Told me not to contact her again."

Jack whistles low. "That's a hell of a shift—from what you had to what she texted."

"None of it makes sense."

Laurelyn shakes her head as she continues looking at my phone. "I'm not sure what happened. All I know is that Magnolia is in love with you. I'm certain. I saw it, and so did Jack Henry. You can't fake that kind of emotion or the look on her face when she was with you."

"She must've changed her mind. It happens."

"Not when it's real," Laurelyn says.

"If we'd known this was going to end with so much pain, Laurelyn and I wouldn't have encouraged you. We hoped that you'd find love the way we did."

"You had no way of knowing that our relationship would go sideways." And even if I had known, I still would've chosen to spend those three months with her.

Laurelyn reaches for her phone on the piano. "She may have blocked you, but she hasn't blocked me. I could call her for you."

It would be so easy to say yes.

One call.

One conversation.

One chance at clarity.

But I shake my head. "No. Don't."

"Alex—"

"She told me to not contact her because we were over. There's no point in calling her."

Laurelyn's thumb hovers over Magnolia's number. "This isn't how someone acts when they're done."

She stares at the phone cradled in her hand, and her eyes flick up at me. "You're still logged in, right? Can you make playlists?"

I shrug. "I don't know. I guess"

"You should make one about her on her account. Give it a name she'll notice."

Jack grins. "Babe, that's kind of brilliant."

Laurelyn nods. "Hopefully, she'll see it and know it's from you. Maybe she'll understand."

"Seems kind of pathetic. Do you think it'll work?"

"Only one way to find out," Laurelyn says. "And you might communicate with her through music."

This isn't really my kind of thing. "What would I name it?"

"Something from your heart." Laurelyn hands me my phone. "Just give it some thought. It'll come to you."

I nod. "I appreciate everything the two of you have done for me."

Laurelyn smiles. "We're still pulling for you two. We haven't given up hope."

Hope is foolish. That's what I keep telling myself. It's just another kind of heartbreak waiting to happen. A softer edge to the same blade. You think it'll save you, carry you, pull you from the wreckage—but most of the time, it just delays the fall.

And yet... it's still there in my heart.

Quiet. Stubborn. Curling around the edges of my chest.

What if she's hurting too?

I don't have proof. Don't have a plan. But I'm not ready to let go. Not yet.

I play Magnolia's playlist again on the drive home, the one titled *Missing Big Guy*. I turn the volume up and let it fill the quiet spaces. Every song feels like a letter I never got. Like she's speaking to me through the lyrics she chose.

I don't know what she's saying with these songs, but I want to understand it.

Before I go to bed, I open her account again.

I don't have a name for the playlist yet. But I'll come up with one. Because if this is the only way I can talk to her... I'm going to say everything I need to say.

Chapter 13

Alex Sebring

I tap through her music account, thumbing a new playlist into existence. It feels stupid and sappy and also like the most important thing I'll ever do. I don't overthink the songs. I just pick the ones that remind me of her: slow, aching ballads; rough-edged rock; even the country tracks she claimed to hate but tapped her fingers to... or shimmied her hips in beat with when she thought I wasn't looking.

When it comes time to name it, I hesitate. This isn't just some random playlist. It's a message. A lifeline. A reminder that wherever she is, I'm still here, still hers, still waiting.

I type the title—*You Are My Everything, Magnolia*—and hit save before I can second-guess it.

Not the most creative, not the most polished. But it's the truth.

Maybe it'll find its way to her heart, the way she's carved herself into mine.

Maybe she'll see it and know.

And if she doesn't?

Well, my heart's already breaking without her.

What's a little more honesty about the wreckage?

Chapter 14

Alex Sebring

MAGNOLIA'S ABSENCE SCREAMS AT ME IN THE THINGS SHE LEFT behind—the pair of unwashed knickers I found in the laundry basket… the half-used strawberry lip balm she'd apply at bedtime… the box of tampons under the sink.

I can't bring myself to throw them out. It's pathetic, I'm well aware. But every time I carry them to the bin, I freeze. Like chucking her cotton rockets means admitting she's never coming back.

So yeah. The tampons stay.

It's been four weeks since Magnolia ended things. Two weeks since I created that playlist for her and got no response. A month since I've functioned like a real person.

I am nothing but a lovesick fool.

My phone buzzes. It's Tinā again, but I don't answer. My family, Jack, Laurelyn—they all mean well. They've all been calling and texting to check on me. And I've ignored every damn one of them.

I don't have the energy to pretend that I'm okay and everything is going to be all right.

Last night, I tried reading Magnolia's journal—the one filled with all her private thoughts from her time in Sydney. Pages of messy loops and coffee stains and pieces of her I thought I knew.

I only read two entries before I had to stop. Not because it was too much work. But because it wrecked me.

He makes me feel so safe. So wanted. I've met no one like Alex. I didn't think I could fall this deeply in love with anyone. But with him, it was inevitable.

She loved me.

With her whole heart.

And then the wind shifted, and she didn't anymore.

A faint beep cuts through the silence—sharp, familiar. The kind that comes from the back door when someone punches in the code.

I don't move. Because I already know who it is. No one else uses the keypad. No one else walks into my home like they own the place.

Only one person doesn't need an invitation.

Tinā.

Her footsteps move through the house with a calm authority, the kind that comes from raising six kids and running a home like a quiet empire. She doesn't call out for me. Doesn't ask permission. She knows where I'll be.

It's late morning, I think, but the blinds are still closed. And I haven't bothered to check the time.

There's a quiet knock, and the door creaks open. She pauses in the doorway, taking me in without a word. I can imagine what she sees. The blankets tangled around my waist. The stubble that's moved past rugged into something closer to despair. My body too still. My spirit gone quiet.

"Oh, Aleki."

I shift my gaze toward her, and the second our eyes meet, I see it in the soft furrow of her brow, in the way her mouth tightens like she's trying not to cry. Heartbreak. Not the loud kind. The quiet, aching kind that mothers carry when they're watching their child slip into something they can't fix with a kiss to the forehead and a warm plate of food.

"You missed Sunday with the family. Again. And church. Four weeks in a row, Aleki."

I shift, pulling the pillow higher beneath my head. "I'm going through a lot right now."

She comes into the room and sits on the side of the bed. "I called you three times yesterday."

Talking is the last thing I want to do. "I texted to let you know I was okay."

Her fingers fold in her lap, tight. "And the day before that? When Jack texted? Or when Sefina found out she landed her dream job and we all gathered at the house to celebrate?"

I glance away. "I'm happy for her."

She hums low in her throat. "You didn't even reply, Aleki."

"I need space right now."

"You've always pulled away when you're in pain. You lock the doors and pretend you're fine when, in truth, you're crumbling."

I blink up at the ceiling, not sure what to say. Because she isn't wrong.

"You've always carried things deeper than your siblings. You hold on longer. Feel it harder. It's your greatest strength—and your greatest burden."

I swallow the lump in my throat, turning my face into the pillow. Her hand comes to rest on my shoulder, fingers warm, grounding.

"I know what heartbreak looks like. I know what grief sounds like. But this is more than that."

I don't respond.

"Aleki."

My throat tightens.

"Are you thinking about hurting yourself?"

Her words land like a stone in my chest. I hate that she's filled with a fear like that.

"No, but I'm tired of hurting like this. It's too much."

Relief flashes in her eyes, and she reaches over, brushing a hand over my hair like she did when I was a boy. "Okay. That's what I needed to hear."

Her hand falls away. "Now, get up. Take a shower. I'm going to make you something to eat. You may not be ready yet, but you still have to show up for yourself."

She doesn't wait for a response. Just leaves the room with the same steadiness she entered, footsteps fading down the hall, leaving behind coconut-scented lotion and the echo of her strength.

I stare at the doorway long after she's gone.

Show up for myself—easier said than done.

But I owe her that. And perhaps I owe it to Magnolia too. The man she fell in love with wouldn't rot in bed. He wouldn't disappear into silence and dust.

A few minutes pass, and I swing my legs over the edge of the bed, bare feet hitting cold floorboards. The effort is monumental, but I do it.

For my tinā.

For the tiny flicker inside me that hasn't gone out.

I shower, standing under the hot spray until my skin turns red and my lungs stop tightening with every breath. I trim my beard, towel off, put on some clean clothes.

Tinā doesn't say a word when I come into the kitchen. She gestures to the chair and sets a plate in front of me like it's any other morning. But this is not my usual breakfast.

It's panikeke, warm and golden, still fragrant with coconut oil. A heap of oka sits beside it along with fried eggs, sauteed taro leaves, and thick wedges of papaya. A traditional Samoan breakfast. The kind that feeds more than your body.

There's no way any of this came from my fridge. I haven't bought groceries in weeks. She had to have brought everything with her.

That's who she is. A woman who shows up. Who feeds you when

you're too broken to ask. Who reminds you where you come from when you've forgotten how to stand.

As I pick at the food, she moves around the kitchen like it's hers. Clearing empty cups from the counter. Wiping down surfaces that don't need wiping. Refilling the fruit bowl, straightening the salt and pepper shakers like symmetry might fix what's broken in me.

Tinā says nothing. Doesn't push. She moves with purpose—a quiet, steady love disguised as tidying up. It's a love you don't earn but shows up anyway.

I watch her for a second, then look back down at my plate. And somehow, keep eating.

"I've been trying to make sense of it," I say, voice rough from disuse.

Tinā pauses mid-wipe, her hand resting on the countertop. "Make sense of what?"

"There's something I want you to read."

It's right where I left it—a small, leather-bound journal with soft, worn edges and Magnolia's handwriting etched on the inside cover. My chest tightens the moment I touch it. I carry it back into the kitchen like it might shatter if I hold it too tight.

I place the journal in her hands, swallowing hard. "Magnolia gave it to me the morning she left Sydney. She said her heart was in it, the parts she couldn't speak out loud."

Tinā takes it, reverent in the way only mothers can be when handling someone's pain.

"She wrote about falling in love with me. About how much I meant to her."

Tinā opens the journal, flipping through the first few pages in silence. She pauses on a page, her eyes scanning a passage. Then she clears her throat and reads aloud.

"*Sometimes I look at him and forget how to breathe. I didn't expect this. I didn't want to fall for anyone. But he makes me feel seen. And safe. And wanted. It's startling how fast I've become his.*"

She pauses again, glancing up at me, but I can't meet her eyes.

Her voice softens as she reads the next line.

"He doesn't even realize how much he's healing me just by letting me in. I don't know how to explain it—but when he looks at me, I feel like maybe I'm not so broken after all."

"I don't get it. How do you go from that to deleting someone from your life like they were nothing?"

Tinā closes the journal, resting her hand on top of it. "You don't write words like those unless you mean them. And people don't lie in ink, Aleki. Her affections for you were real."

"But if it was real—" I stop, tired of asking the same question over and over.

"How do I still love her this much after everything?"

She looks at me like she's seeing right through to the boy I used to be. Then she reaches across the table, her hand covering mine.

"Because when you love someone the way you loved her, it doesn't vanish. Not just because they're gone. That kind of love doesn't disappear, Aleki. It stays. And it changes you."

Her words gut me. But somehow, they also hold me together.

"You need fresh air. Not this grief-soaked Sydney silence you've been sitting in. You need grounding and family and to breathe where the world isn't so heavy."

I glance up, already knowing where this is going.

"Go home to Samoa, Aleki. Let the sea cleanse your hurt and your roots remind you of who you've always been."

I blink hard. "And then what?"

She doesn't hesitate. "Remember who the hell you are."

Chapter 15

Magnolia Steel

THE BLINDS ARE CLOSED, AND THE TV CASTS A DULL GLOW across my living room. I'm buried beneath a mountain of blankets that haven't seen a wash cycle in weeks.

I couldn't tell you when I last stepped into daylight. Sometimes the rays sneak through the cracks in the blinds—too happy, too bright —like they can't understand that I want no part of them.

I'm surrounded by barely touched takeout containers and a trash can overflowing with tissues. So many tissues. An empty wine glass sits on the coffee table—glass number... I'm not sure. Not enough to make me forget him. Only enough to blur the edges.

The TV is on YouTube autoplay, stuck in its current obsession: Alex Sebring's rugby highlights. I've seen this one already. Twice. Doesn't matter. I'll watch him again.

He's electric.

Fast. Brutal. Commanding. Every time he charges down the field with the ball, it hits me right in the chest. He played like he had something to prove—like every second mattered. The commentators call him The Wall. A beast. Unstoppable.

He told me he played professional rugby, and that he was sort of a big deal. But I didn't know I was in love with a damn legend.

To the rest of the world, he's a superstar. But to me, he was... *mine*. And now he's not.

I haven't cried today. That's something at least. But not because I'm fine or getting better. Because there's nothing left in me.

The sadness settled into my bones days ago. I don't notice the sting of tears anymore.

I can't remember the last time I showered, and I've eaten nothing of substance since... well, I can't say when.

Violet brought soup this week. I think. It could've been last week. My stomach growls like it's trying to remind me I still exist, but I ignore it. Everything tastes like nothing.

The front door opens, no knock. Violet stomps into my living room with the energy of a woman on a mission. "I swear to God. I'm gonna have to peel you off that fucking couch with a spatula."

She stops. One sniff of the air and her face contorts like she's stepped into a landfill. I don't turn my head, but I hear the disgusted noise she makes. "Jesus, Mags. You reek like gym socks, old tears, and emotional damage."

"Go away."

"Not a chance in hell."

She crosses the room, yanks the remote out of my hand, and turns off the TV. The silence is deafening.

"Hey! I was watching that."

"No. Enough of this bullshit."

She tosses the remote onto the chair like it personally offended her. "You've been lying here like a corpse for weeks, binge-watching your ex on YouTube like you're getting paid by the hour. Your hair looks like it lost a fight with a squirrel. Your skin is so pale I could cast you in a vampire flick without makeup. And when's the last time you brushed your teeth? Be honest. I can handle the truth."

I don't answer.

"Exactly." She grabs the blanket and rips it off me. "You stink. I'm talking medically concerning levels of stink."

I recoil like she's yanked off my security blanket. "Violet, stop."

She doesn't. She grabs my arm and hauls me up. I'm so weak, I can't even fight her. My body flops forward like a rag doll.

"What's the point? Everything I love is gone."

Violet's face softens, but only a little. "*You're* not gone. *I'm* not gone. And you don't get to disappear because he did."

She shoves me into the bathroom and turns on the shower. "Bathe. Now. Or I will scrub you myself, and I promise you *will not* enjoy it."

The door closes behind me, and I stand motionless for a long time, staring at the tile like it might give me answers. To be clear, it doesn't.

I peel off Alex's oversized T-shirt I've been living in, step out of my leggings, and reach up to touch the diamond pendant hanging around my neck.

My fingers close around it, and for a second, I can't breathe. It's like tearing open a wound I've been trying to pretend had healed.

I stare at the pendant and the way the diamonds catch the light even in this dim bathroom. It still looks beautiful. It still looks like hope. But it's not. Not anymore.

Alex... it's beautiful. I'll never take it off. I meant those words. But how was I to know that things would go this way?

My chest aches as I unclasp the chain, like I'm letting go of something precious.

Because I am.

This hurts. And it's not closure, but it's a beginning. A crack in the armor I've wrapped around my grief. The first step toward accepting that our forever isn't happening.

Hot water scalds my skin when I step into the shower, but I don't flinch. I stand there, letting it burn, letting it rinse away the pieces of myself I no longer recognize.

I wash my hair. Shave my legs. Brush my teeth at the sink.

Who is this hollow-eyed girl in the mirror? I don't recognize her.

I shuffle out of the bathroom in clean pajamas with wet hair clinging to my shoulders. The steam did something to my brain—shook a few cobwebs loose. I'm still hollow and exhausted but less like a ghost.

Violet's in the kitchen, sleeves rolled up, standing over my panini press like it's a power tool. The aroma of melted cheese and toasted bread fills the air as she glances over her shoulder, a relieved expression on her face as I pad in on bare feet.

"Well, look who survived basic hygiene."

I grunt something that might be a thank-you and sink onto the barstool, pulling my knees up to my chest.

She plates a grilled cheese cut into two triangles, sliding it in front of me. "With Wickles pickles, the way you like it. Eat."

My stomach twists at the sight of food. "I'm not hungry."

She crosses her arms. "Well, I don't give a damn. You're eating it anyway. You look like someone photoshopped your body smaller and forgot to adjust your head."

"Gee, thanks."

She points at the plate. "Chew. Swallow. Repeat. That's how it's done."

With a sigh, I pick up half the sandwich and take a bite. My stomach clenches like it's not sure what to do with actual food, but the buttery crunch hits my taste buds and something in me stirs.

"Good girl," Violet says.

I chew, forcing down another bite. Then another.

She stands across from me, watching with those sharp eyes of hers. "You've lost too much weight."

I shrug. "Breakup diets work."

"Breakup spirals don't. You scared the shit out of me."

My eyes fall to the half-eaten sandwich on my plate, my fingers curling around the crust. "I think I was born with a broken heart, like there's something in me that's always going to be cracked."

Violet doesn't flinch. Doesn't give me pity eyes or rush to fill the silence. She watches me for a beat and leans in with something softer in her eyes. Something fierce. "Possibly, but you were also born with teeth."

I blink at her, confused.

"You were born tough. Even when you don't want to be. Even when it hurts. That heart of yours might've come with fractures, but it also came with fire. And you're still here. That counts for something."

"I'm not sure how to stop hurting like this."

Violet reaches across the counter, her voice gentler than it's been all day. "Maybe today isn't about not hurting. Let's shoot for... feeling different."

I swallow hard, blinking against the sting in my eyes. "How?"

She looks thoughtful for a moment. "Start by doing the thing that always makes you happy."

I furrow my brow. "Work?"

Violet nods. "You've always come alive when you're creating. Designing. Organizing. Making beauty out of chaos. That's your thing. And if there's anything that'll remind you who you are, it's that."

I stare at her for a long moment, then look down at my hands. They're trembling. But maybe—just maybe—they still remember how to build something.

Violet clears the plates and tidies my kitchen while I stay perched at the counter, still bundled in clean pajamas, damp hair, and a raw heart.

She half turns, her gaze catching mine. "How is your money situation?"

I arch a brow. "You want a breakdown of my net worth?"

She tosses a dish towel at me. "I wanna be reassured that you're not one missed-rent payment away from sleeping on my sofa."

"I'm fine. You know me. I've been smart. I have investments. Decent savings. I won't be on your couch anytime soon. Promise."

Violet nods, satisfied. But I can tell the what's coming next before she ever opens her mouth.

"And work?"

I wince. "No clue. I haven't looked. I know I need to, but I—" I trail off, trying to find the right words.

She picks up the thread for me. "You're afraid of giving your heart to another company, another boss, only to be tossed out again like you never mattered."

I nod. "Right."

We're quiet for a beat, the soft hum of the refrigerator the only sound.

Violet leans forward on the counter. "It could be time for you to stop giving your heart away and build something that's yours."

I blink. "Meaning what? Start a business?"

She shrugs. "Why not?"

"Because I've just emerged from my own personal apocalypse?"

She points at me with a smirk. "Which makes it the perfect time. You've already hit rock bottom, and the only direction is up. Now you get to build with no fear of falling."

I roll my eyes. "Thanks for the reminder."

"You know what I mean."

I chew on the thought, unsure. "It's not like I have a business plan just waiting in a drawer."

"No, but you've got talent. Vision. A killer work ethic. Connections. And don't even get me started on your style choices. People would kill for your eye, Mags."

I let the silence stretch for a long moment. And then, with hesitation, I say what's on my mind. "I could pull from my retirement. The tax hit would be a bitch, but it's the only way."

Violet's eyes light up. "Now that's the Magnolia Steel I love."

A tiny ember of purpose glows inside me. I shake my head, the confession falling from my lips before I can filter it. "I don't know where to start or what the hell I'm doing."

"But you want to figure it out, don't you?"

I hesitate for half a second... then nod. "Yeah. I do."

"That's all you need."

Violet leaves just after nine, promising to check in tomorrow and threatening bodily harm if I don't text her back. She kisses the top of my head, pulls on her sneakers, and disappears into the hallway like a woman who knows the battle isn't over—but maybe the tide has shifted.

The apartment is quiet again, but it's different now. Less haunted. Like something might be stirring in the ashes.

A phoenix.

I pad back into the living room, curling up on the couch with a blanket that smells like detergent instead of depression. The TV screen isn't black anymore. Violet switched it off YouTube while I was in the shower. Now, the screen saver displays a photo of a baby polar bear sprawled belly-up in the snow, one paw in the air like it's waving at the camera. It's peaceful. Ridiculously cute. And somehow exactly what I need.

It shouldn't make me feel anything, but it does.

A small tug in my chest. A flicker of quiet.

The tiniest breath of peace.

I don't turn Alex back on. I don't reach for the remote. I sit there for a moment, listening to the quiet. Letting it settle.

And then I reach for my laptop.

No more ghosts tonight.

My fingers hesitate over the trackpad before I open a blank browser and start a search: how to start your own interior design company.

It seems stupid at first—silly, even. But I keep going.

A new tab opens. Then another. And another.

I jot down notes. Ideas. Names. Words that spark. I start a Pinterest board, pinning color palettes and spaces I love. Mood boards. Branding ideas. Nothing structured, nothing permanent— just little pieces of who I am, and who I hope to become.

The wound inside me still aches—tender and bruised—but it's not the only thing I feel anymore.

Movement.

Hope.

I click on a spreadsheet template, half-smiling as I plug in the beginnings of a budget. The numbers blur, and my hand trembles over the mouse pad, but I force myself to focus.

After a few rows, I open a new tab and begin a new search: commercial spaces to rent in Charleston. It's ridiculous—I don't even have a name for the business yet. But scrolling through photos of empty storefronts and airy lofts does something to me.

I imagine color palettes on blank walls. Fabric swatches fanned across sleek worktables. My name on the door.

It's too soon. Too uncertain. But at least the ache in my chest isn't only grief. It's a possibility.

Morning's approaching by the time I close the laptop.

I'm not okay. Not yet. But I will be.

Chapter 16

Alex Sebring

Copper and gold streak the sky, warmth blooming at the edges of the world. The sun here doesn't simply rise; it breathes, stretching its light across the sea and the hills.

I haven't slept. The bed in my grandparents' fale is firm and familiar, but the ache inside me isn't something this place soothes.

I'm here, like Tinā suggested. Breathing fresh air. Letting the ocean salt soak into my skin. Letting silence speak louder than the noise I left behind in Sydney.

It's been days since I arrived. I've spent time with my grandfather, sat with my grandmother. I've eaten warm taro and drunk from fresh coconuts and watched the way the waves kiss the shore.

And today, I'm doing the thing I came here to do.

The tattoo fale is tucked behind the village, shaded by palms and thick with history. Ink and coconut oil linger in the air, their scents woven into the thatched roof and mats. The man inside is old now, older than I remember, but his eyes are still sharp—still seeing more than they say.

"Aleki," he greets me, using my Samoan name, voice gravel-thick. "You've come to bleed again."

I nod, my chest tight, words barely clearing my throat. "This pain hasn't passed. It's too deep. I think it belongs on my skin."

He studies me for a moment, then gives a slow, solemn nod. "When the heart carries too much, the body must help. Ink is not just art, Aleki —it's memory. It's truth. It's how we survive what tried to break us."

He gestures for me to sit and motions toward the tools. Not a machine. Not a sterile gun in a sterile shop. These are the au tapulu— the handmade combs. Bone and wood and ink.

Tradition. Pain. Honor.

"Where will we place this one?"

I tap my chest, just over my heart. "Here. This is where she lives."

He doesn't ask who. Maybe he already knows. Maybe heartbreak looks the same in every man who's sat on this mat.

His fingers trail over the spot, mapping it with a quiet understanding.

"What will you carry here?"

He isn't only asking about the design. It's about the wound it covers.

"The manumea. The ghost bird that mates for life."

His eyes flick up, something ancient and knowing shining in their depths. "Endangered but not extinct."

He nods slow and solemn. "The manumea sings for only one mate. And if that mate is lost to him, he sings anyway."

This man has known me all my life. He's carved my story into my skin. And today, he's about to hear a new chapter. "She has become lost to me."

I lie back, the woven mat biting into my skin as he mixes the ink, calls for his apprentice, and begins the blessing. I let my eyes drift shut, and the first strike lands like thunder. Sharp. Deliberate.

He works with slow, meticulous hands. The tapping sound

echoes in my bones. Each line and curve that will become the manumea is placed with care.

As the ink sinks deeper, my thoughts drift.

To Magnolia's laughter—how it started soft and built like a swell, always louder than she expected.

To the way she looked at me when we made love. Or when we fucked hard.

To when she said 'I love you.'

I think about her journal entries. Her handwriting. The parts of her she never meant for anyone else to see but gave to me. And how I read those words with shaking hands and couldn't reconcile them with the cold text that came weeks later.

I feel every inch of this pain. And somehow, it feels earned.

"This bird never stops searching for its mate," the tattooist says, not looking up from his work.

I close my eyes again, swallowing the lump in my throat.

This ink isn't for anyone else. It's not for show, not for meaning wrapped in metaphor. It's all mine.

My scar. My vow. My proof that she existed.

That I loved her.

That I still do.

He works in silence for a long time, the only sound being that of the rhythmic tap of bone against skin. My breath pushes through clenched teeth, each strike etching her deeper into me.

When it's done, he leans back, eyes scanning the ink like it's a story now told in full. His apprentice hands him a small bowl of oil— thick and fragrant, the kind his father used, and his father before him.

He rubs it into my skin, a balm over the fresh wound. Then he places a folded strip of tapa cloth across my chest, the oil darkening the edges as it sinks in.

"To protect what's sacred," he says.

I nod, my throat thick. Because she was. She still is.

He rises and gives me a nod that says we're finished but not done.

The pain hasn't left—but now it has a place. Something I can see and touch. Something that won't fade.

I sit up, ribs sore, breath thin. But there's something different in my chest now. Not lighter, not healed. But anchored.

I gather my shirt but don't put it on. The cloth presses over the tattoo, soothing and stinging all at once. I step out of the fale into the late afternoon sun, where the air smells like salt and soil and stories passed down.

And for the first time in weeks, I inhale a full breath.

The sky is streaked in hues of twilight when I return to my grandparents' house. The village has stilled, the hush of evening settling over the trees and rooftops like a blessing. Even the breeze moves slower now, as if it knows the world needs peace and quiet.

My chest aches with every step, the sting of fresh ink pulsing in time with my heartbeat beneath the cloth. But it's a good ache.

Their simple house is tucked into the hillside with wide open shutters and the smell of something sweet still lingering in the air. Tinā always says this is where we come when we lose ourselves. And I think she's right.

I toe off my sandals at the back door and step inside. Tui is seated on the front porch watching the ocean. Nana hums as she moves through the kitchen. She doesn't ask where I've been for so long. She knows.

I ease into the rocking chair beside him, its wooden frame creaking beneath me. We don't speak at first. Just sit together, letting the rhythmic hush of waves meeting the shore fill the quiet between us.

After a while, Nana joins us, a woven blanket draped around her shoulders despite the heat. She eases into the chair beside me, eyes on the horizon. "What did you mark yourself with this time?"

I swallow hard, eyes still on the sea. "The manumea."

She's quiet for a beat, then nods, understanding. "The bird that mates for life."

"I thought I had as well." My voice cracks a little, and I hate it.

Tui doesn't speak often, but when he does, his words are wise. "The manumea is still out there. Searching. Singing. Even alone, it doesn't stop. Not because it's desperate—but because it remembers the sound of being found."

She reaches over and brushes a strand of hair from my forehead, like I'm still five years old. "Pain tells you what mattered. And if it mattered this much, it's not finished yet."

That undoes me a little. I allow their words to settle into all the places still raw and open.

"I don't know how to move forward without her."

"You don't have to know right now," Nana says. "You just have to move. The rest will come."

We sit together for a while longer in a silence that feels full rather than empty. A breeze rolls off the sea and kisses the wound beneath the cloth. It stings, but I welcome it.

Because pain that has meaning hurts less than pain that has none.

SYDNEY FEELS COLDER WHEN I RETURN. NOT THE WEATHER, but the air inside this house. The silence I used to drown in doesn't sting as much—it just hums low, like a sound I'm learning to live with.

I drop my bag inside the door. Kick off my shoes. The house looks the same. but I'm not sure I do.

It takes a while to move. To shower. To eat. But eventually, I step into the one room I've avoided the longest.

The gym.

It still smells like chalk and steel. Like discipline.

I stand in the doorway for a beat, heart thudding for reasons that have nothing to do with cardio. Then I cross the threshold, my feet finding familiar grooves in the mat.

The speakers come on with a slow beat—something low and pulsing. I stretch, stiff and unsteady, but I move. I lift. Slowly at first. Then heavier. Harder.

And when I catch my reflection in the mirror—sweat beading at my brow, muscles straining under weight—I see the edge of the tattoo peeking through the neck of my T-shirt.

A reminder of a love that still lives under my skin. Of a woman who cracked me open... and the man I'm trying to become because of it.

My grip tightens on the bar. And just like that, her voice finds me. Not real—just words written in her journal about us. About me.

I thought I'd be ready to go home after this trip. But all of a sudden, nothing about leaving feels right. I'm not ready to go. I'm not ready to leave him. I don't think I ever will be.

I lift again. And again. Until the ache in my body drowns out the one in my chest.

It's not redemption. It's not closure. But it's something other than dying a slow death.

She may not be mine anymore...

But I'm still here. And I'm not done with me yet.

Chapter 17

Magnolia Steel

A SOFT BEAM OF MORNING LIGHT FILTERS THROUGH THE FLOOR-to-ceiling windows of my new office, casting a warm glow over the space I've worked to create. The scent of fresh flowers from the small arrangement on my desk mingles with the rich aroma of my caramel latte, marking my new beginning.

My own design firm wasn't part of the plan. Then again, neither was being fired from Soul Sync in the middle of what should've been the peak of my career. But here I am, standing on my two feet. The exhaustion that clings to me is the good kind that comes from long nights poring over business plans.

Today, it all becomes real. My first official client meeting.

I straighten my blouse for the third time, a nervous energy humming beneath my skin. There's something thrilling about the unknown—about diving headfirst into a future I'm still figuring out.

The chime of the office doorbell pulls me from my thoughts. I straighten, plastering on the practiced smile I've been perfecting for weeks. "Here we go, Magnolia Steel," I say under my breath, adjusting a stack of fabric swatches on my desk for the hundredth time.

When I look up, my breath catches for a split second.

My client fills the doorway—no joke. Broad shoulders that seem to stretch wider than the frame itself, a towering presence with a muscular build that speaks of years of rigorous training. Everything about him exudes power, from the way he carries himself to the confident smirk playing at his lips. His tailored charcoal suit molds to his form with perfection, the crisp white shirt beneath hinting at wealth that doesn't need to be flaunted.

He's not just large. He's commanding.

I step forward, smoothing my expression into something polished and professional, and extend my hand. "Hello, I'm Magnolia Steel. You must be Mr. McRae."

His handshake is firm, his palm warm against mine. "Tyson," he says, his deep voice laced with an unmistakable Australian accent.

That accent. It slams into me with the force of a wave, and for a moment, the world around me blurs.

My heart stutters in my chest, but I school my expression, refusing to let anything show. "It's a pleasure to meet you."

He nods, his sharp gaze sweeping across the office with a quick assessment. "Nice place. New?"

"Very new."

His gaze sweeps over the room, a slow smirk tugging at his lips. "Classy and sophisticated. Just what I expected."

"Chic is my style."

I gesture toward the sleek leather chair across from me. "Please, have a seat."

As he settles in, I take a breath and launch into my spiel. "I'd love to hear more about your vision for the project. What are you looking to achieve with the space?"

He's filled with easy confidence as he launches into his plans— the boutique hotel, the concept, the luxury touches he wants to incorporate. He talks a good game, throwing around words like exclusive and bespoke, but there's something about the way he speaks that comes off as calculated.

That voice—*his* voice—keeps replaying in my head like a terrible song I can't shake. The cadence, the confidence, the arrogance. And his face.

And then it hits me.

Tyson McRae.

Not just any Tyson McRae. *That* Tyson McRae.

The one from Sydney who sent Alex over the edge that night at the wedding. The one always provoking him. The one who hates him so much that he intentionally hurt him, ending his career.

How did I not recognize him sooner?

In my defense, I only caught a glimpse of him that night. It was dark, and my focus wasn't on Tyson. It was on Alex—on holding him back, on stopping him from making a mistake he couldn't undo.

Now he's sitting across from me, larger than life, taking up space in more ways than one.

I force my lips into what I hope is a smile, but inside, my mind is spinning.

What the hell is he doing here?

Tyson leans back in the chair, stretching in a way that feels deliberate—like he's casually putting all that broad-shouldered, muscled-up physique on display for me. "I want it redone top to bottom. And I'd like you to be the one to handle it."

Suspicion prickles at the edges of my thoughts.

Charleston is brimming with seasoned designers who've spent years establishing themselves. Designers with bigger portfolios, stronger connections, and an entire team at their disposal. If money's no object for a man like Tyson McRae—and I know it isn't—why would he come to me?

There's only one answer.

My fingers tighten around the pen I've been twirling, the motion a poor attempt at grounding myself. "That sounds like an exciting project. But I have to ask—why me? There are a lot of established firms in Charleston that specialize in boutique spaces."

His lips curve, but the smile doesn't quite reach his eyes. "I've done my research, and I know talent when I see it. Your designs are fresh and uncomplicated. I'm not interested in a stale, cookie-cutter hotel design. I want something unique... with soul."

I nod, feigning calmness. "I appreciate that. It's always my goal to create something personal and meaningful for my clients."

"Which is why I came to you."

I force a polite nod, but suspicion needles at me. Of all the designers in Charleston, he walked through *my* door? A door I didn't even have two months ago. A door I'm terrified won't stay open if I don't make this work.

Despite the warning bells in my head, I flip to a clean page in my notebook. "Tell me more about the space."

"Luxury with a twist of charm. Filled with Charleston's history but not outdated. Sleek and inviting. Modern with touches of tradition. I want a place people walk into and instantly know they're somewhere special. A place they'll never forget."

He's saying the right words, but I can't shake the feeling that this, whatever it is, has nothing to do with hotels and everything to do with me.

A nagging unease creeps in, the same feeling I get when something is too good to be true.

"This is an enormous investment. You could've chosen any designer, not someone whose firm is in its infancy. I think we both know this is about something else."

Tyson's brow lifts, that damn smirk never wavering. "What do you mean?"

My gaze meets his head-on. "You and Alex have history—and not the good kind. I'm his ex."

There it is—the flicker in his eyes, the faint twitch at the corner of his mouth that tells me I've hit the mark.

His laughter is a rich, indulgent sound that grates against my nerves. "So what? You think Sebring would care? Hate to break it to you, Miss Steel, but he's moved on."

My stomach drops, but I do my best to not let it show. "Moved on?"

Tyson nods, his smirk widening, like he's enjoying this far too much. "Heard through the grapevine he's in a serious relationship. Lucky bastard found *the one*. He'll be marrying her any day now."

The one.

He'll be marrying her any day now.

It takes every ounce of willpower not to react, not to let the sharp stab of pain show on my face. Instead, I force out a laugh that sounds hollow even to my own ears. "Good for him."

Tyson watches me with something that almost looks like amusement. "Alex is all about marriage. Family. Stability. He's getting exactly what he wants... *again*. He's always been pretty good at that––getting what he wants."

A lump rises in my throat, and I swallow hard, refusing to give him the satisfaction of seeing how much his words hurt.

"Look, Miss Steel. There's no scenario where taking this job would hurt Alex. You aren't a thought in his mind anymore." He waves a hand in a dismissive manner. "This is business. That's all."

I nod, but deep down, my heart is splintering. "Right. Business is business."

A sharp ache settles in my chest, heavy and unrelenting.

You aren't a thought in his mind anymore.

It shouldn't hurt this much. I should have been prepared for this —for the possibility that Alex wouldn't cling to the wreckage of what we had the way I have. But hearing it spoken aloud, in such a blunt manner, makes it real in a way I wasn't ready for.

"Good for him," I say a second time, but the words taste bitter, like regret and humiliation.

Alex doesn't care about me. Maybe he never did. Because how else could he move on this fast? How could he replace me with such ease, slipping into someone else's life––and bed—like I was nothing more than a passing fling?

A fool. That's what I am. A complete and utter fool.

Love is a foolish game. Play foolish games and win foolish prizes. And a broken heart is the fool's ultimate prize.

And damn, did I win big.

My grip on my pen tightens until my knuckles ache.

I won't let Tyson McRae see me crumble. I won't allow him to see he's struck a nerve.

Smoothing my features into a practiced mask of indifference, I sit up straighter and force a smile. "I wish him nothing but the best."

Pain doesn't pay the bills. No matter how much my heart aches, rent still needs to be covered, and my business will not build itself. I can't afford to wallow in my history with Alex Sebring.

Tyson is watching me, his lips twitching like he's debating if he'll call my bluff. But I don't give him the chance.

I flip to a new page and poise my pen over it. I force a bright smile and shift gears. "Do you have a projected timeline in mind?"

"I'm hoping for an aggressive schedule. Six months would be ideal."

My head shoots up. "*Six months?*"

"Yes, Miss Steel."

Tell me you've never done a renovation in historical Charleston without telling me you've never done a renovation in historical Charleston.

"That's more than ambitious. More like impossible."

"Nothing is impossible when you have the budget to get the job done."

I beg to differ.

"Permits can take time, especially in historic districts. There are a lot of restrictions with renovations—materials, structural changes, even paint colors. The review process alone could push your timeline back."

He grins, unfazed. "I like the ambitious timeline."

Of course he does. "We'll need to prioritize securing those permits early. Some approvals can take many months depending on the scope of work. Are there elements you want to preserve?"

Something flickers behind his eyes. "I trust your judgment on that."

"You mentioned wanting modern comforts without losing the charm. Are you thinking about incorporating—" I pause, blinking down at my notepad, the words evaporating from my mind.

Shit. What was I about to say?

Tyson leans forward, his eyes watching me with something too close to amusement. "Are you all right, Miss Steel?"

I nod quickly, too quickly. "Yeah, of course. I was thinking out loud."

A slow smirk spreads. "Right."

He taps a finger against his thigh, studying me like he's unraveling a puzzle piece by piece. "Listen, I didn't mean to rattle you. I assumed you already knew about Alex's marriage."

I swallow hard, forcing a tight smile. "It's fine."

"I don't think it is, and I'm sorry for that. I can see it's shaken you." His voice takes on a soft, empathetic tone.

I refuse to let him see just how deep his words have cut. "It's just surprising. That's all. I'm fine."

He watches me. "Maybe we should meet another time and give you a chance to process."

"No." Panic flashes through me at the thought of losing this opportunity.

I sit up straighter, forcing a steadier tone. "That's unnecessary. We should keep going."

"Only if you're sure."

Right now, work is the only thing keeping me from falling apart. I can't let this slip through my fingers. No matter who Tyson McRae is to Alex—no matter what history lingers between them—this is too important.

Clients like him don't walk through the door every day. I need this.

I nod, plastering on a smile that I hope doesn't look forced. "Let's talk about the lobby."

Tyson studies me for a beat. "I have an idea. Why don't we take this discussion somewhere more relaxed?"

I blink, surprised. "More relaxed?"

He shrugs, his broad shoulders shifting beneath his tailored jacket. "Dinner. Tomorrow night. We'll talk through the details over an elegant meal."

Dinner with Tyson McRae—the idea shouldn't make my stomach twist the way it does.

Alex has moved on, leaving no loyalty or devotion behind for me. But somehow, mine for him remains—twisted up inside me, stubborn and aching. I shouldn't still feel it. I don't want to. But it's there, rooted so deep I can't seem to break free.

A setting outside these four walls, with drinks, might help me shake off the weight of everything he's just dumped on me. I need time to think, to gather myself, but I can't afford to hesitate for too long.

I force a polite smile. "A dinner meeting sounds good."

Tyson's grin widens just a fraction, and something about it makes my skin prickle. "Perfect. I'll text you the details."

He stands, adjusting his jacket like a man who is used to getting what he wants. "I look forward to it, Miss Steel."

"Me too."

The door clicks shut behind him, and my entire body sags like a marionette whose strings have been cut. A raw, broken sob rips from my throat as I slide down the wall, landing hard. I curl in on myself—knees to chest, arms locked tight around them—like I can hold everything together if I just squeeze hard enough. But I can't. I'm unraveling, thread by thread, and there's no stopping it.

My chest heaves, and the tears come fast, spilling down my cheeks in a flood I have no strength to hold back. I press a trembling hand to my mouth, but it does nothing to muffle the broken sounds escaping me. The weight of everything—losing Alex, losing my job, losing the future I thought I had—presses down, crushing me beneath it.

He's moved on. He's happy. In love. Getting married.

The words replay in my head, stabbing deep, each repetition twisting the knife a little more. Alex doesn't think about me. I'm nothing more than a footnote in his story, a passing memory he's long since left behind. And here I am, shattered to pieces on the floor of a rented office, drowning in the wreckage of something that never belonged to me.

My head falls back against the door, the cool wood grounding me for a fleeting second before another sob wracks my body. I thought I was moving on. Thought I was building something new, something solid. But one conversation with Tyson McRae has me crumbling to pieces again.

This can't be my life. I won't let it be.

I press my palms to the floor and push myself up. My legs are unsteady, like they don't quite belong to me anymore, but I force them to hold me.

One foot in front of the other. One day at a time. That's how you survive heartbreak.

Flicking on the bathroom light, I take a long, shaky breath, forcing myself to meet my reflection.

Red-rimmed eyes. Blotchy cheeks. A mess.

I splash cold water onto my face, letting it wash away the evidence of my breakdown—at least on the surface. I smooth my hair, straighten my blouse, and press my lips together until they stop quivering. Bit by bit, I put myself back together.

Chapter 18

Magnolia Steel

CHARLESTON'S EVENING AIR CLINGS TO MY SKIN AS I STEP ONTO the sidewalk, gliding my hands down the sleek lines of my black dress. Professional, yet elegant. A calculated choice. Tonight is about business—nothing more, nothing less. I remind myself of that with every click of my heels against the sidewalk leading to the front of the restaurant.

Inside, the low hum of conversation and the clinking of glasses weave together with the soft strains of jazz. The lighting is dim, golden, casting a warm glow over the rich mahogany furniture and deep velvet booths. It's the kind of place where people whisper promises and share secrets over wine priced like mortgage payments.

A place of Tyson McRae's choosing.

And there he is.

Tyson McRae is dressed in a tailored navy suit, crisp and sharp, his broad shoulders cutting an imposing figure. His signature smirk plays on his lips the moment his eyes find mine, and he strides forward with the ease of a man who's never known rejection.

"Miss Steel." He leans in and presses a kiss to my cheek.

Bold move.

I don't like it.

"Mr. McRae."

The scent of his expensive cologne surrounds me—something dark and spicy. My spine stiffens at the uninvited display of intimacy, but I force a polite smile, brushing it off as though I'm unbothered.

Like it doesn't make my skin crawl.

I step back, creating a space between us, but his grin only deepens, as if he enjoys the game already in motion.

We're seated at a private table tucked away in a secluded corner, candlelight flickering between us. Very romantic. Not the type of setting for talking business.

Tyson McRae settles into the chair across from me, his eyes lingering on me for too long.

What is he playing at?

The setting makes me hyper-aware of him—the way he leans in, the deliberate slowness of his movements, the weight of his gaze like he's already peeling back my clothes. I square my shoulders and reach for the menu, putting it up as a shield between us.

I'm here for business. And that's all.

But the intimacy of the atmosphere says otherwise, like this meeting isn't about interior design and hotel renovations. There's an undercurrent of something else—something personal. And that's dangerous.

I need this deal. I have no choice but to entertain it, even if it feels like playing with fire.

Tyson's eyes flick to mine over the top of his menu and I force another smile, ignoring the unease twisting in my stomach. Deep down, I know nothing about tonight is going to be business as usual if he has anything to say about it.

Tyson orders a bottle of red. Expensive. *Very expensive.* I wouldn't have known that six months ago, but one becomes acquainted with the finer things in life when you date a billionaire for three months.

"Only the best for this beautiful woman," he tells the server, handing him the wine list.

I press my lips together, swallowing the irritation rising in my throat. Flashing his wealth, his dominance—it's his way of setting the tone. But I won't let him steer this evening off course.

"I appreciate the gesture, but I'm fine with water."

Tyson waves a dismissive hand. "Nonsense. You'll love this one."

His gaze lingers, dark and assessing. "I love a woman who knows what she wants, but tonight, let me spoil you."

Behind my tight smile, frustration simmers, but I bury it deep. "I'd prefer to talk specifics about the hotel."

I reach into my bag for my notepad, flipping it open to my prepared list of questions.

He leans back in his chair, watching me. Amused. "Always straight to business with you, huh?"

"That's what this dinner is about—business."

He shakes his head, a low chuckle escaping him. "No wonder your work is so bold. Unforgettable... just like you."

My spine stiffens.

Compliments from clients aren't unusual, but the way he says it—like it's not my designs he's talking about—makes unease creep under my skin.

I meet his gaze head-on, offering a polite smile. "Thank you. I take a lot of pride in what I do."

"Pride. Focus. Dedication. You leave little room for distraction."

I keep my grip firm on the pen in my hand. Stay cautious, Magnolia.

Alex's warning echoes in my head—his gritted words about Tyson's reputation, his games. He doesn't play fair. He'll come at you from every angle. I know that much.

My guts say I should run far and fast from Tyson McRae, but I need this job.

He tilts his head, watching me with something too sharp, too interested. "Tell me, Miss Steel... are you always this serious? Or are you just playing hard to get?"

Any time a man says the words *playing hard to get,* I see one thing.

Red. Fucking. Flag.

I don't flinch, but I feel it—alarm bells ringing loud in my mind.

I offer a cool smile and close my notebook. "My work is important to me, Mr. McRae. If that's a problem, let me know now."

His eyes gleam with something that resembles a challenge. "Not a problem at all."

I take a steady breath, reminding myself why I'm here. Stay focused. Stay professional. Stay in control. Even if Tyson McRae seems determined to blur those lines by slipping in flirtatious remarks between sips of wine and bites of steak.

His confidence is suffocating.

"Tell me, Miss Steel—do you always keep people at arm's length, or am I just special?"

I offer a polite smile, refusing to engage with his game. "I keep things professional with clients."

"Do you now?"

If I didn't know better, I'd think he was taking a jab at me—implying that I didn't keep things professional with Alex. But that makes no sense. Tyson doesn't know Alex was ever my client. Or at least he *shouldn't* know.

Celeste also wasn't supposed to know.

Still, there's something in the way he looks at me that says *we both know better than that.*

He leans in, his cologne wrapping around me like a subtle trap. "There's more to life than business. What do you do for fun?"

"I design. It's what I love, so it doesn't feel like work. I'm lucky I've been able to make a career out of my passion."

He watches me for a beat, his lips curling at the edges. "Passion. I like that."

I sip the wine he insisted I have, buying a moment to steady myself. "Speaking of passion, let's talk about yours—your vision for the hotel."

He chuckles. "We'll get around to that."

Tyson McRae is a man used to getting what he wants—whether it's business or pleasure. And right now, he's making it very clear which one interests him more.

"What about your personal life? Any room in that curated schedule for a little fun?"

I glance down at my plate, appetite long gone. "My business takes up most of my time these days."

"That's a shame. You should let yourself enjoy life a little."

"I enjoy life."

He hums, swirling his wine again. "You might enjoy letting someone else take the reins."

Take the reins? Sounds like there's a whole dump truck's worth of meaning buried under those words.

God, I don't know what he's trying to say.

Am I dealing with another Andrew Tate wannabe, looking for a woman to command like some trophy on a leash?

Maybe he means it sexually—some dominance kink wrapped in polite conversation.

Or maybe he's just a run-of-the-mill control freak who needs everything and everyone dancing to the beat of his drum.

Whatever it is, it's a no from me. A hard, resounding no.

This is a precarious situation I've gotten myself into. I'm trapped between wanting to shut him down and needing to keep him interested enough to sign the contract.

The expensive food, the luxurious setting, the way he watches me like I'm some prize to be won—I'm not about to play his game.

"How are you holding up now that you've had a little time to absorb the news?"

I blink, my spine straightening. "What news?"

"Come on, Miss Steel. Don't make me spell it out."

I shrug, pretending to not know what he's referring to.

He leans in, eyes glinting with something dark and knowing. "Sebring's engagement."

The air in my lungs turns to lead, and I grip my wine glass tighter to hide the way my fingers tremble. "I told you. I'm happy for him."

Tyson studies me for a beat too long, his smirk deepening. "Right."

The fucker needs to get off my case about Alex. "In case you missed it, I'm the one who left Alex. Not the other way around."

Not a lie. But also not the whole truth.

There's a new crack forming in my armor, and I can't let him see it. "I guess he found what he was looking for."

"A blonde." He hums in amusement, sitting back in his chair with the air of someone who knows what he's doing. "Sebring always had a thing for fair ladies."

Alex never told me that was his preference, but I suppose there could be some truth to it. Celeste is a blonde.

"I'm surprised he dated someone like you."

The words land like a slap, hot and stinging. *Someone like you*—as though I'm some kind of cautionary tale. Like I'm less. Disposable.

I grit my teeth, swallowing the insult like a mouthful of broken glass. "Guess I was the exception for a brief moment in time."

Tyson McRae's eyes never leave mine. "What a shame he couldn't see what he had right in front of him."

"Alex and I wanted different things. It would never work between us."

The weight of my lies presses against my ribs, suffocating and inescapable, but I keep my composure. I have to. Tyson McRae is circling like a shark, and the last thing I need is for him to see blood in the water.

"Just so you know... I prefer brunettes."

I take another sip of wine, Tyson refilling my glass without a word, the liquid mercy I'm too worn down to refuse.

His eyes dance with amusement, observing me. "Drink up, Miss Steel. You're too tense."

I glance down at the half-empty glass, my head already feeling lighter than it should. Is he pushing the wine because he wants to loosen me up? Or because he hopes to get me into bed?

Either way, I will keep my wits about me. Because Tyson McRae does nothing without an agenda. And right now, I'm pretty damn sure I'm at the center of his plan.

Dinner ends with a lingering tension, one I can't quite shake as I push my chair back and reach for my purse. He stands first, ever the gentleman, offering his hand to help me up.

Outside, the night air is thick and warm, wrapping around me like a heavy blanket. Tyson McRae walks beside me, his hand resting at the small of my back as we step onto the sidewalk. The intimate touch sends a ripple of unease through me, but I don't pull away. Not yet.

"Please allow me to walk you to your car."

"Thank you, but I didn't drive tonight. Knew we'd be having drinks."

Tyson stops, brows lifting in mild surprise before his lips curve into that same confident smile he's been wearing all night. "I'm happy to give you a ride home."

I hold up my phone, flashing the screen. "Already requested an Uber. Two minutes away."

His gaze flickers to the phone before returning to me, amusement dancing in his eyes. "Efficient as always."

The soft glow of the streetlights casts long shadows between us. I sense him watching me. And then he steps closer—too close—his voice dropping to something silkier, more intimate.

"You're beautiful tonight," he says, his eyes trailing over my face.

I shift my weight, instinct screaming at me to put more space between us.

"Thank you." Now is the perfect time for me to make things clear. "But just so there's no confusion... this is a business relationship. I'm not looking for anything. Building my business is my entire focus, and I don't have the time for anything else."

His grin doesn't falter. If anything, it deepens. Like he expected my rejection. Like he enjoys the challenge.

"I'm a very patient man, Magnolia."

Not Miss Steel, but Magnolia. Too intimate. Too presumptuous. He's trying to step into a space that isn't his—and he won't find a welcome waiting for him.

Before I can respond, headlights sweep across the sidewalk, and I spot my Uber pulling up to the curb. Relief floods me like a tidal wave, and I take another step back.

I lift a hand toward the approaching car. "That's my ride."

"Allow me." He steps forward, pulling the car door open for me.

"Thank you." I slide into the back seat. "Goodnight, Mr. McRae."

"Call me Ty."

His hand lingers on the doorframe, waiting.

"Goodnight, Ty."

I sink into the back seat as he closes the door. He steps back, watching the car pull away.

I glance back at him, my pulse still racing. He stands beneath the glow of the streetlights, hands in his pockets, that damn smirk still playing on his lips—like he's already won.

Chapter 19

Magnolia Steel

THE DESK CHAIR CREAKS AS I SHIFT, MY FINGERS GLIDING OVER the trackpad, scrolling through fabric samples. Sunlight filters through the sheer curtains, illuminating the room's worn elegance— the faded wallpaper, the antique moldings, the heavy wooden furniture that's seen better days. The hotel is old, but in the best way—rich with history and potential. It just needs a careful hand to restore its grandeur.

My habit has become working from different rooms in the building, letting myself settle into the space, absorbing its atmosphere before I attempt to reshape it. This particular room has a ton of charm, but it's stiff and uninviting. The bones are good, but the life is missing. That's what I need to bring back.

I reach for my tape measure, snapping the metal out as I stretch it across the bed frame, making a quick note in my notebook. My pen glides over the page, listing details: plush bedding, warm lighting, deep navy and brushed gold accents. Classic, but not suffocating. Sophisticated, but livable.

I return to my laptop and study the images I've collected on my mood board. This project is more than a job—it's my chance to prove myself, to establish my name in this new-to-me industry.

To remind myself that I haven't lost everything.

The soft hum of Madonna's "Love Don't Live Here Anymore" drifts from my laptop speakers, blending with the scratch of my pen against my notebook. The melancholy melody fills the room, wrapping around me as I fine-tune the details of my design.

Absorbed in my work, I drag and adjust the placement of an accent chair in my rendering, considering how it would look against the restored paneling. The hotel's history deserves to be honored, but it needs to be functional too. Modern luxury with a soul. That's what I'm aiming for.

The door swings open and I jolt, my heart slamming against my ribs as I snap my head up. Ty stands in the doorway, his presence as commanding as ever.

The dark suit molds to his tall, athletic frame, the sharp cut emphasizing his broad shoulders and trim waist. His crisp white dress shirt is unbuttoned just enough to give the impression of effortless confidence—controlled, never careless. Dark hair, styled but not overdone, adds to the easy arrogance he wears so well. And then there are his eyes—icy blue, sharp, assessing, always watching.

Chiseled jaw, the perfect amount of scruff, and a presence that demands attention without him having to say a single word.

What a breathtaking display of arrogance in a suit.

Yeah, he's good-looking. And it annoys the shit out of me.

"I've been trying to reach you."

He steps inside like he owns the place... which he does.

Frowning, I blink at him. "Trying to reach me?"

I grab my phone from the desk and flip it over. The screen lights up with several missed calls and unread messages from him.

Shit. "Sorry. Guess I got caught up in my work."

He waves a dismissive hand, letting the door swing shut behind him. "It's all right. You're dedicated. I'm okay with that."

He steps further into the room, his gaze flicking between my laptop screen and the open notebook beside it. "What are you working on?"

"Building a mood board for the guest rooms." I scroll through my favorites giving him a quick preview. "I like to work in the space I'm designing so I can visualize the end result. Helps with scale and material choices and making sure everything fits the energy of the hotel."

He moves closer. "And what energy did you decide on?"

"I like your original idea—timeless elegance. A blend of the hotel's history with modern luxury." I glance up at him—and realize too late just how close he is.

Our faces are inches apart, his sharp blue eyes locking onto mine with an intensity that sends a flicker of heat down my spine. The air between us feels charged, humming with something unspoken. Close enough that if I moved a hair, my nose might brush against the edge of his jaw.

"Like you said... a place people want to come back to."

Ty's eyes shift and he stares at my mouth. "That's the idea, isn't it?"

His presence is impossible to ignore when his scent wraps around me.

Our shoulders almost brush, and the heat rolling off him makes the air feel hotter.

I click through the images, shifting the laptop toward him. "So, this is what I'm thinking for the furnishings. Rich upholstery. Warm wood tones. I want it to feel classic but still inviting. Like... tufted leather armchairs in that deep cognac color, with brass nailhead trim. Dark-stained mahogany desks—something with a little bit of carving detail, a nod to the old craftsmanship the hotel was known for. And I'm picturing floor-to-ceiling drapes in deep jewel tones, framing those huge windows so the afternoon light spills through. I want to keep the old-world charm but polish it up. Think velvet settees with turned legs, clawfoot coffee tables, antique-style sconces throwing off this soft, cozy glow. A mix of heirloom and high-end."

He nods in approval, his gaze lingering on the screen before shifting to me. "You're good at this. I can already picture it. But there's one thing that concerns me."

I glance up, brows lifting. "Oh?"

His lips twitch into something just shy of a smirk. "It's easier if I show you."

He steps back from the desk and gestures toward the bed. "Come here."

I hesitate for a fraction of a second before standing.

He crosses the room, stopping at the foot of the bed and motioning for me to sit.

I give him a questioning look as I lower myself onto the edge. "Okay?"

"Tell me what's wrong with this bed."

I press my palms into the mattress, testing the feel beneath my fingertips. Then I shift my weight and give a small bounce. "It's too firm to suit me."

"What else?"

I bounce again, and the bedsprings protest with an unmistakable squeak. I wrinkle my nose. "Loud. Guests don't want to feel like the whole floor can hear them rolling over—or doing anything else, for that matter."

His lips twitch like he's holding back a laugh. "Good point. What else?"

A checklist spins through my head, but nothing feels wrong. Lifting my gaze, I meet his eyes. "I'm not sure."

He watches me for a moment, then exhales, shaking his head with something that looks a lot like disappointment. "Let me show you."

He lowers himself to his knees in front of me, the movement slow and deliberate. My breath catches, every muscle in my body going rigid.

"Imagine this room, this bed... and the way your lover would worship every part of you until you forgot your own name."

A warning bell chimes in my head, but I don't move. I can't speak.

His hands ghost over my knees. "May I?"

I blink, my brain cells scrambling. "May you what?"

His lips curl at the corner. "Show you the problem with the bed."

I hesitate, uncertain of where this is going, but nod.

"Easy," he says, his voice low and maddeningly calm. His hands slide from the tops of my knees to the insides of my thighs, coaxing my legs apart with a touch that's too careful to be truly innocent.

"I know what you're thinking, but stay with me so I can show you what I mean."

"You've got about ten seconds to make your case before my better judgment shows up."

"I'm being serious here." He leans in closer, his eyes pinning me in place. "Imagine me as your lover and I'm going down on you."

What the actual hell?

Every rational part of me screams to be offended, to shut this shit down.

But betrayal simmers low in my gut because his words send a flash of heat straight through me.

God, I hate that my body responds to him before my mind can.

"Do you see the problem with this?"

There's a whole lot of problems with this. Not just one.

His grip is firm, his palms warm against my skin. The space between us smaller than it should be, the air charged with something I don't want to name.

"Let me be more specific."

He lowers his head and places a kiss on the inside of my thigh, his eyes locked on mine, looking up at me as he does it.

Oh fuck.

"Now do you see the problem?"

I swallow hard, pulse hammering in my ears. "The bed is too low. It makes positioning... difficult." My voice comes out embarrassingly breathless, like it belongs to a woman who hasn't had a man go down on her in months.

A slow smile tugs at the corner of his mouth. "Bingo."

"You realize that not all of your guests will be on their knees, right?"

Something dark flickers in his eyes. "The fun ones will be. And the ones, like me, who know how to take care of a woman."

Fucking knew it! I should've become a nun.

I should get up. Walk away. Remind him this is a business relationship, not whatever dangerous game he's turning it into. But my body won't move, frozen in the space between common sense and the heat crawling over my skin. I need this job—desperately—but the air between us crackles with something dark, undeniable, and I hate how much a part of me aches for it.

I need to get control of this situation—fast. Before it goes too far.

Hell, it's already gone too far.

His fingers flex against my skin, and his voice drops lower, rich with confidence. "I'm a man who enjoys giving a woman pleasure. And I'm very good at it."

A sharp breath catches in my throat. Logic screams at me to get away, to remind him this is business. But my body betrays me, rooting me in place, frozen.

"Fuck, you smell good." His eyes lock onto mine, a slow smirk tugging at the corner of his mouth. "I bet you taste sweet."

A shiver rolls down my spine.

His gaze drags over me like he's already undressing me in his mind. "You can close your eyes and pretend I'm him."

Him.

My stomach tightens. "Ty—"

His eyes are locked on mine. "I don't mind."

My fingers curl into the bedspread beneath me. Every nerve stretched taut, the slow, traitorous thrum of arousal sparks low in my belly. I don't want to feel this. I don't want to want this. But it's been so long since anyone touched me—and my body longs for pleasure even when my mind protests.

Ty's body is like Alex's, a rugby powerhouse—tall, broad, solid muscle. I wonder—if he pressed me into this mattress, would it feel the same? Would his weight settle over me the way Alex's did, grounding me, making me forget everything but the way he felt, the way he moved?

The thought sends a jolt of something sharp through me.

No.

No one could ever feel like Alex.

But Alex isn't in my life.

And he never will be again.

A sharp knock at the door shatters the tension, followed by a muffled voice. "Housekeeping."

Ty lets out a quiet curse, the frustration rolling off him in waves. The intensity in his eyes flickers but only for a second.

I move, pushing to my feet, desperate for the space, for the air that feels too thick.

I straighten my clothes, willing my heartbeat to slow. When I glance back at Ty, he's still sitting on the bed, jaw tight, his hands clenched into fists.

"I'll get it."

"Please do. Because I can't go to the door like this."

We both know what he means.

I crack the door open. "Hi. No service needed, thank you."

The woman gives a polite nod and wheels her cart down the hall, oblivious that her new boss is in this room with a raging erection.

I close the door and exhale.

What the hell am I doing? I need to get my head on straight. Now.

The door clicks softly behind me. Ty leans forward on the bed, forearms balanced on his knees, his gaze pinned to the floor. For once, the relentless arrogance in his posture is gone.

He rubs a hand along his jaw. "I shouldn't have done that."

I stand across the room from him, keeping my distance. "No, you shouldn't have."

He looks at me for a long moment before shaking his head, a rueful smile tugging at the corner of his lips. "Bloody hell, Magnolia. You're so fucking beautiful, and—"

He stops, like he's contemplating his next words, and shoves a hand through his dark hair. "I don't know what Sebring was thinking. He was a fool to let you go."

"Alex had a differing opinion."

How many times will talking about this cut me to the bone?

Ty shakes his head. "I'll never understand it."

Neither will I.

I'm so damn tired.

Tired of wondering what went wrong.

Tired of replaying every moment, every conversation, searching for some hidden clue I missed.

Tired of waking up every morning with the same hollow ache in my chest, knowing that no matter how much time passes, it still hasn't gone away.

I just want it to be over—the pain, the questions, the what-ifs.

"The point you were making about the bed is valid. I'll choose thicker mattresses and taller bed frames." My voice is all business as if the last ten minutes never happened.

"I'm glad you understand the logistics."

The insinuation hangs between us, heavy and electric. I tear my gaze away, pretending to return to my laptop, feigning focus. But my hands move without purpose, my mind too tangled in the direction that conversation nearly took. I can't sit here and talk about lovers who take pride in a woman's pleasure—especially when the man sitting across from me looks like he could teach master classes in it.

Not when I haven't had that since the last night I spent with Alex many months ago.

Ty stands, adjusting his trousers. "You're doing a great job. This place is going to be special."

"I'm happy you're pleased with my work."

He checks his watch and glances at me. "I have somewhere to be."

Relief flickers through me. "I'll reach out when I finish the sample board."

"Look forward to it."

He reaches for the door handle but hesitates, throwing a glance over his shoulder. "I know Sebring didn't paint me in the best light. I can only imagine the things he's told you."

My brow arches in silent response, the words kept locked behind my teeth.

He exhales a quiet laugh. "All I'm saying is I'd like it if you gave me a chance. Perhaps begin with friendship?"

"Let's start with a designer-client relationship and see how that goes."

He nods, his blue eyes locked onto mine. "Fair enough but remember this: I'm more than happy to help you forget Sebring if you ever change your mind."

The door clicks shut, and the silence that follows is deafening.

What the hell just happened?

One minute, I was reviewing fabric swatches and debating headboards. The next, Ty was on his knees, demonstrating why the beds need to be taller.

Of course, he wouldn't just look at my mood board and call it a day. No, he had to make it an immersive, hands-on kind of experience.

The bed is too low for eating pussy—they don't teach you that problem-solving skill in interior-design classes.

The real joke is on me. Because for a second—one fleeting, reckless moment—I allowed myself to wonder what it would feel like to let go. To give in. Close my eyes and pretend.

Imagine he was Alex.

Maybe a meaningless fuck would help—a way to silence the ache, to feel something other than this endless, hollow pain. But even that feels impossible. My body might crave the distraction, but my heart isn't ready. Not yet.

Chapter 20

Magnolia Steel

My laptop is open, the guest room mood boards pulled up. Images stare back at me, but my focus is shot. My mind is tangled up in something I shouldn't be thinking about.

It's been two days since the close-call-cunnilingus incident. Not long enough to forget the way Ty's lips pressed against my thigh, the way his breath was hot against my skin, the way my pulse thundered in my ears when his mouth hovered there.

Well, hell—if this ain't a damn clusterfuck, served up hot with a buttered biscuit.

I snap the laptop shut, wishing it were that easy to shut down my mind too.

Ty and I haven't talked since. Haven't acknowledged the moment we crossed a line. Maybe that's for the best. Maybe silence is the best way to move forward.

Except, are we moving forward? Or are we waiting for it to happen again?

The shrill ring of my phone slices through the silence. I glance at the screen, and my stomach tightens.

Tyson-fucking-McRae.

I hesitate, my pulse kicking up. I should let it go to voicemail. Keep things easy and safe.

But apparently, I'm a closet masochist.

What the fuck am I doing?

"Hello."

"Good morning, Magnolia. How are you?" His voice is deep, smooth, like nothing is out of place between us. Like he isn't the last person I should speak to right now.

"I'm good." I hesitate for half a second. "Doing a little work."

"What are you working on?"

I glance at my closed laptop. "Still on guest-room designs. Lots of decisions to be made while we're waiting for the historical preservation board to approve the plans we submitted."

It's not a lie—I am working. But that's not what's consuming me. My mind has been looping all day, trying to make sense of what happened between Ty and me.

The way he touched me.

The way I almost let him take it further.

The way I might have wanted him to keep going.

I should've drawn a hard line. Should've put distance between us. But I didn't.

I still haven't.

And now, he's calling me like everything is normal. Like we didn't almost crash and burn in guest room 112.

Ty's voice pulls me back. "Take a break from work and come out with me tonight. There's a gallery opening I want to go to."

Not a call, not a text. Now, out of nowhere, he's asking me to a gallery opening as if nothing happened?

I should say no, make an excuse. But that's not what I do.

"You like art, huh?"

"I do, very much, and I want to buy some for the hotel. It's a talented artist. I believe you'll like his work."

"Who's the artist?"

"William Bloom."

Wow. I'm shocked that he would have an interest in William Bloom. He doesn't seem the type. "I love his work."

"You're familiar with him?"

"Absolutely."

"Is that a yes?"

"Is it a formal event?"

"It is. Do you have a dress?"

My stomach dips. The dress isn't the problem—I have plenty. Too many, if I'm being honest. Most of them bought in Sydney, for glittering nights with Alex—nights wrapped in silk and his arms, when I was his in every way that counted.

I shake off the memory. "I have a dress."

Bad idea. Bad idea. Bad idea.

But I hear myself ignore my own advice. "Sounds fun."

"Perfect. I'll pick you up at seven."

"I'll be ready."

The call ends, and I stare at my phone.

What the hell am I doing?

Assisting my client in buying art for the project we're working on. Totally legit. That has to be what I'm doing. Because no other answer is acceptable.

THE LOW RUMBLE OF AN ENGINE ROLLS THROUGH THE QUIET night, smooth and unmistakably fast. Ty pulls up in a car that looks like it belongs on a magazine cover—sleek, black, and made for people who have more money than they know what to do with. A car that turns heads simply by its existence.

My posture is perfect as I step outside, heels clicking against the pavement. A cool breeze blows up the skirt of my dress, whispering over my bare skin, but the chill disappears the second our gazes meet.

His eyes drag over me, slow and unhurried, dark with something unreadable. "Fuck, you're a stunner." The rough edge to his voice sends a ripple through me.

Fuck, you're a stunner. God, I miss hearing those words.

I swallow, my grip tightening around my clutch. I know what's on his mind. Hell, I know because it's on my mind too.

I fight a smirk... and lose. "You clean up well, Mr. McRae."

He smirks back. "Admit it. You think I'm hot."

I roll my eyes, releasing out a dry laugh. "You're insufferable."

He chuckles, reaching for the passenger door handle. "That wasn't a no."

I step past him, sliding into the leather seat as he closes the door behind me.

The banter does what I hoped it would—lift the awkwardness—at least a little. But as he rounds the car and slips behind the wheel, one thing's for sure.

This night is going to be precarious.

Because Tyson McRae is dangerous.

Music hums low through the car's speakers, a steady pulse under the quiet. I glance at the display panel, seeing the song title on the screen. "I'm God" by Clams Casino & Imogen Heap. The ethereal melody fills the space, a strange contrast to the tension between us.

"I don't recognize this song," I say, half to myself.

Ty shifts gears, his eyes flicking to me before returning to the road. "That's not surprising."

I arch a brow. "You think you've already got my music taste all figured out?"

He smirks, tapping a rhythm against the steering wheel. "Not yet. But I'm getting there."

Something about the casual way he says it makes my stomach tighten, but I shake it off, looking out the window at the city lights flashing past. My gaze drifts back to him. "How'd you hear about the William Bloom show?"

"I keep up with artists I like. Would've been criminal to be in the

States and not catch one of his shows—especially with it happening right here in the city I'm in."

Tyson McRae—a cocky, unpredictable force of nature—appreciates fine art. Surprising.

"I own one of his pieces."

He glances at me, interest flickering in his eyes. "Yeah?"

I nod. "Bought it a few years ago. His work is raw. Layered. I'm not sure how to explain it, but it makes you think on a deeper level."

"I agree with that."

Ty stares ahead, but his gaze keeps flickering to me, like there's something he wants to say.

I shift in my seat, overwhelmed by the tangle of emotions clawing for a way out.

It's reckless, it's stupid, but I can't stop myself. Or my mouth. "Why do you hate Alex so much?"

The mood shifts in an instant.

A muscle tics in his jaw, but there's the flash of something darker that flickers across his face and makes my stomach twist. "You want to get into this now?"

"Yeah. I do."

Ty exhales hard, his hands white-knuckling the steering wheel. "I grew up with nothing, Magnolia. No privilege. No money. No safety net. Pure survival."

There's a razor-sharp edge beneath his voice.

"I worked my ass off. Every damn day. Pushed harder than anyone. Scraped by on talent and grit alone. And I made it—my dream position, my shot. But Alex-fucking-Sebring-the-third walked in and took it from me like it was nothing."

I hear the bitterness in his voice, the raw resentment pulsing beneath his words.

"I can take not being the best, but here's the thing. He was born into privilege and money. Had the best coaches. The right teams. Everything I had to fight tooth and nail for was handed to him on a silver platter."

There's fire behind his frustration, but beneath it, there's something else. Something deeper.

Ty lets out a bitter laugh. "But you wouldn't understand that."

My brows knit. "What does that mean?"

He glances at me, his gaze assessing. "You have no idea what it's like to come from nothing."

I let out a short, humorless laugh. "You think you know me?"

He doesn't answer, just keeps driving, waiting for me to prove him wrong. So I do.

"My parents didn't give a damn about me. I raised myself. I didn't come from nothing—I came from less than nothing. You aren't the only one who worked their ass off for every single thing they have. So don't tell me I don't understand."

Silence swallows the space between us as Ty's hands flex on the wheel. I sense him processing, recalibrating.

"You and I have far more in common than you and Alex ever did. I'm sorry that I assumed otherwise."

For the first time, I might understand Tyson McRae a little.

The gallery is a world of its own—high ceilings, soft classical music floating through the air, and the low hum of cultured conversation. The scent of polished wood and expensive wine lingers, wrapping the space in quiet sophistication.

Ty walks beside me, hands in his pockets, scanning the room with a calculating interest. We weave through the crowd, stopping in front of the first piece that catches our attention.

It's bold—shadows and sharp edges, a story trapped beneath layers of paint. I tilt my head, studying it.

"I like the movement in this one. I think it's my favorite piece."

"The Unseen Queen." Ty leans in, tilting his head. "You can't see her face, but you can tell she's fierce. That's real power. Not needing to be perfect to own the whole damn room."

I glance at him beside me, surprised to hear him say that. He understands more about art than I expected. "Exactly."

"Should I buy it?"

"I don't think you have a choice. It would be perfect surrounded by the colors and fabrics I've chosen for the hotel."

We move through the gallery, lingering on the same pieces, drawn to the same styles. It's an odd realization—our tastes align.

"You have a great eye for this."

"That's high praise coming from you."

He listens as I explain what I love about certain pieces and the artist's use of light. His attention doesn't waver, not even for a second. It's unnerving, the way he seems to listen with his whole body, like every word I say matters.

He leans in, a half-smile playing at his mouth. "You're even more beautiful when you talk about what sets your soul on fire."

The compliment is unexpected. I try to brush it off with a small shake of my head, but my pulse betrays me, quickening.

We aren't moving on from what happened in that hotel room. Not really. It's still there between us, crackling under the surface, daring one of us to be reckless enough to reach for it again. This—whatever this is—is not business. It's a slow flirtation with disaster, and we're both playing along like we don't know better.

I give him a look that's intended to be stern, but I think it comes off more like playful. "You're terrible at keeping things professional."

"You're not exactly discouraging me, sweetheart." He smirks, not even pretending to apologize. "If you really wanted me to stop, you wouldn't be smiling right now."

He's right, and worse? He knows he's right.

We linger a moment longer at the last canvas, both of us quieter now, something unspoken hanging between us.

Ty clears his throat and shifts into business mode, pointing out the pieces he wants to purchase for the hotel. I keep my focus sharp, professional, helping to handle the arrangements without missing a beat.

Transactions are handled, signatures scrawled, everything finalized.

We step out of the gallery, and I still feel the buzz of the evening clinging to me. The night air is crisp, a stark contrast to the heat simmering beneath my skin.

"That was productive."

"It was. Thank you for coming with me."

"Thank you for inviting me."

He walks beside me, his hand settling at the small of my back. It's a quiet, possessive touch that sends a ripple of awareness through me. I should pull away, but I don't.

We turn to walk down a side street, the quiet stretching between us like something tangible, something waiting to break. The city hums in the distance, but here, in the dim light between buildings, it seems like another world.

Then he stops.

Before I can react, his fingers curl around my wrist, tugging me back. My breath catches as he pulls me into the narrow alley between two buildings, pressing my back against the brick wall, the rough texture biting through the thin fabric of my dress.

He's close. Too close. The air between us turns electric, humming with something unspoken, something inevitable.

His eyes flick down to my mouth. "You want me to stop?"

My pulse pounds, my body betraying me.

I shake my head... because I can't form a single word.

His lips crash against mine, claiming, devouring. Heat surges through me, curling low in my belly as his hands grip my waist, pressing me closer. I melt into him, into the sharp angles of his body, the rough scrape of his stubble against my skin.

I close my eyes, and it's not Tyson McRae kissing me.

It's Alex.

My own mind turns traitor, conjuring memories of his touch, his mouth, the way he used to hold me like I was something breakable. But Ty isn't Alex. His touch is different—rougher, more demanding.

I force my eyes open, and his gaze locks with mine. There's something dark and unreadable flickering in his eyes as his hands slide up my thighs, slipping beneath the hem of my dress.

His fingers brush against my panties, pushing them aside with an ease that makes my breath hitch. I gasp as he strokes me, slow, deliberate. My body arches into him, a treasonous reaction I can't control.

His lips trail down my neck, his breath hot against my skin. "So bloody beautiful," he says, his voice thick with something I can't name.

I clutch at his shoulders as he slides two fingers inside me, curling them just right. My head falls back against the brick, a strangled moan escaping my lips as pleasure crashes over me. He doesn't stop, doesn't look away, as he watches me fall apart in his hands.

The tension coils, tightens—then shatters. I tremble against him, breathless, dazed. Ty pulls his fingers from me slowly, deliberately. And then—

He brings them to his mouth.

Tastes me.

"Fuck." His eyes lock on mine. "You taste so sweet."

I can't breathe. Can't think.

What the hell have I done?

The night air presses in, thick with something unspoken. The moment stretches between us, taut as a wire pulled too tight. My breathing is uneven, my pulse still thundering in my ears.

Ty stands steady, his gaze locked onto mine, waiting for me to react.

I don't. I can't. My mind is a storm, thoughts colliding in a messy, tangled wreckage.

I should move. I should say something. But all I can do is relish the sensation of pleasure still pulsing through me, feel the ghost of his fingers inside me, carry the weight of everything I let happen.

A part of me is sick with guilt. But then, just as quickly, I shove it down. Bury it.

I haven't betrayed Alex. He ended things with me. He's with someone else. He's marrying another woman.

The one.

I don't owe him my loyalty or fidelity. Yet something inside me twists, sharp and unforgiving.

Why does it ache like I just crossed a line I can't come back from?

Ty watches me, unreadable, but there's something in his expression—something satisfied, something knowing. He lifts a hand and brushes his thumb over my bottom lip, his touch deliberate and possessive.

"You don't have to think so hard with me, Mags." His voice is smooth, confident, like he's not the least bit uncertain about what just happened between us.

My stomach tightens. Because that's the problem. I wasn't thinking at all.

I was letting go. And if I keep allowing myself to play with this fire, I will get burned. Maybe not today, maybe not tomorrow—but the flames will find me.

I swallow hard, stepping back, putting distance between us even as my body protests the loss of heat. My fingers tremble as I adjust my dress, as if I can erase what just happened, as if I can make myself believe that I'm still the same person I was before he pulled me into this alley.

Ty doesn't stop me. He doesn't say a word. He just watches, his smirk lingering.

The silence stretches, suffocating me.

I force a breath. "We should go."

His smirk deepens, but he nods. "Whatever you say, Mags."

He steps back, giving me space, but the damage is already done. My skin still burns where he touched me. My mind is branded with the way he looked at me, the way he pressed against me.

I don't look at him as we walk toward the car, my pulse still hammering in my throat.

This was a mistake. And deep down, I know something else.

It probably won't be the last.

The drive back is suffocating. The silence stretches, thick and heavy, filling every inch of space between us. Ty's hands grip the steering wheel, his posture relaxed. But I know better. His restraint is a tangible thing, pressing against the tension that lingers between us.

My mind betrays me, flashing back to the alley. The rough brick against my back. The way his fingers slid beneath my dress, parting me with ease. The way he worked me, his touch unyielding.

My breath increased and my body arched into him, desperate and wanting. He watched me unravel, eyes locked on mine, consuming me whole.

I will the memory away, staring out the window at the blur of city lights. Every second is like an eternity.

I need to say something. Anything.

"What are you doing in the U.S.?"

He smirks but keeps his eyes on the road. "You mean besides making women come hard in dark alleys?"

I roll my eyes, but the corner of my mouth twitches. "I mean why did you buy a hotel here?"

"Why not?"

"I'm serious, Ty. Tell me the reason."

"I'm playing one last season of rugby. After that, I'm done. Out for good." He flicks a glance at me before turning his attention back to the road. "Rugby's been my life, but I need something else. The hotel's an investment for the future."

"Why not buy a hotel in Sydney?"

"So I can continue competing against the Sebrings? Nah, I'm done with that. I'm done with Sydney."

My pulse jumps at the mention of Alex's family. He and I may be over, but I still care very much for the Sebring family.

"Did you know what you were doing when you injured Alex?"

He chuckles. "Wasn't trying to end his career... but I wasn't exactly trying not to, either. Just how it played out."

I should be angry. I should tear into him like a tornado through a trailer park.

But I don't.

My bond with Alex isn't just broken—it is severed, clean and final, the moment he ended us with a heartless text. Just icy words on a screen where love used to be.

And yet, as I sit here, I still can't help but wonder...

If our bond is truly severed, why do I still feel the pain?

Chapter 21

Alex Sebring

THE RESTAURANT LOOMS AHEAD, A COZY SPOT TUCKED BETWEEN towering high-rises, its warm lighting spilling onto the street. As I walk through the entrance, a strange mix of anticipation and apprehension coils in my chest because I haven't seen Kye in months.

Kye Bennelong. My former agent, my friend—one of the few people who knows me beyond the headlines and statistics. We are more than client and rep; we are mates. He was the first to see the fire in me, the one who fought like hell to make sure my career became more than potential. And I owe him for that.

As I weave through the path around the tables in the restaurant, I realize how much I've missed him. The easy camaraderie, the way Kye grounds me with a simple look, a joke, a well-timed kick in the ass when I needed it. Rugby gave me more than a career; it gave me an extended family. And Kye? He was a big part of that.

Maybe it's because we share a unique understanding—me with my Samoan roots, and him with his Aboriginal heritage. I often feel like an outsider in certain circles, caught between cultures, never quite fitting into the mold the world has laid out for me. Kye understands that without me ever having to explain it. He understands what it's like to walk into a room and feel you have something to prove—like you have to be twice as good to be considered equal.

I spot him before he sees me, sitting at a corner table, his head bent as he talks into his phone, his deep voice carrying over the soft hum of conversation. He's always been larger than life, a towering presence in any room, an easy smile and a laugh that could shake the walls.

He hasn't changed—broad-shouldered, sporting the same signature short fade hairstyle, dressed in a killer tailored suit.

Kye looks up, spotting me. His face splits into a grin, wide and welcoming, like no time has passed at all.

His phone is pressed to his ear, and he signals, the way he always has, to give him a minute.

"No, babe. I swear, I'm leaving as soon as Alex and I are done. Just keep everything... *ready* for me."

Pause.

"Yes, I'll bring your favorite sushi."

Pause.

"I know salmon is full of omega-whatevers. Babe, I'm on it, all right?"

His jaw tics and he wears the strained look of a man clinging to his last thread of patience.

"Yeah, yeah, I know it's the right time. The test said so."

Kye's gaze snaps to mine, amusement flickering in his eyes. "I'll be there soon, all right? Just... light a candle or something."

Pause.

A slow grin spreads across his face.

"Lucky me."

I shake my head, smirking as I slide into the seat across from him. He hangs up and tosses his phone onto the table. "Marriage, mate. It's a beautiful thing."

I arch a brow, settling back in my chair. "Didn't realize marriage came with sushi orders and omega-whatevers."

Kye groans, rubbing a hand over his face. "It does when you're trying to have a baby. Apparently, there's a perfect time for everything, and my wife's got it down to a science. Peeing on sticks, tracking charts, monitoring temps—you name it, she's on it. And if I screw up the sushi order, I might as well not bother going home."

I chuckle, shaking my head. "Never thought I'd see the day—Kye Bennelong, tied down and trading in late nights for early-morning feedings and nappies."

"Oh, it's happening, mate. Full speed ahead. My missus has me on a game plan tighter than pre-season training. But hey, at least the drills are fun."

"The legendary Kye Bennelong—reduced to ovulation sticks and sushi deliveries. You are living the dream."

Kye laughs, the deep sound filling the space between us. "Yeah well, I'm almost forty. It was a good run while it lasted."

"A great run."

His expression turns softer, more sincere. "Truth is I love it. Being a husband is great. Wouldn't trade it for anything. Can't wait to be a dad."

Kye—one of the wildest blokes I've ever known—has slipped into marriage and family life like it's the role he was born to play.

And me? My life has gone in the complete opposite direction.

I force a smile, reaching for the menu and flipping it open, hoping he doesn't see the shadow that passes over my face. "If the agent thing doesn't work out, at least you've got a promising future as an expert in fertility tracking."

Kye chuckles. "That's me, mate. A man of many talents."

I nod, but my mind is elsewhere—drifting to everything that's slipped away from me. But Kye has it figured out—a wife, a family in the making, a solid future.

And here I am, more lost than ever.

He flags down a server, ordering a round of old-fashioneds. Doesn't ask what I want. He just remembers.

Some things never change.

"So, what've you been up to? Last I heard, you were taking the fancy hotel business by storm and living the good life."

I shrug, offering a half-smile. "Living the good life—that's debatable. It's been fine, I guess. Keeping busy."

He takes a drink of water while we wait on the good stuff. "You were always shit at lying, Sebring. Anything exciting going on in your life? Or is it all work and no play?"

"Does trying every old-fashioned in Sydney count as play?"

He chuckles, shaking his head. "Sounds thrilling."

His eyes soften, and I see concern beneath his usual swagger. "You miss it?"

I know what he's referring to, but I play dumb. "Miss what?"

He gives me a pointed look. "Come on, Sebring. The field. The game. The rush."

"I miss it every damn day."

Kye nods like he already knows the answer. "Figured as much."

The old-fashioneds arrive, and Kye wastes no time diving into rugby talk. "Have you been keeping up with the boys? Seen how things are going without you?"

I shake my head. "Not really. I hear bits and pieces here and there, mostly from Nate."

"I'm going to fill you in, but you got to keep this on the down-low."

"Sure."

"Your replacement isn't working out."

That's unexpected. "I was under the impression that David was satisfied with him."

He shakes his head. "Nah. Kid's got talent, sure, but he's no Alex Sebring."

A strange mix of pride and regret tugs at me. "So what's the plan? They looking to trade him?"

Kye nods. "That's the word."

My stomach knots. I shouldn't care, shouldn't ask, but I can't help it. "Please don't say they're looking at Tyson McRae."

I brace myself for the answer.

Kye chuckles. "You'd rather set yourself on fire than see McRae in your jersey."

I shake my head. "I couldn't take that shit."

Kye's expression shifts into something more serious. "You don't have to worry about that. They're looking at you."

I let out a short laugh, leaning back in my chair. "Good one, mate."

But Kye doesn't laugh. "I'm not kidding."

The humor drains from my face. "I'm going to need you to explain what that means."

"They want you back. Management's been talking, and they're interested."

I blink, trying to process his words. It makes no sense. "They all know my injury never healed."

Kye leans forward, his eyes locked onto mine. "But what if it could? What if your days on the field weren't over?"

The weight of his words settles over me, and something stirs inside me.

Something dangerous—hope.

I look at Kye, searching his face for any hint that he's having me on. But there's nothing—just steady, unwavering certainty in his eyes.

A slow exhale leaves my lungs as I shake my head. "The ankle's done. My playing days are over."

The words taste bitter, even after all this time. Saying them out loud doesn't make them any easier to accept.

Kye's expression is unreadable. Then, that infuriating smirk of his spreads. "But what if those days weren't over?"

I blink, surprised. "You've lost me."

"Hypothetically speaking... if the injury was a non-issue, would you come back?"

No hesitation. "Of course I'd come back. I never wanted to leave. You know that."

He nods. "That's what I thought, but I wasn't sure if you'd met the love of your life and moved on from it."

I met the love of my life. And I lost her.

There's a hollow space inside me that no amount of winning, no amount of moving on, will ever fill. You can't patch up and forget some things. They carve their mark so deep that pretending you're whole again just feels like lying.

I shake off the thought before it can drag me under. "Is there a point to this conversation about me returning?"

He grins, leaning back in his chair like he's been waiting to drop this on me. "There's a doctor in the States who specializes in sports medicine injuries, and he has a remarkable talent for Achilles repairs."

"Kye—"

He holds up a hand, cutting me off. "Hear me out. This guy is a miracle worker. He's getting athletes back to playing in record time, stronger than before. Your injury might be bad, but it's not impossible. You just haven't had the right medical team working on you."

A war wages inside me.

The last surgery didn't fix me. The rehab, the endless PT sessions, the hope—none of it was enough. And the risk of going through it all again only to end up back at square one scares the hell out of me.

"David is asking you to do this."

"David?"

"He wants you back. Bad."

David isn't only the team's owner—he's the pulse behind it. Ruthless when he has to be, loyal when it counts. He doesn't throw second chances around like confetti. If David's asking for me, it's because he believes I still have something worth fighting for.

"Think about it, Alex. You could have another chance."

Something twists in my gut. "I have to think about this."

"Go see the doctor for a consultation. What's the worst that can happen?"

"The worst? I let myself hope for something that's never gonna happen."

Disappointments have dominated my life the last few years. I don't want to go through another.

The last one almost killed me.

Kye's gaze softens, and for a moment, he's not just my agent—he's my mate. "At least you would walk away knowing you tried everything."

I nod, my mind already running in a dozen different directions. This could be something... or it could be nothing. But Kye's words echo in my chest, steady and relentless.

What if there's still a chance?

Kye turns up the last of his old-fashioned. "Want me to set up an appointment?"

"I guess a consultation wouldn't hurt." I play it cool, but it hits me harder than I want to admit.

Kye smirks, seeing straight through my bullshit. "Right. Just an inconsequential consultation. No big deal."

He takes out his phone. "Any dates we need to work around?"

I shake my head, the answer coming too fast. "No."

Nothing. No obligations. No one waiting on me.

"Claire. Hey, love. Do me a favor, and call Dr. Tate's office first thing tomorrow and book a consultation for The Wall."

He pauses, listening for a moment before adding, "The Achilles specialist in Dallas. Priority booking, whatever it takes to get Alex in with him ASAP."

Dallas, Texas.

The United States.

The words hit me square in the chest. Texas is in the South. And Charleston...

How far is Dallas from Charleston?

My jaw clenches, annoyed at myself for even wondering it. Months have passed. I should be over this. Past her. But Magnolia's never left my thoughts. She's there always, woven into the quiet spaces of my mind.

Kye carries the confidence of a man who's got life figured out. "Three years... I reckon you've got at least that much left in you if you get healthy again. I wouldn't say that about just anybody. But you... you're built different."

Three years.

For the first time in a long while, something flickers inside me.

Three more years on the field. The roar of the crowd, the rush of adrenaline, the bone-deep satisfaction that comes from doing what I love most. It's a future I hadn't dared to consider since my injury.

It's been two years. The road back won't be easy—hell, it'll be brutal. I'll have to fight harder than I ever have, push my body past limits I haven't tested in a long time. And even then, there's no guarantee I'll make it.

The idea gnaws at me, refusing to let go. The possibility that I'm not done yet.

I swirl the last sip of my drink, staring at the amber liquid as if it might offer some kind of answer.

Rugby would give me purpose, something to focus on besides the emptiness Magnolia left behind. If I can't have her, this might be the next best thing.

"You get this surgery, you put in the work, and you'll be back on the field. Trust me, when you're out there again, everything else fades away."

Everything else.

Magnolia.

The ache that never quite leaves me.

The thoughts that haunt me late at night when I'm alone with nothing but the weight of what could've been.

Kye's unwavering belief in me stirs something in my chest. "It'd be good to play again."

"Damn right, it would. You're not done yet, Sebring. I know it. You know it."

I let his words settle, rolling them over in my mind. He's right. I'm not done yet.

For now, the thought of stepping back onto the field and getting that rush is enough to get me through another day. Even if it's temporary, it's better than nothing. And right now, I'll take it.

Chapter 22

Alex Sebring

Dr. Harrison Tate studies his computer screen, his eyes scanning the images of my ankle with a focus that makes my stomach twist. The large monitor casts a cool glow over his face, highlighting the lines of concentration etched into his features. He's one of the best in the world—people fly from all over the globe just to sit in this chair.

I've been in Dallas for two days, going through one test after another. Now comes the part I've been dreading.

The verdict.

He clicks through a few more scans before giving me his attention.

"Alex." He exhales, folding his hands together on his desk. "Your injury is more extensive than we first expected."

The words hit like a wrecking ball to the gut, but I keep my cool, my hands gripping the armrests a little tighter. "How bad?"

His lips press into a thin line. "It's obvious that the injury didn't heal as it should. There's extensive scar tissue, and the alignment is off."

He turns his monitor around, and points to the glaring problems on the 3D scan, explaining a lot of medical terms I remember from before but still don't understand.

"There was never any real chance of you returning to play rugby with your ankle in this kind of condition."

The weight of his words hits like a physical blow. A part of me wants to argue, to push back, to tell him I'm a hard worker and this won't keep me down. But the evidence is staring me right in the face.

"I don't have to tell you that rugby is a demanding sport," he says.

The last thread of hope I'd been holding on to frays and snaps. I should've known better. Should've listened the first time they told me it was over.

A bitter laugh escapes me, hollow and resigned. "Guess I was foolish for hoping I could make a comeback."

"Hope is never foolish."

So this is it. I'll go back to Sydney and manage hotels for the rest of my life—take over my father's dynasty and give up on mine.

The truth hurts—my time on the rugby field has ended. I had my glory days, but they're gone. Reality is staring me down in high-definition clarity on his computer screen.

"With that being said, I believe I can fix this."

My head snaps up. "Wait... what?"

He swivels the monitor again and clicks through more images. "Don't get me wrong. It will not be easy. The damage is significant, and the recovery will be grueling. But with the right surgical approach and proper rehabilitation, I believe you can make a full recovery."

I stare at him, waiting for the catch. The fine print. The inevitable *but* that always follows statements like that. "You're telling me I can play again?"

He nods. "It's one of the worst I've ever seen, but I love a challenge."

Good news is what I'd hoped for, but this seems almost too good to believe. "I don't know what to say. I'm speechless."

"Surgery is only the first step. Rehab will push you harder than anything you've done before. And if you're not committed, if you don't follow the protocol to the letter—"

"I'm one hundred percent committed." The words leave my mouth before I put any thought into them. If there's even the slightest shot at getting back to the sport I love, I'll take it. No hesitation. No second-guessing.

I won't blow this again.

Dr. Tate nods, satisfied with my response. "Good. Because this isn't only about getting you back to rugby, Alex. It's about making sure your ankle holds up for the long-term. You'll be in pain the rest of your life if we don't fix this. Not just in a game, but every day with walking, running, even standing too long. It will lead to impaired mobility."

This is my first time hearing that prognosis.

It's a real kick in the twig and berries.

After all this time, something stirs inside me. Not the hopeless longing I've been drowning in for months, but something sharper. Stronger. The spark I'd lost.

And just like that, the impossible becomes real again.

Dr. Tate taps a few keys to pull up a detailed recovery timeline on the screen. "Let's talk about what recovery looks like. This will not be a quick fix. We're looking at a structured, phased approach over the next several months."

I nod, my eyes skimming the outline he's handed me, though the words blur together almost immediately. I clear my throat, pushing down the old instinct to fake it. Not today. Not when everything about my future is on the line.

"Just so you know, if it looks like I'm not reading this properly, it's not because I don't care. I've got severe dyslexia. Reading's always been a bitch for me."

Dr. Tate's gaze sharpens, but not with judgment. With understanding. He gives a quick nod and starts explaining instead.

"For the first six weeks post-surgery, you'll be in a cast or boot with minimal weight bearing. Then we'll get you back on your feet, focusing on mobility and strength over the next few months. At the six-month mark, you'll start working on more sport-specific training— jogging, controlled exercises, agility work. Full-contact play, though? You're looking at anywhere from nine to twelve months before you're cleared to play."

Nine to twelve months. Up to an entire year of my life facing rehab, of waking up every day and fighting for something that isn't guaranteed.

"It's a long road, but if you put in the work, you can come back stronger than before."

"And if I rush it?"

He gives me a pointed look. "You *don't* rush it. Not unless you want to risk blowing it all over again."

Reality sinks in. This isn't only about getting back on the field. It's about doing it the right way, about giving myself the best shot at a future I thought was out of reach.

"Brutal truth... what are the odds of success?"

"Stay committed, follow my instruction, and I'd say your odds are damn good. At least ninety percent."

Hope flares in my chest.

It's going to be hell. But for the first time in almost three years, it feels like there's a way forward.

"There are conditions about signing on for this that you may find difficult."

Okay, here we go.

"You must stay in Dallas for the first twelve weeks post-op. No exceptions. The success of your recovery depends on doing proper therapy. I don't trust that task to anyone other than my team."

Twelve weeks. Three months away from home. I let that number settle in for a moment.

Being here all alone is daunting, but what other choice do I have?

"It's a lot to take in. If you need time to process, discuss with your people—"

"I don't need time. Let's get it done as soon as possible."

A flicker of satisfaction crosses Tate's face. "All right. I'll have my assistant put you on the schedule."

I shift forward, resting my forearms on my knees. "How soon can we do this?"

He turns his attention to his computer and makes several clicks. "Looks like I can get you in next week."

Next week. I nod, rolling the possibility over in my mind. It's enough time to get my head straight and tie up loose ends.

He stands, offering his hand. "This won't be easy. But it'll be worth it."

I leave the clinic with a weight heavier than hope. After swinging by the hotel to grab my bag, I head straight to the airport.

The hum of the jet engines fills the cabin, a low, steady vibration threading through my chest. I stare out the window, watching Dallas shrink below me, anticipation flickering to life in my gut.

The road ahead looks different. But as the plane climbs higher, darker thoughts creep in, coiling tight around my heart. No surgery, no miracle fix, can heal the part of me that's still broken.

Without giving myself time to second-guess it, I press the intercom button. "There's been a change of plans."

A crackle, then the pilot's voice cuts through. "Yes, Mr. Sebring?"

"We're going to Charleston instead."

A beat of silence. Then, "Charleston. Copy that. I'll need a moment to adjust the flight plan."

Charleston.

Magnolia.

Closure.

That's the lie I sell myself—that this is about getting answers so I can finally move on.

My therapist once told me closure isn't about fixing the past; it's about finding a way to live with it. Maybe that's true. Maybe I need to see her one last time. Hear it from her own lips.

Because if I don't, I'll stay stuck in this purgatory forever—halfway between healing and heartbreak.

And that's no way to live.

Chapter 23

Alex Sebring

THE WHEELS OF THE PRIVATE JET TOUCH DOWN WITH A SOFT jolt, and the unfamiliar Charleston skyline stretches beyond the window.

My phone is heavier than usual as I dial Magnolia's number. One ring, and straight to voicemail.

> Hey. I'm in town. I need to see you. It's important.

The text sends, but there's no read receipt. No dots appearing to tell me she's typing. Only silence.

I try again.

> Please. Just five minutes of your time. That's all I'm asking for.

Still nothing.

The texts continue to sit there, unread, glaring back at me. And now there's no doubt—she's blocked me. Not that I didn't suspect it months ago.

One thing about Magnolia—she never does anything halfway.

When she decided she wanted me gone, she made damn sure there was no coming back.

I shove my phone into my pocket. "Fuck! I didn't come all this way just to hit another roadblock."

With no other option, I grab my bag and head for the waiting taxi. Sliding into the back seat, I give the driver the address to Soul Sync, the one place I can find her.

As we weave through the streets of Charleston, I watch the city unfold around me—colorful buildings with intricate ironwork balconies, cobblestone streets lined with trees swaying in the warm breeze. It's picturesque, the kind of place Magnolia would thrive in, full of charm and old-world elegance.

But right now, it's a beautiful maze keeping me from what I came here for.

I drag in a slow breath, tapping my fingers against my knee as the taxi pulls up to Soul Sync's office. I step out, staring up at the building, my pulse hammering in my ears. Months have passed, but standing here now, it feels like no time at all—like I'm right back where I was when she walked away.

My chest tightens at the thought of seeing her again, the weight of everything left unsaid pressing down on me. Part of me wonders if she'll let me get a word in. Or will she turn and walk away the second she lays eyes on me.

Maybe she should. I'm fucked up in the head, even more so since I lost her.

But another part of me—one that's louder, more desperate— clings to the hope that I might get something out of this.

A moment.

A conversation.

A chance to make sense of what happened.

I roll my shoulders, forcing down the nerves clawing at my throat. I can't turn back now. Whatever happens, I'll face it.

I step inside Soul Sync, the cool blast of air-conditioning hitting me like a welcome reprieve from the thick Charleston heat. The lobby is sleek and modern, similar to the one in Sydney. For a moment, it feels like I've stepped back in time.

Before I can take another step, a bright, cheerful voice calls out from behind the reception desk.

"Well, look who it is—Julius Caesar."

I turn toward the voice, and there she is—the same client specialist rep from Sydney. "What a surprise seeing you here."

My pulse kicks up, but I force a polite nod. "Yeah. Thought I'd drop in."

She tilts her head, eyes sharp and curious. "I take it you're here to see Magnolia?"

She knows about Magnolia and me.

This is bad.

My stomach flips. "Can I see her?"

Her smile slips, and it's enough to tell me something's off. I'm not going to like what's coming.

The warmth in her eyes dims. "I'm sorry, but that's not possible."

She pauses, glancing around the lobby, before lowering her voice. "Magnolia doesn't work here anymore."

My heart sinks, heavy and certain—this is worse than I imagined. "Since when?"

"A few months ago."

Right around the time she cut me off.

I stare at the client specialist rep, searching her expression for some kind of explanation, but she's all polished professionalism now, her service smile back in place.

"Why?" The sound of it is all wrong—too raw, too exposed—but I can't pull it back now.

A flash of sympathy crosses her face. "I'm not at liberty to discuss that. But I believe you already know the answer."

There's only one explanation, and it sinks into my chest like a lead weight.

Me.

I'm the reason Magnolia lost this job—the job she loved and

worked so damn hard for. And just like that, the guilt I thought I'd buried months ago comes rushing back, sharper than ever.

These things always have a way of coming out. Whispers in the right ears, a few too many coincidences lining up. And despite the obscene amount of money I paid Celeste to keep her mouth shut, somehow, it still wasn't enough to protect my girl.

Frustration simmers beneath my skin. "I just need to talk to Magnolia. How can I get in touch with her?"

Her professionalism doesn't budge, but there's something in her eyes—compassion, maybe. "I'm afraid I can't help you with that."

"Please. I'm on my way back to Sydney, and I need to see her before I go."

She hesitates for a second, and I think she might cave. But then she shakes her head, her expression turning apologetic. "Soul Sync's privacy policy is strict. There's no wiggle room."

Her voice drops to a softer tone. "I've seen what happens when people break the rules, and I can't risk my job. Please don't ask me to do that, even for Magnolia, whom I love dearly."

Fuck my life.

"I get it. But leaving the States without seeing her isn't an option."

"I'm sorry."

"She's moved on—I'm not here to interfere with her life. I just need one chance to look her in the eye and say what I should've said months ago."

She offers the faintest of smiles. "I hope you find her and say what needs to be said, for both of your sakes."

She leans closer, her voice low. "It's Thursday. There's a great aerial dance studio in Charleston called Elevate Aerial Arts. They hold classes every Thursday at six o'clock."

What the hell is she talking about? "Thanks, but I'm not interested."

Her lips twitch with something that resembles amusement. "You should check it out tonight at six o'clock. Elevate Aerial Arts. I think you'd enjoy it."

She glances at her watch, a subtle smile playing at the edges of her mouth. "It's almost five, and the studio is across town. You better get a move on."

I stare at her, realization creeping in. I nod once, the weight of unspoken words hanging between us. "Right. Thanks for the suggestion."

As I turn to leave, her voice follows me, softer now. "For what it's worth, we all knew she was seeing someone while we were in Sydney."

I freeze, my feet rooted to the spot.

"She was in love, and it was obvious. She was so damn happy. I'd never seen her like that before. She didn't want to come home—it was clear she was leaving someone behind who had her heart."

A dull ache settles in my chest. "You think so?"

She nods, offering a small, sympathetic smile. "I know so."

I give her a tight nod before pushing through the door and stepping into the sticky Charleston heat.

If Magnolia was so damn happy, how did we end up like this?

Chapter 24

Alex Sebring

THE DANCE STUDIO'S BRICK FACADE BLENDS WITH THE ROW OF historic buildings on a quiet Charleston side street. A small brass plaque by the door reads Elevate Aerial Arts.

Students gather around the edges of a padded large mat, their gazes fixed upward. Wide silks hang from the ceiling in thick, cascading sheets of white, their length pooling where they meet the mat.

A woman steps into my line of sight. "Who are you here to watch?"

I blink, confused. "Watch?"

"Which student did you come to see?"

"Magnolia Steel."

The woman's eyes widen with recognition, and she nods toward the silks hanging in the middle of the room, gesturing toward the mat. "You made it just in time. Magnolia's performing next."

My pulse kicks up a notch as I scan the studio in search of her.

My American beauty is here, across the studio, standing near the silks draped from the ceiling.

Magnolia moves with a quiet grace that punches the air out of my lungs. She hasn't seen me yet—thank God. I need a second to pull myself together, to breathe through the ache clawing its way up my chest.

She's wearing a white fitted top and yoga pants that hug every line and curve. Her hair twists into a bun at the crown of her head, loose wisps escaping to frame her face.

She's always been beautiful, but now, wrapped in silk and bathed in white, she looks less like a woman and more like an angel carved from pure light.

My angel.

Or at least she was.

I swallow hard, my fists clenching at my sides as I take her in, piece by piece. Every inch of her is a painful reminder of what I lost. The sight of her hits like a hammer, cracking open the place inside me I've tried so hard to keep locked up.

For a second, I wonder if it was a mistake coming here, if seeing her again is only going to rip me apart even more. But I know the answer.

I have to see her.

Even if it destroys me.

The soft hum of the speakers crackles to life, and her routine begins. A familiar melody drifts through the studio, wrapping around me like a ghost from the past. "All Cried Out" by Allure and 112.

I know this song. It's on the playlist. I've been listening to that music for months, trying to decipher what it means to her.

Hearing the song now feels like a punch to the gut. Each note slices through me with surgical precision, carving into places I thought had scarred over.

The universe continues to fuck with me.

Her performance begins, and she moves with effortless grace, wrapping herself in the white silks. Unease curls in my chest as she climbs.

Magnolia grips the silks and looks like she's preparing to take flight. I'm rooted to the spot, every muscle in my body taut as I watch her, afraid to even blink.

A soft conversation behind me drifts forward to my ears.

"She has the musical taste of a sixty-year-old woman."

"I like her songs. She always picks one with meaning behind it. I love watching her. She looks like a graceful ballerina taking flight."

"Yeah, a ballerina dancing to sad-as-fuck songs."

"I think something sad happened to her."

"Oh for sure. You can tell that someone did her dirty."

With a dancer's ease, Magnolia winds herself into the silks, her body weightless against the fabric. The world around me dulls, but the sting of her classmates' words anchors itself in my chest.

I think something sad happened to her.

You can tell that someone did her dirty.

Magnolia moves like she was born for this—every motion seamless as the silks twist and coil around her body. The white fabric clings to her limbs, wrapping and unfurling in perfect synchrony, each movement a blend of strength and elegance. She bends and stretches, every extension a breathtaking display of control and grace, impossible to look away from.

When her feet meet the mat again, she takes off running. She leaps in one seamless motion, catching the silk mid-stride. The fabric snags around her waist, spinning her into a perfect circle as she leans back, arms outstretched. The motion is effortless, the momentum carrying her like a bird catching the wind, weightless and free. For a moment, she looks like she's soaring.

She wraps one leg around the silk, her arms lifting above her head as she twists, spiraling higher with an effortless ease that makes it look too simple, too safe. But I know better. A single misstep, a slip of focus, and she'll come crashing down.

My fists clench at my sides, tension winding tight in my chest as she releases her grip, allowing her body to tumble downward in a sudden drop. The air leaves my lungs in a sharp exhale, my stomach plummeting right along with her.

The silks catch her at the last moment, halting her fall with a gentle sway. A collective gasp echoes through the studio, followed by a burst of applause that fills the space.

I can't move, my heart lodged in my throat.

Magnolia stays suspended for a beat longer, her head tipping back, eyes closed, a serene expression softening her features. She makes it seem effortless.

Beautiful.

Dangerous.

Her performance ends and I step outside, leaning against the wall just beyond the door, where I wait for her. Minutes drag by, each one longer than the last, and doubt creeps in.

What if she slipped out another way?

Just as the worry takes root, the door swings open. She steps into the night, laughing at something the guy beside her says. He's too comfortable in her space. The easy way he walks next to her, the familiar brush of his arm against hers, the smile he throws her way—it all sets my teeth on edge.

Is this him?

Is this the fucker she's moved on with?

My jaw clenches, hands balling at my sides as a bitter edge settles into my chest.

I don't like it.

Not one damn bit.

Magnolia's eyes lift, our gazes locking, and everything changes. Her smile and laughter die, and her entire body goes stiff. Her lips part, and those hazel eyes widen in disbelief... then narrow with something.

What is that? Shock? Anger? A little of both?

She stops mid-step, staring at me. For a split second, I swear I see something softer—something like longing—but it vanishes as quickly as it appears.

He looks between us, his brow furrowing. "Everything okay, Mags?"

Mags.

I hate that too.

Magnolia blinks, her expression shifting into something flat.

"Yeah. He's just someone I used to know."

Damn. That stings.

She stops a few feet away, arms wrapping around her torso like she's bracing for impact. "Alex."

I nod, shoving my hands into my pockets, unsure what to do with them. "Magnolia."

Her classmate lingers a step behind her, eyes bouncing between us like he's watching a tennis match.

"I need to talk to you."

Her brow lifts, and for a moment, she just stares at me. "So *now* you want to talk?"

Her tone is sharp, edged with something that digs under my skin and festers. It sounds like she's implying *I'm* the one who went radio silent, the one who disappeared without a trace.

Frustration bubbles up inside me, but I force it down. "I've wanted to talk to you for months."

She lets out a humorless laugh, rolling her eyes. "*Right.* You sure have a funny way of showing it."

I blink, thrown off by the bitterness in her words. "What's that supposed to mean?"

She shakes her head, looking away, jaw tight. "You know what? Don't worry about it. Not that you ever did."

I step closer, lowering my voice. "Don't tell me not to worry about it. Not after everything."

Her eyes snap back to mine, blazing with anger. "I can't believe you have the nerve to come here... or to say that to me."

Her words land like a slap. How does she get to be the one who's angry when *she's* the one who cut me loose?

What the fuck is happening here?

This is not my Magnolia.

It's like I'm talking to someone else.

Her eyes lock on mine, challenging me.

My gaze drops for half a second—just enough to confirm what I already suspected. She isn't wearing the pendant I gave her. The one she said she'd never take off.

A sharp pang hits me right smack in the center of my heart. I'm not sure why I hoped she would still wear it.

"Can we go somewhere and talk?"

Magnolia's lips press into a thin line, her chest rising and falling in fast breaths. Her hands tremble, but she squares her shoulders, meeting my gaze head-on with defiance burning in her eyes. "Sure. Might as well clear the air so you can move on guilt-free with your life."

The guy steps between us, his posture rigid, blocking me from her like I'm a threat. "You okay?"

Magnolia's expression softens for him. "I'm fine, Colton."

Colton doesn't seem to be convinced of that. And neither am I.

"Are you sure? Because you don't seem fine."

His gaze flickers to me, his posture stiffening like he's ready to do something about it if necessary.

As if.

I size him up with a glance. Next to him, I look like I was built for war, and he looks like he got lost on the way to yoga class.

He's pretty. And blond. Not her type.

But maybe her type has changed.

Her eyes flick to me, sharp as glass. "He won't hurt me... *physically*, at least."

His eyes sweep over me again, lingering a second too long on my frame. It's clear he's weighing his odds—and not liking them. Still, he gives a tight nod.

"You've got my number if you need me."

She gives him a fucking smile. "Thanks, Colton."

It pisses me off, watching them talk about me like I'm some threat she needs guarding against. Like I'm the villain skulking in the shadows, ready to hurt her. Once, I was the one she trusted to keep her safe. Once, she looked at me like I was her shelter from every storm.

Now I'm the threat she needs saving from?

Magnolia jerks her chin toward the parked cars. "Let's get this over with."

I brace myself for a drive thick with silence and tension, already steeling my nerves for it. But no. The second she shifts into gear, her phone connects to the speakers, and music fills the car almost instantly.

Of course there's music. This is Magnolia. She's never been one to sit in silence.

The opening notes of "How Could an Angel Break My Heart" float through the car. Her hands tighten around the wheel, spine stiffening, before she reaches over and kills the volume. Without thinking, I reach for the knob and turn it right back up.

"I like this one."

"Since when?"

"Since the first time I heard it on the *Thinking About Big Guy* playlist."

She doesn't look at me, doesn't say a word.

But when the streetlights wash over her face, I see it—the rapid blinking, the tight mouth, the tears she tries so hard to hide.

And it guts me. Because I realize what those tears mean.

She's not okay.

And neither am I.

Chapter 25

Alex Sebring

HER APARTMENT DOOR CLICKS SHUT BEHIND US, AND SHE TOSSES her keys into a small bowl on a table by the door. I take in my surroundings, every inch of the space marked by Magnolia's touch. I've never been here before, but somehow, it's familiar—like stepping into a place I've known all along.

It smells like her, that same soft, feminine scent that clung to my bedding long after she was gone. It messes with my head more than I want to admit.

Without a word, I pull my bag from my shoulder, unzip it, and take out the leather-bound journal, tossing it onto the coffee table. The soft thud echoes in the room louder than I expected.

"Figured you might want this back. It's a great work of fiction. You should publish it."

She stills as her eyes drop to the journal, something flickering in them.

What is that? Hurt?

No, can't be.

She lifts her chin, lips curving into something that isn't quite a smile. "Does that mean you finally got around to reading it?"

"I read it. Took everything I had in me to get through it, but I did."

Her chin quivers as she folds her arms. "I'm sorry that giving you a piece of my heart turned out to be such a hassle for you."

Nah, I won't allow her to pin this on me like I'm the bad guy. "I have severe dyslexia."

Placing my hands on my hips, I stare at the floor, unable to meet her eyes. Shame creeps in, the same old insecurities clawing their way to the surface. "I wanted to read the whole thing the day you gave it to me. But I couldn't because I'm not able to."

My chest tightens, and I force out the words I hate admitting. "Even at thirty-three-fucking-years-old, I still struggle to read a damn sentence."

"Alex." The softness in her voice almost undoes me. "I didn't know."

"Because I hid it from you." I shrug, trying to make it seem insignificant, like a reading disorder isn't something that has shaped my entire life every damn day.

She studies me. "Why didn't you tell me?"

"I don't tell anyone unless I have to." A humorless chuckle escapes me, and I shake my head. "Doesn't fucking matter now, does it?"

"I wasn't just anyone." Her voice splinters, and she clears her throat. "At least that's what I thought."

The journal sits between us, a tangible reminder of everything we were—everything we lost. And it kills me.

I turn away from Magnolia... because it just hurts so damn much to look at her.

My gaze drifts around the room, soaking it all in. Her apartment looks just like I imagined—elegant in every detail, with a warmth that makes it hers. Sophisticated, but stamped with her imprint in every corner.

It's very Magnolia.

And there are the photos—dozens of them. Some in frames,

others pinned to a wire grid near her desk. Magnolia with Violet, both of them laughing, arms wrapped around each other in a way that speaks of years of friendship. Magnolia with a group of women I don't recognize, all in dance attire, mid-pose and beaming.

But the one that stops me cold is a picture of us. Me and Magnolia. Together.

It's a shot of us in Sydney—her tucked under my arm, grinning up at me like I'd hung the damn moon. I remember that day, the way she laughed at something ridiculous I said, the way I kissed the top of her head without thinking twice.

What kind of man lets his girlfriend, or fuck buddy, keep a photo like this out in the open? What kind of guy is fine with a constant reminder of her ex?

My focus shifts, and that's when I see it—a basket in the corner, filled with rolled-up Samoan mats, one half-finished and draped over the edge like she abandoned it mid-weave. Next to it, a shelf stacked with books about Samoa and its culture. A map of the islands hangs on the wall, surrounded by small artifacts that are too specific to be mere decoration.

I step closer, my brows pulling together. "What's all this?"

She glares at me, silent.

"Tell me, Magnolia."

"What do you think it is?"

My eyes move over the intricate patterns on the mat, the careful stitching she did by hand. "I don't know."

I'm confused.

Her fingers brush over the half-finished mat like it's something precious. "I was immersing myself into the culture of the man I loved."

Loved. Past tense.

Her hand flattens over the woven strands. "This was going to be a gift for your birthday. Because in Samoan culture, when you give someone a mat you've made with your own hands, it's not just a gift.

It's a piece of yourself—something sacred, something you only give when it truly matters."

I'm lost for words. The weight of it, the care, the meaning—it's too much.

It hurts.

Magnolia clears her throat. "I need a drink. Do you want one?"

I huff out a short laugh, relieved by the distraction. "Yeah. I'll take a double of whatever you're having." I meet her eyes, letting the corner of my mouth lift. "Hell, make mine a triple."

A hint of a smirk flickers across her lips before she turns toward the bar cart in the corner. "This reunion is worthy of a tall one, don't you agree?"

"Understatement."

She moves, graceful and deliberate, pulling out a bottle of bourbon and taking out the ingredients. The familiarity—the way she measures, stirs, and pours with practiced ease—takes me straight back to that day on the yacht.

The ice clinks against the glass as she hands me the drink, her fingers brushing mine. Even that slight, fleeting contact sends a jolt through me, a stark reminder of just how long it's been since I've touched her.

"Old-fashioned just the way you like it."

The amber liquid burns its way down my throat. "Still the best I've ever had."

Hell, *she's* still the best I've ever had.

"Glad to hear that I've still got that special touch."

We sit in silence, both sipping. Both avoiding.

The drink goes down easy—too easy. The burn barely registers before I'm tipping back the glass again, draining it faster than I should. But fuck it. After everything, it's warranted. The last swallow hits hard, and I set the empty glass down with a dull thud.

Magnolia arches a brow. "You slammed that."

I lean back, running my hands through the top of my hair. "Long day."

She hums in agreement, staring down at her drink. "A long day? Hell, it's been a long six months."

I'm not sure what she means by that, but I'm not confused about what it's meant for me—six long fucking months of trying to erase her from my skin, my mind, my soul—and failing at every turn.

"Are you at least happy?"

Magnolia's head snaps up, her eyes narrowing with something sharp... something that looks a lot like anger. "Why would you ask me that?"

I shift forward, elbows digging into my knees. "Why wouldn't I ask?"

She glares at me. "How could I be happy?"

"Because you're the one who called the shots. You moved on, commitment free, just like you wanted."

Her eyes widen, disbelief flickering into something closer to outrage. She slams her drink down with a sharp clink, and delivers a scowl that hits somewhere deep, tightening everything inside me. "What the hell are you talking about? I haven't moved on. Not even a little bit."

My brain scrambles, trying to piece together the shattered fragments of this conversation.

If she hasn't moved on, then what the hell has all of this been for?

I'm so fucking lost.

It's like we're speaking two different languages—living two different stories—and for the first time, I'm not sure what's real anymore.

"Are *you* happy?" Magnolia spits the words out, sharp and bitter, her eyes flashing with a fury I've never seen in her before.

"Am I happy?" I bark out a humorless laugh, the sound scraping my throat. "How the fuck am I supposed to be happy?"

"Because you fucking got what you wanted!" Her chest heaves with the force of her frustration, shoulders tense and trembling.

"What is it you think I want?!"

"You found *the one*. You're getting married... and I'm sure a house full of perfect little Samoan babies won't be far behind. Congratulations."

Her words hit me like a freight train. "I don't know where you got that from, but it's not true. Not even close."

I can't make sense of the pieces scattered between us, but I'm certain of one thing straight away—someone has poisoned her against me.

"Who told you I was getting married?"

No hesitation. "Tyson McRae."

The name slams into me like a wrecking ball, hollowing me out and lighting me up at the same time.

My hands clench into fists, every muscle in my body wired tight, rage rising.

"When did you talk to that fucker?"

"He's my client. I talk to him almost every day."

"Your *what*?"

There aren't words in existence that describe my state of mind.

"You're working with that bastard?"

"I own a business, and he's a paying client. My *only* client. My rent gets paid and there's food on my table because of him."

I shoot up, dragging my hands through my hair, trying to process what I'm hearing.

This isn't a coincidence. Tyson McRae didn't just wander into Magnolia's life at random, needing a designer. No—this has calculation written all over it.

There is some fuckery afoot here.

"I told you how much Tyson hates me. How could you believe anything that came out of his mouth about me?"

A whisper slips from her lips— "Shit" —so soft I almost miss it over the pounding in my ears. Her eyes squeeze shut, like she's trying to block out the mistake she's just realized she made. A shaky breath escapes her, and when she lifts her gaze to mine again, the fury is gone, replaced by something raw and aching.

"You aren't marrying anyone?"

"No. Of course not."

She covers her mouth with shaking fingers, her gaze locked on mine like she's seeing me for the first time. "Oh my God, Alex."

She sees it now. She knows the truth.

We're standing here, both gutted, both raw—and somehow, we're not part of the same story.

I pull my phone from my pocket and go to the last message from her. "Did you send this breakup text to me?"

She takes my phone, eyes widening. "I did not send this to you."

The shit just keeps getting deeper.

"I called you the second I saw this message. I must've called you a thousand times, Magnolia. No answer. Straight to default voicemail every time. No replies to my texts, nothing. You disappeared on me."

"Oh fuck." If regret had a face, this would be it. "I blocked you."

Disbelief floods through me. "Why would you do that?"

She fetches her phone from her purse and begins reading. "This relationship isn't working for me. I've had time to think about this, and I've made some decisions. I need a woman in my bed every night. My sex drive can't handle the distance between us. If I don't end this relationship now, I'll end up cheating on you, and I don't want to hurt you in that way. I need a woman who's wife material. And that isn't you. Don't call or text me again. That would only make this worse. This relationship is over."

She looks up from her phone, her voice shaking at the edges. "I called you. Over and over. After I got that message, it was obvious you'd blocked me. So I blocked you back."

How could she believe I'd do that? "I didn't send that message. I would never say those things to you, not in a million years. And I never blocked you."

Her laugh is short, bitter. "I called your office when you wouldn't answer. Courtney told me you wouldn't take my calls."

My stomach drops. "Courtney said that to you?"

She nods. "Yeah. And she wasn't polite about it either. After that... I blocked you for good."

Fucking Courtney. What has she been up to? I'm mad as hell I have to tell Leilani she was right about her.

"I never told her not to put your calls through. Not once."

Her mouth presses into a thin line, and she fumbles with her phone, unlocking it with shaking fingers. "I'm unblocking you and calling you right now."

We listen in tense silence.

No ring. It dumps straight to voicemail.

"That's what it started doing after I got your breakup text."

I drag a hand through my hair, groaning. "Let me say it again, favorite, I didn't send you a breakup text or block you."

Her eyes snap to mine, something raw flashing through them.

For a beat, something flickers—something soft—and a tiny smile tugs at the corner of her mouth. It's not much, but I catch it. And in that sliver of a moment, I see the shift—the part of her that still knows me.

She blinks hard, shoving the emotion down, but it's too late. I've already seen it.

"Show me your blocked numbers."

I hand my phone to her, a sharp breath escaping her lips. "That's my number... blocked." Her voice cracks on the last word, and it cuts me down to the bone.

"I didn't do this." My voice is rough, desperate. "I swear to you. I don't have a clue how this happened."

Her eyes, wide and wounded, lift to mine.

"Show me my contact in your phone."

I hand over my phone without hesitation, offering her full access —proof I have nothing to hide. She wastes no time navigating to my contacts, her fingers sure even though her hands are still shaking.

After a beat, she stiffens. "Alex... the number saved under my name isn't mine."

Ice crawls through my veins. "What? It has to be."

She turns the screen toward me. "It's not even a U.S. number... it's Australian."

I stare at the screen, my mind racing to make sense of what I'm seeing. "I didn't change your number."

"Well, someone did."

A thick, stunned silence settles between us.

Magnolia's hand tightens around the phone as she looks back up at me, her voice cracking. "I couldn't reach you because my number was blocked. And even if I hadn't blocked you, you still wouldn't have been able to reach me—because whoever did this changed my number in your phone."

The full weight of it crashes down on me like a landslide—violent, unstoppable.

Someone did this, plotted this, wanted us torn apart.

"This isn't a tech glitch. Someone made sure we lost each other. Someone who had access to your life and your phone."

The pieces lock into place with brutal clarity, and anger crawls under my skin, hot and sharp. "Yeah. They did."

Her eyes widen with something that looks a lot like realization. "Someone leaked your emails to Celeste. Stands to reason they had access to your texts as well."

"I got rid of my personal assistant. The texts would've happened long after she was gone." Was I wrong about her? Was she telling the truth when she denied leaking the emails?

A sharp bitterness rises in my throat. "My texts sync to my work computer. If someone got into it, they could've sent the breakup text."

Magnolia shakes her head, her brows knitting together. "To change my contact number, they would've needed access to your actual phone. Once they swapped the number, they controlled everything. They could send messages that looked like they came from me—and send you ones I never even wrote."

She's right. And the worst part? My carelessness made it easy for them.

I'm not a guy who's glued to his phone. I leave it lying around—on my desk, Courtney's desk, the conference room, the break room.

Hell, just last week, it went missing for a whole day before we found it.

Self-loathing simmers just beneath my skin. I made it too easy. I was too trusting, too distracted. And now all I can do is sit here and face the wreckage of what I allowed happen.

"It wouldn't have been hard for someone to grab it while it was unlocked and swap your number."

The reality of it crashes down, the guilt running deep.

"I never checked your number. Never thought to. Hell, favorite —" My voice cracks, and I hate it. "I haven't memorized your number, so I wouldn't have noticed when someone changed it even if I had looked."

"I never memorized yours either. There was no need because your contact was saved in my phone. People don't do that these days, so don't beat yourself up over it."

Maybe not but the guilt gnaws at me. I trusted all the wrong people. And now we're left standing in the wreckage, sifting through the pieces of everything we lost.

"Who in your life would've done this to us?"

"Two people come to mind—Celeste and Tyson. But apparently Courtney played a role as well. I'm not sure what that means."

For a long moment, all she does is stare at her hands, like the words she needs are hiding somewhere in the lines of her palms.

"Alex." Her voice cracks when she says my name. "I didn't let you go."

My heart fractures all over again. "I didn't let you go either."

We've been pacing the floor, pushing each other's boundaries, testing old wounds. Now, side by side on the sofa, there's nowhere left to run.

Neither of us speaks. Neither of us moves.

We just sit there, caught in the weight of everything we've lost— months of heartache, anger, confusion—all because of someone's twisted interference.

I've loved Magnolia from the second I laid eyes on her, and if it's possible, I love her even more now. Maybe because I experienced what life looks like without her in it—and I know I can't survive it again.

But I need to know the truth.

The question burns my throat on the way out. "What is going on between you and McRae?"

Her entire body tenses at the sound of his name. "Tyson McRae is the last thing I want to talk about right now."

My blood roars in my veins. "I don't want to have this conversation either. But I won't give that fucker the satisfaction of twisting the knife. Tell me the truth—have you fucked him?"

Her head snaps back. "No, Alex! I haven't fucked him."

Relief slams into me, fierce and fast—but the anger rides its heels. "Did he try?"

Her hesitation is enough to make my blood curdle.

"I need to know what's happened."

Magnolia's hands twist together in her lap. "I'd be lying if I said nothing has happened between us."

Rage surges under my skin, hot and uncontrollable.

"Fuuuck!" The word rips from my throat as my fist slams into the cushion beside me, rattling the frame of the couch.

Magnolia jolts. "I'm so sorry! I thought we were over and you'd moved on with someone else. That's what Tyson told me. Think about it from my point of view. I believed you'd broken up with me in one of the cruelest ways possible. And you told me multiple times that you wanted a wife and family. There was no reason for me not to believe him."

Nothing happened between us. That's the only right answer. The only one that would let me breathe again. But now my mind is a fucking battlefield, a war zone littered with images I can't stop seeing.

Fuck.

"What happened between you?"

She opens her mouth—but I lift a hand, cutting her off, the regret already crawling up my throat. "I don't know if I can hear this."

A surge of rage shoots through me, and I'm on my feet before I even realize it, pacing across her living room like a caged animal. "Is he in Charleston right now? Because if he is, I'm going to fucking kill him."

"Well, you're gonna have to get in line."

Magnolia pushes off the couch, moving toward the bar cart with clipped, angry steps. She pours herself another drink—heavy, reckless —and tosses it back in one long swallow. The glass hits the cart with a sharp clink.

"What the hell were you thinking? *Tyson McRae?*" The words rip out of me, raw and furious. "Even if we were over—you know what kind of man he is. I told you about him."

"I needed clients, Alex. I had just opened my firm. There was a ton of money going out and nothing coming in. He was a steady paycheck."

Her voice shakes, but she doesn't back down. Doesn't sugarcoat it. She lays it out plainly, like ripping off a bandage neither of us wants to deal with.

"You've always had money. You've never woken up one morning and lost your financial security. My safety net was gone. I didn't have the luxury of falling apart. I was scared."

Hearing her admit that she was scared hits me harder than anything else tonight. Magnolia Steel doesn't lean. She doesn't crumble. She's always been strong enough to carry the weight of the world on her back without asking for help. Vulnerability isn't something she wears easily.

And the fact that she's letting me see it guts me.

"He swooped in the second you were vulnerable and took advantage. Because that's what he does, Magnolia. That's all he's ever done—hurt people."

She may hate me for this—but she'll just have to. Because protecting her will always come before keeping the peace.

"You're done working with him. I don't care what it costs for you to break the contract. It's over. Done! And if I have any say in it, you'll never see him again."

The words leave my mouth without hesitation, firm and absolute. Over the top and I don't give a fuck.

But even as I say them, I know Magnolia. She's independent—and fiery—and she won't be happy about me telling her how to run her business.

I'd never do that to her without a damn good reason. She's achieved too much to let someone else make decisions. But this isn't about control. It's about survival.

And the threat isn't some faceless risk—it's Tyson-ruthless-fucker-McRae.

Magnolia doesn't know who she's dealing with. She doesn't see the calculated moves he makes, the way he always plays the long game. But I do. I know what he is capable of, and I'll be damned if I let him sink his claws any deeper into her.

She straightens, her chin lifting, but there's no fire behind it—no true defiance. Only a quiet resignation that twists something deep inside me.

"Let's be clear about a few things. This is *my* business. *My* decision. *I* decide."

A beat.

"And I choose to not work with him anymore. He lied to me. I can't move forward with a client who does that."

Magnolia Steel has never been a woman to bow to pressure, not even from me. But this time, she doesn't argue.

"I should've never taken him on. But when everything crumbles around you, desperation makes you stupid."

"You did what you had to do. You were trying to build something for yourself after Soul Sync... after everything fell apart... because of me."

A crushing pressure builds in my chest, making it hard to breathe. My skin feels too tight. My head's too full. My heart pounds like it's trying to crack open my ribs just to escape.

The weight of it all—what we lost, what we uncovered—it's too much, pressing down on me, threatening to split me wide open.

"I need a minute."

Magnolia's head snaps up, confusion flashing across her face. "What?"

The panic in her voice cuts into me like a blade.

"I just need a minute to myself."

Her hands curl into fists at her sides, her eyes bright with something raw. Something desperate. "No, we just found each other again. You can't leave. Not now, Alex."

It guts me. The broken way she says my name feels like she's handing me her heart all over again. And I'm too weak to even hold it properly.

I can't breathe.

I claw my hands through my hair, inhaling like I've been underwater too long. "There are things you don't know about me. I understand it makes no sense right now. But I swear to you—I will come back."

I choke on the next breath. "I just need a second to fucking breathe."

She blinks, a tear sliding down her cheek, her body trembling like she's barely holding herself together. "Alex—"

I can't stay. If I stay, I'll shatter.

I turn toward the door, my feet heavy, my lungs burning.

"Alex... where are you going?"

"I don't know."

"When are you coming back?"

A beat of silence that feels like a lifetime.

"I don't know."

I open the door and step through it.

The moment it clicks shut behind me, I sag against the wall outside, bracing myself with one hand, my forehead resting against the cool surface.

My chest heaves with the force of it all—the anger, the heartbreak, the love.

Always the love.

Even now, when everything feels like it's ripping apart, that part never wavers.

I just need a minute to breathe.

A minute to catch my breath and be strong enough to go back in there—to her.

Because walking away from Magnolia Steel has never been an option.

Not then.

Not now.

Not ever.

Chapter 26

Magnolia Steel

THE SILENCE IS SUFFOCATING.

I stand frozen in the middle of my apartment, staring at the door Alex walked out of. The sound of it closing behind him echoes through my bones. My chest is hollow, scraped clean, as if he took everything vital with him.

A shuddering breath pushes past my lips, and I press my fingers to my temples, trying to make sense of everything that happened. But there is no making sense of it.

Alex was here. And now he's gone.

I had to tell him about Ty. Hiding it would have been worse. But now I wonder if the truth broke us as surely as a lie would have.

A wave of nausea rolls through me, my stomach twisting as I replay the way Alex looked at me—the storm in his eyes, the tension coiled tight in his jaw. I saw the moment it hit him, and my words settled deep into his bones.

He left. And I don't know if he's ever coming back.

I try to pull myself together, but it's useless. My hands are shaking. My heart is still racing.

Anger pulses in my veins, thick and wild.

Ty—that fucking bastard.

He poisoned me against Alex, feeding me lies until rejection became the only thing I could feel. He made me believe Alex had moved on with someone else.

And I believed him.

I let his lies sink into my skin, let them reshape the way I saw Alex, let them push me straight into the arms of a man who only ever wanted to use me as a weapon against the man he hates.

It's disgusting.

I scroll through my contacts until I find his name. My thumb hesitates for a second before I make the call.

Ty picks up, his voice smooth, oozing satisfaction. "Hello, beautiful. How's my favorite designer this evening?"

He sounds like my call has made his night. Fuck that. I'm about to ruin it.

"I'm not doing so great."

"What's wrong? Let me guess—having a hard time choosing between white and off-white for the bedding?"

"I have a question for you."

"Okay. What's up?"

My question isn't for information. It's a razor—and I'm aiming straight for the jugular. "What's the latest on Alex?"

Ty is quiet for a second too long, and I can imagine the gears turning in his head. "Why do you ask about him?"

"Answer the question."

"In case you forgot, I'm in Charleston. It's impossible for me to keep tabs on Sebring from here. Not that I care enough to bother. Not interested in what he's up to these days."

I let the lie sit there, thick and rotting, giving him just enough rope to hang himself.

"How did you know he was getting married... since you're in Charleston and don't keep up with him?"

Another beat of silence.

"I don't recall who told me."

"You didn't hear a damn thing. You invented it, played me."

Another pause—stalling—because he's trying to gather the pieces slipping through his fingers. "Just because I don't remember who told me doesn't mean I played you, Magnolia. You're reading too much into this."

"Lies and manipulation, all of it. And you're still doing it now."

"Mags—"

"Only my friends get to call me that. And you are *not* my friend." My voice drops to a deadlier, quieter place. "Alex was right about you. You're the parasite he always said you were."

"Will you just listen to me for a minute?"

"And what—set myself up for more lies? No, thanks."

I end the call with a single flick of my thumb. Quick. Final. No second-guessing. No regret. Just silence—and the pounding rush of fury in my veins.

The phone buzzes in my hand almost immediately—Tyson McRae. Incoming Call.

I hit decline without a second thought, my thumb moving faster than instinct.

The phone lands on the couch with a dull thud, like it burned my skin to touch it. My pulse hammers in my ears, my chest tightening under the realization.

How could I have been so blind?

Alex warned me—again and again—and I ignored everything he had told me.

I let Tyson McRae slither into my life, into my business, into my trust.

Almost into my bed.

Worse—I let him touch me. More than touch.

That conversation with Alex is coming. And it's going to tear him apart.

A violent shudder rolls through me, nausea knotting in my throat as I think about it.

I should've seen it—the arrogance, the charm-covered lies, the way he played at every angle like he'd rehearsed it a thousand times. It was all a game to him, and I walked right into it.

God, I hate him.

My head throbs with the weight of too many emotions crammed into too little time. I sit there, numb, while the pieces of tonight grind against each other inside me.

A knock on the door snaps through the quiet.

My heart jolts. Alex... he came back.

I'm on my feet in an instant, rushing toward the door. I yank it open, and my stomach drops.

Ty's expression is hard, blue eyes drilling into mine. "We need to talk."

Fury coils inside me, tight and lethal, a snake ready to strike. "Are you out of your damn mind? Leave."

He reaches out for me, and I step out of his grasp.

"Please, Magnolia. I have to explain."

"You don't have to do anything except go. Now."

His jaw locks. "Mags, please—"

"Don't call me that. You lost that right when you lied and manipulated me. You don't get to stand here like you deserve anything from me."

"I don't deserve anything, but I'm asking, begging, for five minutes." Desperation flicks across his face.

I tighten my grip on the door, every muscle screaming for him to leave. "You can't be here when Alex comes back."

His mouth opens, but no sound comes out. For once, his quick wit abandons him.

"The answer is yes. Alex is in Charleston." I fold my arms across my chest. "He'll be back any minute, and he's furious, Ty. If he sees you here" —I shake my head— "I'm afraid of what will happen."

Ty scoffs, a weak smirk tugging at the corner of his mouth. "I'm not scared of Sebring."

I lean in, my voice dropping to a quiet warning. "You *should* be."

Ty doesn't understand. He didn't see Alex's face when he left, or the way his hands shook, or the raggedness in his breath, his control slipping thread by thread. He doesn't understand the storm brewing inside him, the sheer force of a man who looks like he could lose it at any moment.

And if Alex walks through that door and finds Ty standing here? God help us all.

"I'm serious. Alex isn't in a good place right now. It will not end well if he finds you here."

"Did you tell him about us?"

"Some. It didn't go over well."

Ty's grin is slow, smug. "I want him to know everything that's happened between us."

My body shakes with the effort it takes not to kick him in the dick. "Leave! Now."

I push against the door, trying to close it, but Ty moves fast. One broad hand slaps flat against the wood, stopping it cold. The other braces against the frame, caging me in with nothing but his presence. He doesn't shove, doesn't force—just holds steady, unmoving, his strength a quiet warning.

"You can shut the door in my face if you want, but I'm not leaving. I'll be right here waiting when he gets back."

My breath catches. "Please don't do that."

"Then let me in. Give me five minutes." His voice softens, almost pleading. "That's all I'm asking for. Let me explain and I'll go."

My head spins.

Alex will lose it if he finds him at my apartment. I can predict how that would end, and I don't need more destruction tonight.

I step back, pulling the door open enough to let him pass. "Make it fast."

Ty slips inside, and I close the door behind him, dread curling in my stomach. "Say what you need to say."

"Healthy relationships are built on a foundation of truth and trust. And I want you to know the truth."

A sharp, humorless laugh escapes me as I cross my arms. "That would be a first for you."

His usual cocky smirk is nowhere to be found. Instead, he looks wired—like a man realizing too late that he bet everything and is about to lose it all.

"I'm the one who reported you to Soul Sync." His words are clipped, low and fast, like he's ripping off a bandage.

The blood in my veins turns to ice.

"Please hear me out." He takes a step closer, holding up his hands. "I needed your life to fall apart... so I could be the one waiting in the wings to help you pick up the pieces."

I stare at him, the betrayal sinking deep, like cold steel sliding between my ribs. "You needed my life to fall apart? Jesus, Ty. Who does something like that?"

"I had a plan. I was going to win you over. Seduce you. Make you forget about Sebring. Because nothing—and I mean nothing—would hurt him more than seeing you with me."

Disgust curls in my stomach. My skin feels too tight, like it might split open from the pressure of my rage.

His composure slips at the edges. His usual smugness flickers—just for a second—before something else takes its place. Something... raw.

"At least that was the plan. Destroy Alex by taking the one thing he couldn't stand to lose. Make him suffer." He lets out a humorless laugh, shaking his head. "But something unexpected happened."

His gaze lifts, locking onto mine, and his next words hit me like a wrecking ball.

"I fell in love with you."

I stare at him, stunned into silence. My pulse pounds in my ears, drowning out the words that just came out of his mouth.

Love? That's not what this was.

It was strategy. Control. A game he thought he could win.

He steps closer, searching my eyes. "I love you, Magnolia."

His throat bobs as he swallows hard, shaking his head like even he can't believe what's coming out of his mouth. "I've never said those words to a woman before. Not once. But with you, I mean them."

I stare at him, my heart hammering.

"I said it would be okay for you to think of him if we were together, that I didn't mind. But I did mind. I was desperate for you to want *me*." His eyes burn into mine. "And you did, didn't you? You wanted me."

I'm not a liar, and I won't become one today. "I admit that something was happening between us. But it never would've happened if I'd known the truth. All of it was built on lies."

"I'll do anything, Mags. Tell me how to fix this, how to fix us."

"There is no fixing this because there is no us."

His face twists, and for the first time, I see genuine pain in his expression. Yes, he is a manipulative liar, but I believe his anguish is real.

I take a step back, putting distance between us. "I love Alex. It'll always be Alex."

A sharp knock at the door jolts me out of my haze, and my stomach drops.

Shit.

I squeeze my eyes shut for half a second, willing this moment to disappear. Wishing I could erase the last few minutes, hell, the last six months. But I can't. And there's no time to think.

I swallow hard and turn toward the door, my pulse hammering as I reach for the knob.

Alex stands on the other side, eyes stormy, chest rising and falling like he's one breath away from coming apart. His jaw is tight, his hands clenched into fists at his sides.

"I'm sorry, favorite. I just needed a minute to get my head straight."

Relief crashes into me like a wave. But before I can respond, he shifts forward—and sees him.

His entire body stiffens, his control snapping like a live wire.

"Alex—" I step in front of him, my hands coming up to his chest in an effort to defuse the explosion I can already feel coming. "Please. Just—just calm down."

His dark eyes cut to mine, wild and unyielding. He shakes his head. "Don't ask me to calm down, Magnolia. I've been calm for far too long."

His gaze locks back onto Ty, and I know that the time for calming down is over.

Alex steps inside without hesitation, his body coiled tight like a predator about to strike. The door slams shut behind him, rattling the walls, but his gaze remains locked on Ty.

His voice cuts through the thick tension like a blade. "The breakup texts." Alex studies Ty, his gaze cold, calculating—like he's deciding whether to rip him apart with words or with fists. "That was you."

Ty shrugs, unbothered. "Yeah, with Celeste's help. And your secretary's."

"And pairing Celeste with me at Soul Sync?"

"That was her idea. She's still desperate to get you back."

"You're the one who paid for Celeste."

"I did. And that shit isn't cheap. You must be desperate for a wife."

Alex's nostrils flare, his hands flexing at his sides. "You did all of this to hurt me?"

Ty smirks. "Of course, it was to hurt you. Everything I do is to hurt you. Just like my relationship with Magnolia."

My stomach twists into a knot.

Shit, what is he about to say?

His expression shifts, something flickering in his icy blue eyes. "At least that was the initial plan. But sometimes, plans have a way of changing."

I suck in a breath, bracing myself.

Please don't say it, Ty.

Please don't say it.

Ty's lips curl into something that almost looks like triumph. "I fell in love with Magnolia."

He takes a slow step forward, his gaze flicking to me for a fraction of a second before settling back on Alex. "And she was falling in love with me too."

The room goes deadly silent.

Because all hell is about to break loose.

He's unfazed by the rage radiating off Alex. "I love her, Sebring. I love the fuck out of her."

Alex's nostrils flare, his jaw tight. "Shut your fucking mouth."

Ty takes a step forward, challenging him. "You're out of your mind if you think I'm going to let her go without a fight."

It happens fast—so fast. He lunges, his fist colliding with Ty's jaw with a sickening crack. Ty stumbles back, shakes off the hit, and charges forward.

The full force of two huge, powerful men colliding in my living room makes the walls tremble. The coffee table rattles, a lamp crashes to the floor. I knew this was coming—I felt it the moment Alex laid eyes on Ty—but the sheer brutality of it still shocks me.

A grunt. A fist meeting flesh. The deep, guttural sound of impact as Alex shoves Ty back against the wall.

Ty retaliates, throwing a punch that snaps Alex's head to the side.

I suck in a sharp breath as Alex recovers, the look in his eyes turning lethal. He comes at Ty harder, slamming him against the back of my couch before taking him to the ground. The two of them grapple for control, muscles straining, bodies colliding. It's raw, violent, unrestrained.

Ty flips Alex, pinning him down, his fists landing blows to his face. My stomach twists as blood smears across my hardwood floor.

Ty stops, Alex pinned beneath him. He leans in, voice low, dripping with venom. "I can see why you don't want to let her go. Her pussy tastes so sweet."

Oh. Fuck.

He went there.

The coffee table gives beneath their weight, splintering into pieces.

Alex's roar is pure fury. With a surge of strength, he reverses their positions, straddling Ty and unleashing hell. One hit. Another. And another.

Blood drips from Alex's lip. Ty's face is a ruin of crimson.

Alex won't stop punching Ty. He's a machine.

"Stop!" I scream again, my voice cracking, but he doesn't stop.

I step closer, panic clawing up my throat. "Please, Alex. You're going to kill him!"

Ty groans, his head lolling to the side, but Alex doesn't let up. His fists drive into Ty's face, his knuckles slick with blood. The sickening sound of bone against bone echoes through the room, each impact making my stomach turn.

"Alex!" My voice is desperate now, pleading.

And then something in him falters. His fist hovers midair, shaking. His breath moves in and out of his lungs, his entire body rigid.

Ty's body goes slack beneath Alex's fists, his hands falling to his sides. He's no longer fighting back, no longer throwing punches. He just lies there, his face bloodied, his chest rising and falling in ragged, uneven breaths.

Alex shoves off Ty and falls back against the sofa, dragging his hands through his hair, gripping it.

"Fuuuck!" His voice is a roar, the word ripping through the air like a gunshot.

Ty is motionless on his back, blinking up at the ceiling, blood oozing. His nose is a mess—broken, no doubt. His cheekbone already swelling. But still, after everything, he finds it in himself to smile.

"This changes nothing, Sebring." He coughs, spitting blood onto my floor. "I still love her."

Alex's head snaps toward him, his eyes dark with rage. "Fuck you, motherfucker. You don't know what love is. And you sure as hell don't deserve to love someone like Magnolia."

"You're right. I didn't know what it was to love someone. But that was before her."

Alex's chest rises and falls rapidly, his voice low, guttural. "She is my heart and soul. The air in my lungs. The blood in my veins." His eyes burn into Ty's, deadly and unrelenting. "You will never have her. I promise you that."

I press a hand to my chest as I take in the damage.

My living room looks like a war zone. Shattered glass and splintered wood scatter across the floor, the coffee table demolished beyond recognition. A dented lamp lies facedown, its crooked shade barely clinging on. One of the dining chairs is overturned, and the sofa sits askew, shoved off-center from the rug. Even the armchair by the window is twisted at an awkward angle as if the whole room is still reeling from the chaos.

And in the middle of it all, Tyson lies sprawled on the floor, looking like he just got drop-kicked by karma wearing steel-toed boots.

Karma—she's a salty bitch, that one.

"Ty, you need to go to the hospital."

He coughs, then groans, rolling onto his side. "I'm fine."

A short, sarcastic laugh slips from my lips. "You are most definitely not fine. Your nose is not even in the center of your face anymore."

He drags in a slow breath, wincing as he props himself up on an elbow. "I've had worse."

He inhales before reaching up and gripping his nose between his fingers.

"Oh my God. Don't do it."

An unmistakable crunch reaches my ears as he shifts it back into place.

I close my eyes, a full-body shudder racking through me. "Jesus, Ty."

He exhales, then grins through the blood. "Well, that was unpleasant."

"You should leave." Now. While Alex is catching his breath. I'm not sure he's finished with you.

Tyson pushes to his feet with a groan, wiping more blood from his face as he straightens. He's slower now, stiff, and favoring one side as he makes his way toward the door.

I step ahead of him and pull it open, gripping the knob. He stops just shy of the threshold, looking down at me. There's no smirk, no cocky gleam in his eye. Just something tired. Something raw.

"Pick... me... Magnolia."

My chest tightens. Despite everything, despite the lies, despite the chaos, I can feel the truth in his voice. He means it.

He loves me.

But my answer is still the same. It'll always be the same.

"I choose Alex... every... time."

A beat passes before he nods, slow and accepting, like he already knew what I'd say. "If you ever change your mind, one call. That's all it'll take for me to run to you."

"Wow." Alex lets out a dry chuckle, pure revulsion in his voice. "Didn't think you could be more pathetic, but here we are."

Ty's jaw tightens, his eyes flicking to mine before settling back on Alex. "You've won. For now." His voice is low, edged with something dangerous. "But one fuck-up, Sebring—just one—and I'll be there to catch her when she falls."

Alex leans forward, resting his forearms on his knees, blood still smeared across his knuckles. His eyes burn with absolute certainty. "That'll never bloody happen."

Ty holds his gaze for a moment longer, his expression unreadable. Then he turns back to me. "Until we meet again, Mags."

Chapter 27

Magnolia Steel

THE DOOR CLICKS SHUT WITH A FINALITY THAT ECHOES through the apartment. I press my forehead against the cool wood for half a second before turning back to the man still sitting bloodied on my floor.

Alex leans back against the couch, his broad chest rising and falling in deep, measured breaths. He keeps his hands braced on his thighs, fists still clenched. His knuckles are raw, his lip split, and there's a deep, angry cut just above his eye.

I go to him, lowering myself to the floor. Neither of us speaks for a long moment, the weight of everything that's happened pressing down on us. Everything we've been through. Everything we haven't said.

"I was afraid you were going to kill him."

Alex drops his head back against the couch. "Can't say I wasn't afraid of that myself. I'm still thinking about it."

Who could blame him?

I lift his hand, running my thumb along his knuckles. He watches me, saying nothing, but his body tenses at my touch. His hands look rough—split skin, smeared blood, swelling already forming.

"You need to be cleaned up." I push to my feet. "I'll be right back."

And for the first time since he walked back through my door tonight, I feel like I can take care of him. Make him feel better.

I return with antiseptic and cotton balls, kneeling before him without a word. Antiseptic seeps into the raw cuts across his knuckles, turning the deep scrapes an angry red. Not a flinch. Not a single sound. Just the steady weight of his gaze locked onto my face.

The silence stretches as I clean the wounds and wrap his knuckles. He lets me. No protests, no stubborn remarks.

The cut above his brow is bad. Blood trickles from the deep gash, trailing toward his temple. I reach for another cotton ball, dabbing at it with a softer touch.

"This one's deep. I think it needs stitches."

"It'll be fine."

"With all due respect, you're not the one looking at it right now." I press the gauze and hold pressure to stop the bloody ooze. "It'll scar if you don't get it stitched."

The corner of his mouth twitches—almost amused. "I like scars."

A quiet sigh slips from my lips, but I don't argue. "At least let me cover it with something that'll keep the cut pulled together. It's bleeding everywhere."

He nods. "If it'll make you happy."

I pull the broken skin together and apply adhesive strips. "*Happy* is a stretch, but it'll help to put me at ease."

Something flickers in his expression—something softer. "Do what you need to do."

And I do. Because it's the only thing I can control right now.

My hands rest on my thighs as I kneel before him, searching his face, hoping for something—anything—that tells me we can get through this.

"Please don't hate me."

His head snaps up, his bloodshot eyes locking onto mine. "I could never hate you." His jaw tightens, the muscle in it starting to tic. "But what that fucker said——"

Ty said a lot. But *tasting me*—that's the one that sent Alex into a blind rage, the one tearing him apart.

That part wasn't untrue, but it was misleading. I'm sure Alex must be thinking the worst.

My insides are unraveling. "I will tell you everything, and I won't lie to sugarcoat it. I don't want you to ever have to wonder."

"Never thought you would." He exhales, his nostrils flaring. "This is something I have to hear. I just don't want to."

Understandable. It would gut me to hear details about his sexual encounter with another woman.

"Whenever you're ready——"

He interrupts. "I need this to be over with. Tell me what happened, but with as few details as possible."

"All right."

I clear my throat, summoning the courage to say the words before I lose my nerve. "The first incident... there was some touching—his hands on my legs. He kissed my thigh, just the one kiss though, and offered to go down on me. That was it."

He blows a deep breath between pursed lips. "Okay."

This next one is going to sound a lot worse.

"The second—and final—incident involved kissing and touching." I swallow hard, the shame burning my throat. "How much do you want to hear?"

"The fucker said he tasted you. I need that explained in as few words as possible."

"He didn't go down on me. He tasted me on his fingers... after touching me."

"The thought of his hands on you——" His fists press into his eyes like he's trying to scrub the images from his mind. "Did he make you come?"

I swallow hard, my pulse pounding. "Yes, one time."

"Fuck."

His head drops back. "You can't imagine how much I hate hearing that."

"I'm so sorry, Alex."

His fingers flex against his thighs. "Did you make him come?"

No hesitation. "No."

His shoulders rise and fall with his breathing. "You didn't fuck him or suck his cock or give him a hand job? He kissed you and got you off once with his hand and that's it?"

"Correct."

Something in his face eases—just a fraction—but the torment is still there.

Reaching for his hands, I thread my fingers through his. "He was wrong. I was never falling in love with him, Alex. I love you. Only you."

His chest rises with a deep breath, his grip tightening on mine. "I understand why he fell in love with you. You're so damn easy to love."

His gaze flickers to mine, heavy with exhaustion, pain, and something else—something that looks an awful lot like hope, no matter how fragile.

"Where do we go from here?" His voice is raw, edged with uncertainty.

"I don't know." Fear wraps around my throat like a python that refuses to let go. "What do you want?"

A quiet, bitter laugh escapes him, and he shakes his head. "I want to get in a fucking time machine and go back to six months ago so I can change everything that happened."

If only—

He reaches out and brushes his thumb along my cheek. My eyes flutter shut as I lean into his palm, letting him cup my face, savoring his touch.

"I'm lost without you." His voice breaks, rough with emotion. "I love you. I never stopped. Not for a single second."

A tear slips down my cheek. "I love you too. Every second, every breath, it has always been you."

"We have a lot to figure out."

I nod, because he's right. We have battles ahead of us. "I know."

There are still so many questions, and so many wounds to be healed.

I cup his face, my thumbs tracing over the rough stubble along his jaw. Even with the cuts, bruises, and dried blood, he's still the most beautiful man I've ever seen. I lean in, pressing the lightest kiss to the cut on his face, then another along his cheekbone. A silent apology. A quiet promise.

When my lips brush his swollen mouth, he exhales and pulls back just enough to look at me, his eyes stormy and conflicted. "There's a lot going on in my head. It's... overwhelming."

I nod, understanding. "You need to scream... but not with your voice?"

His throat works as he swallows, his Adam's apple bobbing. He doesn't answer right away, but his eyes darken, heat flickering behind them. "That would be a start."

I slide my hands down to his chest, feeling the steady, heavy rise and fall of his breath beneath my palms. "We both know what you need. It's what I need too."

I clutch his hand, giving a small tug after I rise to my feet. He follows, his grip firm, like he's afraid to let go. Without a word, I guide him through my apartment, past the wreckage of the fight.

In my bedroom, I turn to him, searching his face. His jaw is still tight, his shoulders rigid with the pain of everything still unspoken.

My voice is steady despite the pounding of my heart. "I'm yours, Alex... if you still want me."

"Of course I want you." His fingers tighten around mine. "I've always wanted you. I always will."

I reach for the hem of my top, dragging it over my head before slipping out of my yoga pants, leaving myself bare beneath his gaze. His eyes rake over me, dark and consuming, but he doesn't move.

"Let your hair down," he says, voice low, controlled.

I pull the tie and pins from my bun, shaking my hair loose so it falls over my shoulders.

"So bloody beautiful."

I step closer. "I want you to channel all of it—the anger, the hurt, the hate. Get it out of your system. Like you did in the back of the limo."

His gaze snaps to mine. "Anger, yes. Hurt, yes. Hate, no. Never hate, Magnolia. I love you with all of my heart."

Heart hammering, I square my jaw and lift my chin. "I know you love me, but I also know you're angry. And maybe you'll never admit it, but there's a small part of you that hates me a little for what happened with Ty."

"Stop calling him Ty."

"Okay. Fair."

"It's true that I hate what happened, but that's different from hating you."

I place my hands over the steady, erratic beat of his heart. "Say whatever you need to say, do whatever you need to do. And when it's over, it'll be out in the open and we'll move forward. We'll never speak of it again."

His hands grip my hips, rough and desperate.

"Give me the punishment fuck that you know you want to give me."

He exhales, shaking his head. "I don't want to punish you."

"Yes, you do." I press closer, tilting my head until our lips are a breath apart. "And it's what I want too."

I sink to my knees without him having to tell me.

The moment my hands find his zipper, the tension coils even tighter between us. I work it down slowly, seeing his cock strain against the fabric. His breath hitches—a low, broken sound.

I push his pants down his hips, the fabric sliding over muscular thighs, until they hit the floor. My hands glide up, slipping beneath the waistband of his briefs, relishing his taut muscles quivering beneath my touch. His cock springs free, hard and heavy, and my mouth waters at the sight of him.

"Open your mouth." His voice is low and husky.

I do as he says, trembling with a mixture of anticipation and desperation. He guides himself to my mouth, running the blunt head across my lips, teasing me, punishing me with how slowly he gives me what we both want.

I lick the tip, tasting him, and a ragged sound tears from his throat. His hand tightens in my hair—not enough to hurt, but enough to remind me who's in charge here—and then he pushes deeper, sliding into my mouth with a low curse.

"Eyes up here, babe," he says, voice rough as gravel.

I meet his gaze, hollowed out by guilt and yearning. He rocks into my mouth, slow at first, letting me adjust, letting me take him deeper. His free hand cups my jaw, holding me steady as he sets the pace—demanding, desperate, a rhythm that speaks of all the anger and longing buried inside him.

Tears prick my eyes, but I take it—I take all of him, hollowing my cheeks, letting him use my mouth like he needs to.

"Good girl," he says, stroking my hair. "Fuck, you're so perfect for me."

My nails dig into the backs of his thighs, holding on as he thrusts into my mouth, more ragged now, more broken, his body shuddering with the effort it takes to hold himself back.

"Your mouth is sweet, but it's not where I want to come."

He hauls me to my feet so fast the room spins. His mouth crashes to mine—rough, bruising, desperate. His hands are everywhere—fisting in my hair, yanking me closer, dragging me against the hard lines of his body. I kiss him back with everything I have—the guilt, the regret, the fierce, endless love I carry for him.

He turns me around, pressing me against the wall. His mouth finds the side of my neck, sucking hard enough to leave a mark. Hands slide over my body, worshipping and punishing at the same time—palming my breasts, squeezing my hips, fingers digging into my skin like he can imprint himself onto me.

His voice is a growl against my skin. "You are mine, Magnolia. No one else touches you. No one else hears you come. Ever."

I whimper, arching back against him, needing more, needing him to erase every mistake, every memory that doesn't include him.

He yanks me back by the hair just enough to whisper in my ear, "You're going to take everything I give you. Do you understand me?"

"Yes... sir."

He growls against my ear. "You know how much I like hearing that."

His hand slides between my thighs, rough and claiming, stroking once, twice.

"Already so fucking wet for me," he says, sinking two fingers inside me without warning. "Your pussy never disappoints."

I cry out, my hands flying to brace myself against the wall as he fucks me with his hand, deep and punishing, building me up so fast I'm already on the edge.

"You wanted it rough. You asked for this, favorite. Don't you dare run from it now."

I don't. I can't.

He twists his fingers inside me, hitting that spot that makes me shatter, pushing me over the edge with ruthless precision.

But he doesn't stop.

He turns me to face him, scooping me up into his arms, carrying me toward the bed with a savage tenderness. He lays me down like I'm something precious, like he's staking his claim.

His body hovers over mine, big and powerful, pinning me down without even needing to touch me. His hands skim up my sides, slow, firm, claiming every inch of skin like it belongs to him.

Because it does. It always has.

"Spread your legs for me."

I obey, baring myself for him, trembling with need. His mouth curves into something dark and devastating—not a smile, not exactly. Something more like possession.

He grips my thighs, dragging me to the edge of the bed, lining himself up with my body.

No teasing this time. No slow burn.

Just Alex and...

Raw. Ruthless. Rapture.

The first thrust knocks the air from my lungs. I cry out, arching into him, but he doesn't let up. He drives into me hard, deep, again and again.

"That's it. Take all of me."

I do.

God, I do.

He pounds into me with single-minded focus—like he's trying to erase every trace of anyone else, every doubt, every fucking mistake.

My hands fist the sheets, clutching with desperation, but it's not enough. I need to hold him. Need him closer.

"Alex—" I say, reaching for him.

He grabs my wrists, pinning them above my head with one hand, his other gripping my chin and forcing my gaze up to his. "Eyes on me. No looking away. I want you to know who you belong to."

"I'm yours," I say, the words ripped from some place deep inside me.

His face twists, wrecked and beautiful and so full of love it makes my chest ache.

"You're mine." Each thrust punctuates his words. "Always have been, always will be."

My body clenches around him, spiraling closer to the edge with every brutal, perfect thrust. I'm so close I can sense it vibrating through every nerve ending.

He doesn't slow down. Doesn't soften. He gives me everything. All the anger, all the heartbreak, all the love he's been holding inside.

"I fucking missed you," he says, his voice cracking on the words.

A broken sob rips from my lips. "I missed you too."

He pulls almost all the way out—then slams back inside me so deep I shatter around him, my orgasm ripping through me like a tidal wave, hot and violent, stealing my breath.

Alex curses under his breath, losing the last thread of control, pounding into me as he chases his own release. His body tenses above me, every muscle locked tight—and then he breaks, groaning my name like a prayer as he comes hard, spilling inside me with a shudder that makes it seem like it'll never end.

We stay like that, tangled together, gasping for air, his forehead pressed against mine.

He kisses me—not rough, not punishing— but slow and aching and reverent.

"I love you, favorite," he says against my mouth. "I'll never stop loving you."

Chapter 28

Alex Sebring

MAGNOLIA LIES ACROSS MY CHEST, HER FINGERS TRACING SLOW, lazy circles against my ribs. She's quiet, lost in that hazy place between exhaustion and contentment. Her warm breath whispers over my skin, her body relaxed, melted into me like she belongs here.

Because she does.

My arms tighten around her, an unconscious, possessive act, like my body is afraid she'll slip away if I don't hold on tight enough.

I stare at the ceiling, my mind still reeling.

I was rough with her. Desperate. I can still hear the way she gasped my name, feel the way her body arched beneath mine.

She took everything I gave her—every ounce of anger, frustration, and grief. But also every tangled, ugly thing I've carried since the day he stole her from my life.

Magnolia Steel is the only person who's ever understood me without words. She always knows what I need.

Always.

I press a kiss to the top of her head, breathing in her soft, feminine scent. She smells of barely there vanilla and cherry blossoms.

It's been months since I held her like this, and yet it doesn't seem that long ago. It's as though I never let her go. Like time bent around us, refusing to move forward until we were back together.

Where we belong.

She shifts, her cheek pressing deeper into my chest. My fingers skate across the curve of her bare back, a lazy caress. There's peace in this—in the quiet after the storm.

The wreckage of the night lingers around us, but it's distant, unimportant. Because she's in my arms now.

And Magnolia Steel is my home.

I tighten my hold on her, letting my fingers drift over her spine, tracing the delicate dips and ridges. My body still hums with the remnants of adrenaline, the echoes of everything that's happened tonight.

The fight.

The fury.

The way I took her like I was claiming her all over again.

A thought gnaws at the edges of my mind, clawing its way forward before I can shove it down. "Was I too rough?"

She shifts against me, tilting her chin up so our eyes meet in the dim light. There's no hesitation when she shakes her head. "No. I needed that just as much as you did."

Relief washes through me, but it's tangled with something heavier—regret for the chaos of the night, for the destruction left in our wake. I don't have to be looking at the wreckage to know it's there. I can hear it in my head. The crash of furniture. The shatter of glass.

My throat tightens, jaw clenching at the memory.

I clear my throat. "I'll take care of everything. Get the place put back together. Buy you whatever needs replacing."

She shakes her head against my chest. "I'm not worried about it."

"Not even a little?"

A small smile ghosts across her lips. "It's just stuff, Alex." Then her expression turns serious. "Except my music collection."

That pulls a quiet laugh from me, the first one I've had in a long time. "Your music survived."

"Thank God."

The teasing lilt in her voice makes my chest ache. I love this side of her. The woman who can tease me even after the night we've had. The woman who doesn't care that we destroyed furniture or scuffed walls... as long as her music is safe.

Magnolia Steel. A contradiction in the best way.

And she's mine again. For the first time in months, I'm at peace.

She lifts her head, her eyes focusing on the ink etched over my heart. Her fingers trace the lines, careful and slow.

I say nothing. Just watch her.

She sits up, the sheet falling to her waist, and brushes her hair back as she studies the design. "This is new."

I nod once, my chest tight. "Yeah."

"What is it?"

"The manumea. It's a rare Samoan bird. Beautiful. Endangered."

She stares at it, saying nothing. Just studying.

"I got it for you."

Her lips part, but the words don't come. Her eyes shine, soft and wide.

"After everything fell apart, I didn't know if I'd ever see you again. But I needed to mark what was real, what mattered most. Even if you never came back to me."

She presses her palm over the tattoo like she's trying to absorb it. "Alex—"

"The manumea, even when it's alone, doesn't stop searching for its mate. Because it mates for life."

Her chin trembles, and she ducks her head, blinking fast. "You inked our love on your skin."

"I inked the truth—my undying love for you."

Her hand stays over my heart, and she doesn't move for a long time. When she looks at me again, her voice is thick with emotion. "That's the most beautiful thing anyone's ever done for me."

I slide my fingers along her jaw, gentle. "You were worth bleeding for."

She leans in, her mouth brushing the ink over my heart, and it hits me—every beat, every thud in my chest, belongs to her.

We don't speak for a while after that. There's nothing to say that could top the silence we've earned—thick with meaning, heavy with everything that's passed between us.

For the first time in a long time, I don't feel like I'm bleeding out. I'm full—of her, of the truth, of the staggering relief that she's here.

She shifts, her leg brushing mine beneath the sheet, her palm still resting over my heart like she's reclaiming the piece of me I gave to her months ago.

She lays her head on the pillow beside mine, lashes fluttering as she studies me.

"Something we didn't talk about earlier——"

I tilt my head, watching her. Waiting.

"You thought we were over, so how did you end up in Charleston?"

"I came to Dallas to see a doctor."

Her entire body tenses, and she rolls on her side, pushing up onto her elbow to see my face. "What's wrong? Are you okay?"

I roll and face her, smoothing a hand down her back. "I had a consultation with a surgeon about my ankle."

Her brows pull together, and I can see the concern settling deep. "Has it been giving you more trouble?"

"No worse than before." Except it hurts like hell right now after fighting with Tyson. I think I may've done something to it. But I'm keeping that to myself.

"There's a specialist in Dallas who's renowned for repairing Achilles injuries. He says mine didn't heal right and I need another surgery."

Now isn't the time to bring up returning to rugby. I'll tell her when the time is right. For now, it's just a surgery that must be done regardless—one step in a long line of unknowns. There's no sense in discussing the future when I'm not sure yet if I have a chance at playing again.

"When is the surgery?"

"Next week."

The look on her face says *wow, that's soon.* "Are you going back to Sydney until then?"

"That was the plan. I was already on my way back, but I came here instead."

"What made you change course?"

She may not like my answer, but it's the truth. "Our breakup wrecked me. I thought I might be able to move on if I had closure. But I know now how damn ridiculous that is. I was a fool to think I could ever move on from you."

"How did you find me at the dance studio?"

"I went to Soul Sync. The client specialist assigned to me in Sydney was there. She said I might enjoy the aerial dance studio."

Magnolia's lips twitch. "You mean Whitney?"

"Maybe. I still don't know her name." I smirk. "Due to that strict-as-fuck Soul Sync privacy policy."

"Well, well." She shakes her head, amused. "Didn't think Miss-By-the-Book Whitney had it in her."

"Guess she does." Thank God she wasn't so uptight today.

She lets out a quiet laugh, but it fades as she studies my face. "What are we doing, Alex?"

There's no hesitation on my part. No second-guessing. "Not sure. I only know that I can't be apart from you. I won't do it again."

Relief—I see it in the way her shoulders relax, the way her fingers brush against my chest.

She relaxes, but my pulse ticks faster.

Tyson McRae is in love with her. And I know him. He might back down for now, but he's not finished pursuing her.

"I can't bear to be separated again."

I bring her hand to my mouth, kissing the top. "We'll find a way to make this work."

"Will you stay with me until you go to Dallas?"

"Babe, you couldn't pry me away from you with a crowbar."

A small giggle bubbles out of her, bright and unexpected, and something deep in my chest loosens. God, I missed that sound. I'd forgotten how it could light up every dark corner inside me without even trying.

I brush a strand of hair from her face, tucking it behind her ear. "Skip work tomorrow and spend the day with me."

A regretful smile pulls at her lips. "I can't. I have a new client coming in for a consultation."

"Cancel it."

She lets out a soft laugh, shaking her head. "Tempting, but I can't afford to do that. In case you forgot, I lost my only client."

Her expression sobers. "Starting a business isn't easy. I need this client."

She does. And I hate it. Not because she's chasing her dream—there's nothing I admire more about her—but because if it were up to me, she'd never have to worry about another client again. I'd take care of her. Make sure she had every resource, every opportunity, every single thing she needed to make this business thrive.

But Magnolia Steel isn't a woman who'd ever accept that.

So I just nod. "I get it."

She leans in, pressing a quick kiss to my lips. "My meeting's early. We'll have the rest of the day together."

Kiss.

"And the night."

Kiss.

"And every minute in between."

"That is the best thing I've heard all night."

She settles cross-legged beside me, knees splayed open, her body relaxed like she's not on display. Her bare pussy gleams in the low light, tempting me like a fucking siren call. My fists clench against the need to shove her back onto the mattress and feast on her until she's screaming my name.

"Tell me about your surgery."

I divert my eyes away, running a hand through my hair. "The surgeon is one of the best—he specializes in reconstructive surgeries on sports injuries like mine. I'll have to do my physical therapy there for twelve weeks."

"Twelve weeks in Dallas? Shit."

Fear flickers in her face. "I mean, don't get me wrong, I'm thrilled you'll be in the U.S., but Dallas is so far away. It isn't any better than Sydney. Not being together... is not being together, no matter where you are."

I sit up, reaching for her hand, my thumb skimming over her knuckles. "That's why I want you to come with me."

"Alex—"

"I'm serious."

"I just started my business. Leaving for months would be career suicide."

"I understand, but we've lost so much time. Is there not any way you could come?"

She chews her bottom lip as she turns the idea over in her head. I can almost see the wheels turning, the tug-of-war behind her eyes—her need to be responsible battling whatever part of her wants to say yes.

"I could work remote in Dallas during the designing process. But most things require me to be in Charleston—handling permits, site visits."

"Could you hire an assistant?"

"I could if I had the money, but I don't."

I open my mouth, but she cuts me off. "Don't you dare say you'll pay for an assistant."

God, she knows me so well. "All right. Whatever time you're able to give me, I want it."

Her features soften. I can see the pull in her—toward me, toward us—but also the weight of everything she's carrying. The business she's built. The life she's fought to create.

"You've worked hard to make your own way in the world. I respect that. It's one of the things I love about you. And while I can predict you won't, I wish you'd let me make it easier for you."

Her eyes meet mine, unwavering. "I appreciate that more than you know, but this is something I have to do on my own."

I nod, understanding, even if I don't like it.

This quiet, determined strength is so her.

"All right, but will you please allow me one selfishness?"

"Depends on the selfishness."

"I want to fly you to Dallas to be with me whenever you're free—weekends, weekdays—I don't care when. Even if I can only get an hour with you. Just say the word, and I'll charter a plane to pick you up."

A smile tugs at her lips, small but sure. "Okay, I'll allow you that selfishness."

I shift closer, cupping her face in my hands, brushing my thumb gently along her cheek. "We're gonna make it work this time, favorite."

Because I'll have it no other way.

Chapter 29

Magnolia Steel

THE SECOND THE DOOR CLOSES BEHIND MY CLIENT, I PUMP MY fist in the air, a victorious little jolt of movement I can't contain. I let out a quiet squeal, spinning in a small, giddy circle, wrapping my arms around myself.

I landed the job.

Not just any job. A full-scale design project for a luxury spa.

My dream. The kind of project that puts a designer on the map, that turns whispers into buzz, that takes you from scraping by to being in demand. This is it. The break I've been fighting for—the one that makes every late night, every rejection, every moment of doubt worth it.

I suck in a breath, trying to slow my racing heart. My hands tremble as I grab my phone, fingers moving on instinct. It rings twice before his deep voice fills the line.

"Hey, favorite."

Warmth floods through me at the sound of his voice, wrapping around me like a hug.

God, I missed this. I missed him.

"Hey. Guess what?"

There's a smile in his voice. "Sounds like you're about to tell me something worth celebrating."

I press my free hand to my chest, still riding the high. "I got it, big guy. I landed the client. A full design contract for a luxury spa."

A beat. Then—"Damn right, you got it."

His confidence in me is unwavering, solid as bedrock. It anchors me when I doubt myself. "Congratulations, babe. No one deserves this more than you do."

A rush of emotion rises in my throat. I sink into my chair, twirling as I soak in the pride in his voice. "I'm proud of myself."

"You should be. You did it."

I press my lips together, swallowing hard. He believes in me. Even when I don't always believe in myself. He'll never know what that means to me.

"I wish you were here."

"I am here, remember? And I'm taking you out to celebrate tonight."

A slow smile spreads across my lips. "You are, huh?"

"You, me, good food, a bottle of champagne. What do you say?"

It's a hell yes, but I tease him instead. "Hmm... what kind of champagne?"

A low chuckle. "The expensive kind."

I bite my lip, grinning. "Umm... then I say yes."

"When can you leave?"

I glance around the office, forcing my thoughts to shift out of celebration mode. "Give me a few minutes to straighten up the office."

"It's still early. Want to do some shopping before dinner? Maybe buy replacements for what got destroyed last night? I want to make it up to you."

Home decor shopping—this man is speaking my language. "How could I say no to that?"

"How about I catch a taxi and meet you at your office?"

"Sounds good. See you soon."

I hang up, still smiling, as I clutch my phone to my chest. Life is falling back into place. For the first time in a long time, everything is right.

Still buzzing from my big win, I force myself to refocus. As much as I want to float out of here on a cloud of victory, I need to tidy up for the day.

I grab my preliminary design board for the spa, gliding my palm over the sleek surface before tucking it into my portfolio. This project is going to be everything.

With my presentation put away, I move to the break area, pouring out the last bit of coffee and washing the pot in the sink. A normal task, something I do every day—but there's an extra lightness in my chest now.

This is what I've been working toward. What I fought for. And now it's happening.

Setting the clean coffee pot in the dish drainer, I swipe a towel over the counter, my mind already drifting to Alex. He's on his way. We're going shopping. Then dinner. Then... more.

A slow heat creeps through me.

This day keeps getting better.

I enter my office... and freeze.

Tyson McRae is standing there.

A squeal slips out before I can stop it. A rush of adrenaline surges through me, sharp and immediate. My breath catches in my throat.

His face is a damn mess—bruised, swollen, his left eye black from where Alex's fist connected. There's a splint on his nose, proof that he received medical attention after leaving my apartment last night.

I swallow, my pulse kicking up.

Alex would lose his mind if he knew Tyson was here. He might murder him this time instead of beating the shit out of him.

"Mags—"

"You can't be here."

"I'm sure you don't want to see me right now, but we didn't get to finish our conversation last night."

"There's nothing left to say."

"I meant what I said last night. I love you, Magnolia."

"Stop saying that."

He shakes his head, jaw tightening. "I have to say it because I need you to know."

Anger simmers beneath my skin, rising with every second he stands there, uninvited.

"Let me explain something to you. When you love someone, you put their happiness first. You want them to have everything they've ever dreamed of—even if it costs you everything. Even when I thought Alex had chosen someone else, I still wanted him to be happy. Even as it broke me, I prayed he'd find the life he deserved. Because that's what genuine love is. Selfless. Unwavering. Even when it tears you apart."

I give him a minute to absorb.

"Can you say the same? Do you love me enough to let me go? Enough to want me to be with the one I choose—even if that person is Alex?"

His throat bobs, but he doesn't answer. And that hesitation? It tells me everything.

"Sebring wants things you are not ready to give him."

Who the fuck made Tyson McRae the authority on what I am—or am not—ready to give someone? "What do you think Alex wants that I'm not prepared to give him?"

"A wife. Kids. The whole fairytale ending. That's not you, Mags. You don't want that."

That was the old me—the me who thought love was something to keep at arm's length.

"I wouldn't push you into something you don't want. But that's what Sebring will do."

His words don't shake me or plant the doubt he's hoping for. If anything, they solidify what I already know. Because the thing is... he's got it all wrong.

It's true what they say... you don't know what you have until it's gone.

"I thought I didn't want marriage. But when you love someone, and you lose them, it changes things."

"Sebring is still the same person he was before. What he wants hasn't changed."

"My heart aches for Alex. I never want to live without him again, and I'm not fool enough to believe that doesn't lead to marriage."

A muscle tics in his jaw, the first sign he's beginning to piece it together—and he doesn't like where it's leading. "So you're saying—"

I cut him off before he can try to twist my words. "Like I said... things have changed."

His jaw clenches so tight I'm surprised his teeth don't shatter.

He shakes his head, as if he can will my words away, rewrite them into something else, something that doesn't rip his hope to shreds.

But it's too late. He's lost. And he knows it.

"You've gotta be fucking kidding me."

I shake my head. "I'm not. Not even a little."

His bruised and swollen face twists with frustration. "So that's it? Sebring gets the girl? He wins again?"

"It was never a competition between you and Alex. I am his. I have been from the moment we met."

Before Tyson can respond, a familiar presence sends a shiver down my spine. The hairs on my arms stand on end, and I swear I sense the shift in the air before I even turn.

Alex.

I jolt, my pulse spiking as I glance toward the doorway. He's standing there, broad shoulders rigid, dark eyes locked on Tyson with a look so sharp it could slice through steel.

Shit. This is about to go downhill fast.

Alex steps forward, his voice dripping with irritation. "Jesus Christ, McRae. You're like a fucking pest that won't go away. "

His swollen lips curve into a smirk. "It's not in my DNA to give up on something I want. And I want her."

"Did you not take that ass beating as a hint to leave us the hell alone?"

"You call that an ass beating?"

"Have you seen your face, motherfucker?"

Alex's body is taut, like a predator just waiting for an excuse to strike.

The image of last night's fight flashes in my mind—Alex and Tyson colliding like wrecking balls, turning my living room into a war zone. Bruised knuckles, shattered furniture, and enough testosterone to fuel an entire action movie.

Now they're standing here again, tension thick enough to choke on.

"Please don't destroy my office."

Alex doesn't take his eyes off Tyson. His voice is calm, but the threat beneath it is razor sharp. "Don't worry, love. We won't wreck the place."

I have my doubts. The way his hands flex at his sides tells me he's one wrong word away from doing exactly that.

Tyson turns his attention to me. "We still need to discuss the hotel."

Alex steps in front of me, a human shield between me and Tyson. "Forget it. Magnolia won't be working with you anymore."

Tyson whirls around, pointing his finger at Alex. "Shut up. You don't get a fucking say in our business arrangement."

Alex steps out of the way. "It's your business, babe. Handle it."

I square my shoulders, lifting my chin. "I won't be moving forward on the project with you. You've shown me who you are. I refuse to do business with someone I can't trust."

"You have to. We have a binding agreement. You're obligated."

I shake my head. "Actually, I'm not."

I would say that he looks confused, but it's hard to tell with his face looking like he zigged when he should've zagged. "We have a contract, and there's a clause in that agreement—one you've violated."

"That's bullshit."

I arch a brow, turning toward my desk. "You should've read the fine print."

I pluck a folder from my drawer, flipping it open, my fingers gliding over the pages until I find the clause I'm looking for.

Clearing my throat, I read aloud. "The designer reserves the right to terminate this agreement should the client engage in conduct that is illegal, unethical, or otherwise detrimental to the designer's professional reputation and/or personal values."

I slam the contract on my desk in front of him. "You signed it. Now I'm exercising my legal right to end the agreement."

His jaw tightens. "You think that'll hold up?"

"I don't think, Tyson. I know. You're welcome to fight it, but you won't win. I took special care to cover all my bases with you. My gut told me I couldn't trust you and I was right."

Alex chuckles, full of satisfaction. "Damn, McRae. You got outplayed by the fine print."

The fight in his eyes fades, weakening, until there's nothing left but quiet defeat. "All right then. I guess this is it."

"It is. Goodbye, Tyson."

Without another word, he turns and leaves. The second the door swings shut, I can breathe again. But before I can process what just happened—

Alex is on me.

No hesitation. No patience.

Just raw, unfiltered need.

His hands grip my waist, yanking me flush against him, his body a furnace of heat and coiled power. His ragged breath is heavy with restraint that's hanging by a single frayed thread.

"Damn, babe." His hold on me tightens, his fingertips pressing into my skin. "That was fucking hot."

A breathless laugh escapes me, but it vanishes the second his lips ghost over mine. His eyes are dark, heavy-lidded, devouring.

"Was it?"

"You were such a boss." His fingers skim up my spine, dragging fire in their wake. "Sexiest damn thing I've ever seen, the way you handled him."

I don't even have time to react before his mouth crashes onto mine. There's nothing soft about it. Nothing patient.

Teeth, tongues, lips—everything is fevered, frantic.

His hands are everywhere—one tangling in my hair, angling my head for deeper, hotter kisses, the other sliding down to my ass, gripping hard as he pulls me closer. I feel every inch of him, every solid muscle, every sharp edge that makes Alex Sebring the man who owns me.

His hands slip lower, gripping the backs of my thighs, and before I can react, he lifts me onto the desk.

My breath hitches, a sharp gasp swallowed by his mouth as he steps between my legs, pressing into me, showing me how much he needs this.

"Alex—" I say, but it's more of a plea.

"I loved watching you put McRae in his place."

His lips brush my jaw, trailing lower, his teeth grazing my pulse, sending a shudder rippling through me.

I'm already gone.

Fire pools low in my stomach, coiling tighter, threatening to consume me.

I drag my nails down his back and dig my heels into the backs of his thighs, urging him closer. "Show me how much it turned you on."

A low, dark curse slips from his lips, then he moves.

He shoves my skirt up, bunching the fabric around my hips with rough hands. His fingertips trail a path up my thighs, teasing, claiming. A firm grip on my hips drags me closer to the edge of the desk. His fingers hook under my lace panties, sliding them down, leaving me bare, trembling, aching for him.

A low, guttural growl rumbles from his chest—raw, hungry—and then he's gone, only for a heartbeat. Pants shoved down, he settles between my thighs like he's never letting me go again.

One hand clamps down on my hip, anchoring me. The other guides himself to where I need him most.

With one hard thrust, he's inside me, filling me to the hilt. A gasping cry rips from my throat, my head snapping back as he stretches me, wrecks me, claims every broken, desperate part of me.

His hold on my waist tightens, unrelenting, keeping me pinned to the desk as he moves. Slow at first—teasing, tormenting—drawing out until I'm gasping, until I'm shaking. Then faster. Harder. Deeper. Until there's nothing left but the stars bursting behind my eyelids.

The rhythm turns rougher, more desperate, more unhinged, his control shredding with each thrust, each broken moan. The desk creaks beneath us, rocking with every movement.

"God, you feel so fucking good," he says, mouth over my ear, his voice barely human.

I whimper, clinging to him as he drives into me, over and over, his pace unrelenting.

I'm close. Too close. He feels it.

His fingers find my jaw, forcing me to look at him.

"Eyes on me. I want to watch you come."

And just like that, I shatter.

Pleasure crashes over me in a tidal wave, my entire body convulsing as I cry out his name, fingers digging into his shoulders.

Alex follows with a curse, burying himself deep, his entire body tensing, trembling, before he collapses against me, breathless, spent.

The only sound in the room is our ragged breathing. And for a long moment, neither of us moves. We just exist in this aftermath, tangled, burning, wrecked.

I close my eyes, letting the pressure of him ground me, the steady thump of his heart beneath my palms anchoring me to this moment.

He lifts his head, pressing a kiss to my forehead, my temple, my lips.

"You're incredible."

"You're not so bad yourself, big guy."

His chest rumbles with laughter before he nips at my bottom lip, stealing another slow, lingering kiss.

His grip on my waist lingers, firm and possessive.

A slow breath leaves me, my body still humming, still molded to the hard surface of my desk—the place where I just let him take me, where I gave in to the need that burns everything else away.

His fingers brush over my back, his lips brushing against my temple. "You were made for this."

A shiver rolls through me, not just from his words, but from the quiet certainty in them.

I let my nails drag down his back, anchoring myself to the weight of him. "You enjoy fucking me on my desk, Sebring?"

He chuckles. "Yeah, I love fucking you on your desk, Steel."

I grin, squeezing the muscles in his shoulders. "Good. I like it too."

His thumb brushes over my lips. "You're mine."

The words settle deep, reverberating through every inch of me.

I don't respond. I don't need to. Because we both already know it's true.

Chapter 30

Alex Sebring

LAUGHTER RISES OVER THE CLINK OF ICE AND THE THRUM OF bass-heavy music. Whiskey and beer hang in the air, the lighting low and moody. Normally, I'd love to come and relax, a drink in hand, at a place like this. But tonight, I have bigger things on my mind.

It should be the perfect setting for a casual night out, but there's nothing casual about this. Because tonight, I'm meeting Violet. And according to Magnolia, she isn't just her best friend—she's her other half, her ride-or-die, the person who knows everything about her, including how broken her heart was while we were apart.

This woman isn't just important. She's critical. And if she doesn't like me? Well, that's a problem.

Magnolia's fingers tighten around mine. "You're quiet. Are you good?"

Nerves buzz under my skin, but I shut it down, the way I used to before stepping onto the rugby pitch. "All good."

Magnolia lifts a brow, unconvinced. "You sure? You're doing that thing where you get all broody and silent."

I smirk. "I'm always broody and silent."

She steps in closer, tipping her head up to meet my eyes. "Listen, be yourself, okay?"

"That's vague, lovie."

"Okay, let me be clearer—be yourself, but also maybe brace yourself."

"Very reassuring."

She winks. "Glad to help."

Magnolia tugs me through the crowd, weaving past groups of people pressed around high-top tables, and past the bar where a bartender is pouring a row of tequila shots for a group of friends already swaying to the music.

The further we move into the space, the more my pulse picks up.

It's ridiculous. *I'm* ridiculous. I've played in stadiums filled with thousands of roaring fans, faced down by some of the toughest players in the world. But this meeting? I'm on edge.

This matters. Because, unlike Robin and Charlene, Violet gives a damn about Magnolia.

She was the one checking in on her while she was in Sydney. And she's the one Magnolia was calling, texting, relying on when I wasn't there.

Her approval counts. It's essential.

The usual Friday night chaos fills the bar, and we scan for an open table.

"There." She points toward a high-top table near the back. It's one of the few unclaimed ones, tucked away from the noisiest part of the bar.

"Good find."

A bit of quiet is a good thing—especially considering what's about to happen.

I pull out a stool for her before settling into the one beside her.

Magnolia flags down a passing server. "Want a drink before the inquiry begins?"

"Hell yeah."

"Is it an old-fashioned night?"

"Babe, every night is an old-fashioned night."

Magnolia shifts toward me, her expression softer now. "You know she's going to like you, right?"

"You sound confident."

"I am." She nudges my knee under the table. "No need to stress. Take a breath and relax."

She's trying to put me at ease, and I appreciate that.

"I'm fine."

She watches me for a moment. "Go take a deep breath anyway. Your drink will be here when you get back."

She doesn't say it like an order. It's soft. Steady. Like she's handing me a lifeline without making a show of it.

Magnolia has a way of seeing the cracks before they split wide open—of knowing when the pressure gets too much, when the walls close in. She's the only one who's ever known how to pull me back from the edge without making me feel weak.

God, I love her.

I push away from the table. "Be right back."

The men's room is quiet—thankfully empty—giving me a moment to regroup. I lean against the sink, rolling my neck and shoulders, exhaling a slow breath.

It's a conversation. That's all this is. One woman's opinion.

One *very* important woman.

I shake it off. It'll be fine. Magnolia loves me. Violet loves Magnolia. By default, she should at least tolerate me, right?

...Right.

I push off the sink and head for the door. The second I step into the hallway, a woman appears out of nowhere, blocking my path.

I stop short.

She's wrapped in a dress that clings to every inch of her. Bright red lipstick, eyes flicking over me like she's sizing me up.

This one likes to be noticed.

"Damn. Didn't think I'd get lucky this early in the night."

Here we go.

I shift to move past her, but she mirrors me, stepping right into my path again. I've been in enough bars to recognize the look in her eyes.

"Excuse me."

She doesn't move. Instead, she tilts her head, smiling like she knows something I don't. "You Australian?"

I nod once. "Born and raised."

Her smile curves slow, deliberate. "Love the accent."

I don't react. Not the first time I've heard it, won't be the last. Means nothing.

She shifts, angling her body enough to block my path. "So tell me —what's a guy like you doing here alone?"

"I'm not alone. I'm with my girlfriend."

She steps in closer, a breath too close, dropping her voice to something she thinks sounds seductive. "That doesn't mean we can't have a little fun while you're here."

"It does, actually."

Her grin widens, lazy and cocky. "Can I change your mind?"

"No. Now if you'll excuse me, my girlfriend's waiting for me."

One brow arches high, practiced and sharp. "What are you? Some kind of saint?"

"Not a saint." I meet her gaze, steady and unbothered. "But I am faithful."

She studies me for a beat, head tilted. "Not even tempted?"

This is getting old fast. "Not interested. Excuse me."

A smirk ghosts across her lips—a small, knowing thing.

"See you later," she tosses over her shoulder before pivoting toward the ladies' room, hips swinging like she still thinks she's in the game.

I shake my head once, brushing it off. Don't know what that was about. Don't care.

I've got bigger things to focus on tonight.

Magnolia's scrolling through her phone when I return to the table, glancing up as I slide onto the stool beside her.

"Everything okay?"

"All good." I lift my drink, taking a slow sip.

"You were gone a while."

I debate telling her about the woman—and then decide it might be fun to see her reaction.

"It's nothing. Just some woman trying to hit on me. Wouldn't take the hint."

Magnolia's brows arch. "Oh?"

"Happens all the time."

She grins. "Does it now?"

I shrug. "This one was a 'love your accent' type."

She props her elbow on the table, resting her chin in her hand, eyes glinting with amusement. "I seem to recall being one of those 'love your accent' types."

I tip my glass toward her. "Yeah, but it was different coming from you."

She hums like she's giving it serious thought. "Right. Because I was classy about it?"

I arch a brow. "You told me my accent made you want to climb me like a tree."

Her grin is wicked, unapologetic. "I don't remember saying that, but I do like to climb you like a tree, so—"

I huff a quiet laugh and take a sip of my drink. "Where's your girl?"

"Right here," says a voice behind me.

That voice.

Dread slithers up my spine before I even see her face.

The woman from the hallway slides onto the stool across from me, a smug grin playing on her mouth.

Magnolia, oblivious, beams. "Vi, this is Alex."

Vi.

As in Violet.

As in Magnolia's best friend.

As in the one person whose opinion matters.

I don't move. Don't blink. My mind rewinds, in perfect clarity, every second of that hallway encounter.

She set me up.

She *fucking* set me up.

She watches me like a cat who just trapped a particularly interesting mouse.

"Violet and I already met."

One thing is clear—Violet is going to make me work for her approval.

Magnolia looks between us. "You've already met?"

Violet's smirk sharpens. "Oh, you know. Just a little pregame warm-up."

She leans forward, resting one elbow on the bar. "Had to see for myself what we were working with before we got to this part."

Magnolia's eyes narrow, suspicion sharpening her features. "Violet... what did you do?"

She taps a manicured nail against the bar, slow and deliberate. "Just ran a quick loyalty check."

Her gaze cuts to me. "He was about as tempted as a vegan at a barbecue competition."

Violet lifts the drink I ordered for her and takes a slow sip. "I may have run into him outside the restroom. Recognized him. Pretended to be a random woman trying to pick him up."

Magnolia makes a choking sound. "You did what?"

Violet flashes a wicked grin. "Magnolia, meet 'love your accent' girl."

Understanding dawns on Magnolia's face. "Ohhh. Now it all makes sense."

Violet shrugs, unrepentant. "Had to see how he'd react."

We both know I passed. I just want to hear her admit it. "And?"

She lifts her hand, examining her nails like she's grading me. "Wasn't charmed one bit. Very impressive... for a man."

I don't know whether to feel relieved or insulted.

Magnolia groans and drops her head into her hands. "Vi, you can't ambush people like that."

Violet smirks, unfazed. "I can, and I did. And honestly? If he had hesitated or even thought about it, wouldn't you have wanted to know?"

Magnolia glares at her. "That's not the point."

"It *is* the point."

I try to wrap my head around the madness unfolding in front of me. "Is this normal for you?"

Violet tilts her head like she's considering it. "Only when it's necessary."

"And you decided this was necessary?"

Her gaze cuts into me. "My best friend's heart shattered into a billion pieces. Guess who was there picking up those pieces? Me. So yeah, for me, it's necessary."

Magnolia groans and mutters something under her breath before turning to me, her expression caught somewhere between exasperation and apology. "I swear she means well."

Violet grins, swirling her drink. "I do."

I'm still debating whether I should laugh or just resign myself to my fate, but one thing is clear—this is going to be a long night.

"Can we at least try to have a normal conversation now?" Magnolia asks.

"Sure, but first—" Violet leans in, all faux seriousness. "What are your intentions with my best friend?"

I take a slow sip of my drink, leveling her with a look of my own. "You go for the jugular, don't you?"

Violet nods. "Damn right I do."

Magnolia groans. I just smirk.

Let the games begin.

"Okay, Vi. How about letting Alex breathe for a minute?"

She shrugs, feigning innocence. "I just need to make sure he's the good guy I want him to be."

I bite back a grin. "You could've just asked."

"Where's the fun in that?" She flashes a wicked grin and studies me. "But now that we're here, tell me, Sebring—what are your long-term plans?"

Is Violet her best friend... or a mob boss vetting the guy dating his little girl? Hard to tell. All she's missing is a baseball bat and a couple of goons named Tony and Vinny flanking her.

I glance at Magnolia, but she's not helping me out of this. If anything, she's watching with a mix of amusement and mild horror.

I shift my attention back to Violet. "You want the business proposal version or the emotionally vulnerable one?"

Her eyes light up. "Oh, I love a man with options. Let's start with business and work our way up."

Magnolia groans. "Oh my God."

I smirk, leaning forward. "Fine. Business version? Magnolia is the smartest investment I could make—for my future, my happiness, and everything that comes next."

Violet lets out a hum of approval, nodding. "Not bad. And the emotionally vulnerable version?"

My smirk fades into something more honest, more real. "I love her. Completely."

The words come easy because they're the truest thing I've ever said.

Violet's teasing fades. A flicker of something unreadable crosses her face, something softer. "Good answer."

Magnolia shifts beside me, her fingers tightening around mine under the table.

"Do I have your stamp of approval?"

She chews on the stir stick, like a cat playing with her food. "For now."

She eases off the interrogation—a little.

We settle into something that resembles normal conversation, but there's an undercurrent to it. A constant evaluation. She's still watching me, still testing me, even if it's not obvious.

Magnolia nudges her knee against mine under the table. "You holding up okay?"

She has no idea the things I've endured. "I've survived worse."

"You're a tough one. I'll give you that. And speaking of being tough—" Violet twirls her finger, gesturing to my face. "How's the other guy look?"

Magnolia tenses beside me.

No hesitation. "He looks like someone who shouldn't have fucked with Magnolia."

"You protected my girl. I like that." Violet hums, nodding. "Much respect."

I expected pushback—a lecture about how violence solves nothing or how I'm a walking red flag for swinging first and thinking second.

No reprimand. No judgment.

Only respect.

Violet waves a hand, casual but deliberate. "For the record, I like you. You're good for her."

Winning Violet over feels bigger than any game or championship I've ever won.

"Don't fuck this up, Sebring."

"I won't. Because Magnolia's the biggest win of my life. No offense to my rugby career."

Violet lifts her glass, holding it upwards, and I tap my drink against hers. "Cheers."

And just like that, I'm in with her.

Violet made me work for it, but I passed. And for the first time tonight, my shoulders relax, and I breathe a little easier.

Chapter 31

Magnolia Steel

THE HUM OF THE JET ENGINE FADES INTO A WHISPER AS WE TAXI toward the private hangar in Dallas. Alex's hand is resting on my thigh, his thumb tracing circles over my leg. He doesn't appear nervous on the outside, but I know him. I see the way his jaw flexes, like he's bracing for something.

We've made this trip like a team, the two of us showing up together.

After everything we've gone through, it still amazes me how easily we've fallen into being us again. Like the ache never happened, like we never unraveled, like our love remembered how to—just be.

The penthouse is what I expected—sleek, masculine, understated luxury—with warm wood, rich leather, tall windows that let the Dallas skyline pour in like liquid gold. It smells like eucalyptus and old money.

The bedroom is massive—warm, elegant, and designed to impress.

"I see you went all out," I say, turning in a slow circle.

He shrugs like it's no big deal. "Three months is a long time. I wanted it to feel comfortable... so you'd want to come back. Spend time with me."

I pause, tilting my head. *Odd thing to say.*

"You worry I won't?"

"A little." His voice is careful, almost too casual. "Travel can be exhausting. You've got the business consuming a lot of your time. I wanted to make it easy for you to stay. To work here. To want to be here."

I go to him, putting my arm around his shoulders. "I'm going to be here every minute I can. You got it?"

He nods, the corners of his mouth lifting just enough to soften the tension. "Promise?"

I go up on my tiptoes and press a kiss to his mouth. "Promise."

We spend the afternoon walking around the city. Nothing fancy—a museum, a bookstore, a quiet bench at the edge of Klyde Warren Park where we split a slice of caramel cake we didn't need but definitely wanted.

By early evening, I see it—the subtle shift in his gait. The quiet hitch in his breath when he thinks I'm not paying attention. The way he favors his good ankle.

He hasn't said anything, but I suspect he injured it again when he fought with Tyson.

"Are you okay?" I slow down beside him as we cross the street. "You're limping."

He gives me that signature half-smile that's pure trouble. "I'm fine."

"Alex, you're not."

He stops on the sidewalk and turns to face me. "Listen, babe. I'm about to be in a boot for weeks. I've got days ahead of me stuck in bed with an ankle that'll hate me. The pain is going to be worse than last time and believe me when I tell you it was no walk in the park. So let me have this. Let me have you and Dallas tonight."

"Okay."

"And besides—" He leans closer, voice dropping low enough to make me shiver. "I don't mind being stuck in bed... if you're in it with me."

I swat his chest, laughing as he catches my wrist mid-air and brings it to his lips, brushing a kiss over the inside. His eyes don't leave mine.

God, I love him.

We walk a little slower. His limp worsens, but he doesn't complain. He lets me fuss over him and carry the small bag from the bookstore. He chooses to take the longer route back to the hotel because the light hitting the buildings is beautiful and he wants more time with me before the sun sets.

Oh, how this man loves sunrises and sunsets.

And right now—bathed in gold, his hand wrapped around mine, that crooked smile tugging at the corner of his mouth—I understand why. There's something sacred in the in-between. The hush before the night. The knowing that something is ending, but something else is about to begin.

THE RESTAURANT IS SPECIAL, THE KIND OF PLACE YOU HEAR whispers about—soft lighting and candlelit corners, dark wood floors that hush beneath your heels, a wine list so extensive it reads like a novel written in vintage years and sommelier secrets.

We're only a few sips into the wine when Alex leans back in his chair, swirling the deep red. His smile is slow, a hint of smug beneath the softness.

"How many strings did you have to pull to get us in here tonight?"

He nods, taking a slow sip. "Called in a few favors. Threatened to cry. Whatever it took."

I laugh, adjusting the strap of my dress. "You're ridiculous."

His eyes scan me like he's memorizing every detail. "I wanted our only night in Dallas to be special."

"It is."

He's wearing a slate-blue button-down, the top few buttons undone enough to tease the ink that creeps along his collarbone—bold lines and curves that disappear beneath the fabric like a secret only I know. A navy sport coat hugs his shoulders, tailored but effortless. His hair's still damp from the shower, pushed back in that way that says he tried... but not too hard. Because he doesn't have to. He's all quiet confidence and devastating calm, and somehow, that wrecks me more than anything else.

To anyone watching us, we look like we've had it easy. Like we belong here—two polished people sitting at a corner table, wine glasses in hand, laughing like the world never tried to break us.

But that's the illusion.

Getting here wasn't easy. It was raw and brutal. It was sleepless nights, unanswered messages, and heartbreak that settled deep in our bones.

We clawed our way back to this moment. Back to each other. And now that I have him again, I won't let go. Not this time. Not for anything.

The server refills our wine, and we lift them in quiet unison, fingertips brushing.

"To surviving the worst."

He meets my gaze and taps his glass to mine. "To never forgetting what it took to get here."

Dinner is slow and decadent. He orders the largest steak on the menu—because of course he does. I go for a pasta I can't pronounce with more garlic than should be legal in the state of Texas.

We trade bites across the table like it's second nature, like we've been doing this for years instead of falling back into each other's rhythm after months apart.

Alex cuts a piece of his steak for me and lifts it to my mouth with a smirk. "You'll thank me later."

He tells me about the trouble he and his brothers used to cause Malie growing up—how they'd sneak out to surf before dawn, track mud through the house, and come home with bruises they all swore were from "falling," not fighting. His grin is wide, boyish, when he talks about how Malie once chased them down the driveway with a wooden spoon, yelling in Samoan, because they'd shaved off each other's eyebrows on a dare.

I'm still laughing when I reach for my wine, eyes wet with amusement. "That's wild, but honestly, it kind of makes me think raising a house full of boys wouldn't be the worst thing."

He stills, fork halfway to his mouth. "Yeah?"

I glance up, meeting his eyes. There's something unreadable in his expression—curiosity edged with something softer.

"It'd be pure chaos. Loud. I'm pretty sure, disgusting. But I think I'd love it."

His mouth curves into a slow, thoughtful smile, the kind that lands somewhere deep in my chest.

I smile back. And that moment stretches, filled with everything we don't say.

My feelings have changed. Somewhere between losing him and finding him again, I let go of the rules I'd built around my heart. I want love—real love—and a family of my own.

I want forever, and I want it with him.

And if it comes with little Tasmanian devils... well, okay.

But now isn't the time for that conversation. Not tonight. Not with tomorrow looming. So I take another sip of wine instead and hold on to my secret a little tighter and for a little longer.

His eyes stay on mine, steady as ever, but I can see it—the flicker of something fragile beneath the surface. I notice everything when it comes to him. He won't say it out loud—I've learned that much about him—but he's nervous about tomorrow.

"Everything's going to be fine." My voice is low, keeping this conversation between us in our little corner. "You hear me? You've got this, big guy. And you've got me."

His shoulders ease and that little crease between his brows softens.

"You're not going through this alone."

His eyes flicker with something quiet. Relief, maybe. Love, definitely.

"I didn't realize I needed to hear that. I'm glad it's you who'll be with me."

My foot finds his under the table. "I'll be the perfect nurse and take care of every... single... inch of you."

His jaw tightens, eyes flashing heat.

"And if you're a good patient, I might climb into that tiny hospital bed and make you forget you're supposed to be resting."

"*Take Magnolia three times a day for pleasure.* I like that prescription. I'm looking forward to this surgery now."

ALEX UNLOCKS THE DOOR, AND LIKE ALWAYS, OPENS IT FOR ME. The moment the penthouse door clicks shut behind us, everything changes.

He shrugs off his sport coat, draping it over the arm of the couch before unbuttoning his sleeves and rolling them up, forearms flexing with each motion. His hair's a little mussed from the night breeze, and it's somehow sexier than when we left.

The city glows outside the floor-to-ceiling windows, but all I can see is him.

I toe off my heels, sighing in relief as they hit the floor. My dress whispers around my legs as I cross the room, that silky fabric suddenly too warm.

I glance over at him, and he's looking at me. No—not just looking. Watching. Like I'm something he's been waiting on all night. Like I'm prey, and he's a man who knows how to hunt without rushing the kill.

I reach up and tug the clip from my hair, letting it fall in a slow cascade over my shoulders. The waves loosen, framing my face as I shake them out with a practiced flick, aware—achingly aware—of the way his gaze heats as he watches. Like he's starving. Like I'm already his.

Because I am.

His voice is low, almost a growl. "Fuck, you're sexy."

He crosses the space between us with unhurried confidence, the kind that makes my breath catch. His eyes drag down my body, slow and reverent. But he doesn't touch me. Not yet.

Instead, he stops just short of pressing against me. His hand lifts, fingers teasing the bare skin of my shoulder, light as a whisper. "You did this on purpose."

"Did what?" I ask, feigning innocence even as heat pools low in my belly.

His mouth tilts in a lazy, sinful smile. "Letting your hair down and shaking it out like that."

His knuckle skims down the curve of my arm. "You knew what it would do to me."

"Possibly," I say, heart thudding as I tilt my chin up to meet his eyes. "Or maybe I just wanted to see if you were still paying attention."

His eyes flare. "I never stop paying attention where you're concerned."

He brushes my hair back from my face, fingers lingering at the nape of my neck. Then, with maddening slowness, he dips his head, lips ghosting just beside mine without closing the distance.

"You're playing with fire," he says against my mouth.

"Then burn me."

And then he kisses me. But it's not sweet. It's not soft. It's possession.

It's every promise, every prayer, every plea poured into one searing, consuming kiss.

His mouth crashes over mine, and I melt into it, gasping against the sudden heat of him. His hands find my hips, gripping tight, pulling me flush against his body like he needs me there to breathe.

I wind my arms around his neck, moaning into his mouth as he deepens the kiss, his tongue sweeping against mine with a hunger that makes my knees go weak.

When he walks us backward toward the bed, I go—no resistance, no hesitation, just the pounding of my heart and sensation of his body pressed to mine.

His mouth moves lower, skimming along my jaw, tracing fire across my throat. I tilt my head to give him more, every inch of me aching for his touch.

My hands tug his shirt free from his waistband, already desperate to feel him—skin to skin.

And he lets me.

He groans low in his throat. "God, you undo me."

"*I'm trying to undo you.* But these damn buttons. Where do you buy your shirts? Frustrate-the-fuck-out-of-her-with-difficult-buttons-dot-com?"

He grins, lazy and smug, eyes dark with heat.

"Tailor-made to drive you insane. Buttons are foreplay, babe."

"Yeah? Well, foreplay's taking too damn long."

My fingers fumble once more—twice—and I've had enough. I grab both sides of his shirt and rip it open, buttons popping and bouncing across the floor like confetti.

He blinks, then laughs low and full of heat. "Fuck, that was hot."

I meet his gaze, breathless. "Damn right it was."

Tonight isn't about perfection. It's about need.

I push his shirt off his shoulders, revealing the ink I already know by heart—except now there's more. My eyes drift to the new lines, the fresh tattoo over his heart.

I trace the edges with my finger. "This is for me."

His hand covers mine. "Not *for* you. It *is* you."

I press a kiss against the tattoo. "Mine."

"Fuck," he whispers. "You're unreal."

I slide my nails down his chest as I push his shirt off. "Bet you say that to all the women who drop everything to be your nurse."

He grins, but there's heat behind it. "Only the one I'm still falling for every... damn... day."

For all the teasing and the heat crackling between us—it's that quiet, gruff confession that cuts right through me.

Still falling for me.

Every... damn... day.

Like I'm more than someone he wants at this moment. I'm someone he's choosing. Again. And again. And again.

Something twists in my chest, tender and breathless. The kind of ache that comes with knowing this is real. This is us. And I'm not scared of it anymore.

I blink up at him, heart pounding, throat tight. "Then I guess I better give you a reason to keep falling."

His belt comes next, undone with a practiced flick that earns me a raised brow and a soft, amused grunt. "Seems like you've done that a time or two."

"Only for you."

He leans in, mouth brushing the shell of my ear. "That's right. Only for me."

He kisses me like I'm oxygen—like the world might stop spinning if he lets go. My back hits the wall behind us, and his hands roam with purpose, slipping under the hem of my dress, fingertips grazing the bare skin of my thighs as I gasp against his mouth. But just when I think he'll lose control, he stills.

Then, in one fluid, confident motion, Alex lifts me off the floor.

My breath catches as my legs wrap around his waist, our bodies aligned, tension humming between us. His hands grip me tight, like he can't bear to let go even for a second.

He carries me through the penthouse with slow, deliberate steps, every movement precise, restrained—but barely. He kicks open the bedroom door and lays me down like I'm something sacred.

I sink into the mattress, my dress bunched around my hips, chest rising and falling fast.

And he just looks at me.

His body hovers over mine, arms braced on either side of my head, eyes devouring every detail.

He doesn't touch. Doesn't speak.

Just watches.

I reach for him, fingertips skimming the taut planes of his abs, the trail of ink along his ribs. But he catches my hands, pinning them to the bed beside my head.

"Do you know how many nights I imagined this?"

My chest tightens. "Alex—"

"Not the sex. This—you and me together. No pretending. No countdown. No goodbye."

The emotion in his voice tugs at something deep inside me, and tears prick my eyes—not from sadness, but from the overwhelming fullness of this. Of us. The weight of everything we lost and everything we somehow clawed our way back to.

I reach up, cradling his face in both hands, and pull his mouth back to mine.

This time, the kiss isn't desperate—it's sure. It's steady. It's a vow wrapped in love.

His hands slide down my sides, anchoring me as our mouths devour each other in slow, aching sync. His fingers find the hem of my dress, teasing it upward inch by inch.

"You didn't wear this sexy little thing to dinner, expecting me to behave like a gentleman after."

I smile against his mouth, breathless. "I don't expect you to behave at all."

His laugh is low, wicked. "Good. Because I'm done pretending that I have an ounce of control where you're concerned."

The dress slips over my head in one fluid motion, cool air kissing my skin as he drinks me in. His eyes darken as he takes in the lace beneath—barely there, black, and meant only for him.

His mouth follows every inch he exposes, lips dragging over my skin like he's blessing it. My breath stutters when his hands cup my breasts, his thumbs brushing over my nipples through the lace of my bra.

We take our time, every movement, every touch, laced with reverence and want. There's no frantic tearing, no fumbling. Only hands mapping familiar territory like it's brand new again. Like we're both a little afraid to wake up and find this moment isn't real.

By the time we're skin to skin, my breath is already shallow, pulse racing beneath the press of his hands.

And then—

His hips press against mine as his hand slides up the inside of my thigh, parting me. His fingers move with devastating purpose, and I arch into him, gasping his name like a prayer I never want to stop repeating.

And still, he doesn't rush. Doesn't fumble.

He worships.

Every inch of me, every sound I make, every tremble and whisper of want—I feel it mirrored in him.

When his mouth trails down my body, slow and unrelenting, it's not just foreplay. It's love in its rawest form.

And when he enters me—body-to-body, soul-to-soul—it's not with a groan. It's with a broken sound, like surrender.

My hands clutch his shoulders, and my legs squeeze around his waist. He holds still for a moment, foreheads pressed together, his breath shaky against my mouth.

"This is everything to me, favorite. You are my everything."

My chest tightens, breath catching like his words wrapped around my ribcage and cinched tight.

Everything.

It's not just something he says. It's the way he says it—like a truth that's lived in him longer than he's known how to name it.

I run my fingers through his hair, tugging him closer, our

foreheads brushing. "You don't even know how deeply I'm yours, Alex."

His eyes flicker—heat, hunger, and something close to awe.

I kiss him again, slow and deep. Like I mean it.

Because I do.

God, I do.

He moves, and each thrust is slow, controlled—like he's savoring the feel of me, the rhythm of our bodies syncing. We move together like we've done this in every lifetime before. His hands grip my hips, grounding us both, and when he picks up the pace, my body arches, mouth parting with a soft cry.

He kisses it away. "This... us... it's the only thing that's ever made sense."

His words shatter me.

I come with his name on my lips, every nerve lit like fire, and he follows with a sound that's half-curse, half-confession—like I just undid him from the inside out.

He collapses over me, arms tightening, like he never wants to let go.

And I don't want him to.

We lie tangled in the sheets, bodies slick with sweat, hearts still racing. I rest my head against his chest, listening to the steady thump of his heart.

"I didn't know it was possible to be this close to someone," I whisper.

His arm tightens around me, lips pressing to the crown of my head.

"You're it for me, Magnolia Steel."

The quiet settles in, but it's the good kind—the kind that only exists when you've been undone.

His breathing slows, syncing with mine, and I feel it in my bones —that sacred stillness that only comes after being known in every way a person can be known.

I curl closer, brushing my lips against his chest, right where his heart beats steady and strong. The heart that chose me—again.

For so long, I convinced myself I didn't need this. That independence meant solitude. That safety meant distance. But lying here now, in the quiet aftermath of all the walls we've torn down, I know better.

This man—this love—isn't the end of who I am. It's the beginning of everything I didn't know I could have. And for the first time, I let myself believe in a future that doesn't scare me.

A future with him.

Chapter 32

Magnolia Steel

Hospitals were never part of my story—only backdrops to someone else's battle. The only real time I spent inside one was when Violet's mom was fighting cancer. She survived. She's thriving. Stronger than ever.

Alex will be stronger than ever, too.

He's not here because he's broken beyond repair. Still, it doesn't make this easier.

I'm sitting beside a hospital bed, holding the hand of the person I love while someone prepares to cut into him. I'm smiling like my chest isn't caving in, trying to be brave for both of us. I don't know if I've ever been this terrified in my life. And I swear, it's like I've forgotten how to breathe.

Alex sits upright in the bed wearing a brave face, but I sense the tension beneath his skin. It's in the way his thumb keeps tracing circles against my wrist. The way he hasn't looked away from the far wall since they took his vitals.

I shift in my seat beside him, reaching for the scratchy hospital blanket and tugging it higher across his legs. "You doing okay?"

"Fine," he says, his voice steady. But his eyes flick to mine—and that's where the truth lies.

Not fine. Not really.

"You don't have to pretend with me."

His mouth twitches, a smile ghosting across his lips. "I'm not pretending. Call it compartmentalizing."

I raise a brow. "Sounds like a fancy word for scared."

This time, his smile sticks. "Maybe a little."

He shifts on the bed, glancing down, and grimacing at the IV taped to his arm.

"God, I'm starving."

"You had a massive dinner last night. Your steak was huge. You were still licking your fingers when we got back to the penthouse."

His lips twitch. "That wasn't because of dinner, favorite. It was because my fingers had been inside your sweet pineapple pussy."

"Alex, shh—" I laugh, glancing toward the door. "We're in a hospital surrounded by lots of ears. Behave."

He chuckles, unbothered. "I will never look at a pineapple again and not think of your pussy."

"Omigod, stop it."

His stomach lets out a loud growl, making both of us pause.

"See?" He places a hand over his gut. "I'm dying. That is the sound of suffering."

I lean in, brush a kiss to his cheek. "You're always suffering when you're not being fed. I swear your stomach has a louder personality than you do."

There's a knock, and the door swings open. Alex's doctor steps in, glasses low on the bridge of his nose, looking calm, collected, confident.

"Morning, gang. You ready to get that busted ankle of yours back in fighting shape?"

"That's what I'm hoping for."

The doctor glances at me, a light teasing smile tugging at his mouth. "And who's this? Your post-op nurse?"

Alex smirks. "Best kind—unpaid but highly motivated."

I roll my eyes. "Motivated to smother you with a pillow if you don't behave."

The doctor chuckles. "Looks like you'll be in excellent hands."

He moves to the side of the bed and uncaps a black marker, crouching down beside Alex's leg like it's just another day and not the start of something huge.

"Left ankle, correct?" he asks.

"That's the bloody troublemaker," Alex says.

With a quick swipe of his marker, the doctor draws on Alex's left ankle—black ink against golden brown skin. It's official now in a way it wasn't a moment ago.

"X marks the spot," he says with a wink, capping the marker like it's no big thing.

But to me, it is.

"You've got about thirty minutes before we roll you back and give you the best sleep of your life."

Alex looks at me, smirking. "I could use some sleep."

Me too. We sure didn't get any last night.

The doctor leaves with a nod, the door closing behind him. My fingers reach for Alex's, lacing tight. "You good, big guy?"

He nods once. "Yeah... no. Not really."

My chest clenches.

"I thought I'd be fine, but my anxiety is through the roof. About the surgery, yeah, but more about what comes after. We just found our way back to each other, and already we're staring down another stretch of distance before we've even had the chance to find our rhythm."

I squeeze his hand. "It's temporary, Alex. We've been through worse than distance."

"Yeah, but you're building your life there—your business, your future—in a place that doesn't include me."

His words sink deep into my ribs. Because the truth is that I've been thinking the same thing.

Why am I pouring myself into building a life in Charleston when the person I love will be nine thousand miles away?

I stroke my thumb across the back of his hand. "That's something we're going to talk about. Not today, but soon."

He nods. "Yeah. Soon."

He shifts, reaching for his phone on the tray beside him. "I should call Tinā and Dad before they take me back."

"You better if you know what's good for you."

He unlocks the screen, taps FaceTime, and props the phone up as the call connects. Malie's face appears first, eyes going glassy when she sees him in a hospital gown. "Oh, Aleki—"

Alexander appears over her shoulder, already frowning. "Took you long enough to call."

Alex huffs a small laugh. "What? Miss me already, old man?"

His dad snorts. "Nah, but I miss kicking your ass on the golf course."

Alex scoffs. "Once. You kicked my ass once. And only because I was distracted by this one."

I feign offense. "Hey, don't blame me for your bad golfing skills."

"I have skills."

Alexander shrugs. "Distraction or not, a win's a win."

Malie swats at him. "Oh, stop it, you two."

The laughter continues, and softens into something quieter, warmer. Malie's eyes find mine, and her expression shifts—gentle, full of gratitude.

"Magnolia... thank you for loving my son. And for being the one beside him right now."

My throat tightens. "Loving him is easy. As for taking care of him..." I glance at Alex with a teasing smile. "We'll see how good of a patient he turns out to be."

Alexander laughs. "I'm afraid you've got your hands full with that one. He hasn't been still for more than a minute since the day he was born. Came out ready to fight and hasn't stopped moving since."

Malie lifts a brow, teasing. "I can't wait to hear how the bedpan duty goes. You'll earn your stripes with that one."

I groan. "I'm billing him for every accident."

Alex rolls his eyes, grinning. "I regret this call already."

The laughter lingers long enough to settle everyone's nerves before Malie's smile softens.

"Magnolia, when the doctor comes out and gives a report, please call us right away. Doesn't matter what time it is, all right?"

I nod. "I will. Promise."

Her eyes flick back to Alex, and her smile wobbles. "And remember, if he gives you any trouble, you have my permission to smack him."

I press a hand to my chest. "Noted."

Alexander clears his throat, standing a little taller behind her. "You'll do fine, son. Just wake up with both legs and don't give the nurses a hard time. They're the ones in charge of handing out pain meds."

Alex huffs a soft laugh. "No promises."

His mother blows him a kiss. "I love you, Aleki."

"Love you too, Tinā."

Alexander nods, firm but warm. "Love you, son."

"Love you too, Dad."

Malie's gaze returns to mine one more time. "We love you too, Magnolia."

For a moment, I freeze. The words catch me off guard—not because they're untrue, but because I'm not used to hearing them. Not from anyone's parents. Not even my own. The warmth spreads anyway. Quiet and steady. Like belonging.

"I love you both," I say. And I mean it.

The call ends as the nurse pushes through the door, a smile in place. "It's that time, Mr. Sebring."

She unlocks the bed and adjusts the rails, then glances at me with a wink. "Next time you see this guy, he'll be a little less busted up."

Alex's hand finds mine again, his palm sweaty. I lean in and press a kiss to his forehead, lips lingering just a second longer than they should.

"I'll be here when you wake up."

His eyes meet mine. "I love you, favorite."

My heart clenches. "I love you too, big guy."

He nods, silent now, but something flickers in his eyes—something that says everything he isn't ready to put into words.

And then they wheel him away—his fingers slipping from mine like a tether loosening.

The door shuts behind him, and in a snap, it's quiet.

The waiting room smells of disinfectant and tension. I pick a chair by the window—not for the view, but away from others. Maybe I can get some work done.

Design software loads, blank templates blinking at me. But the only thing I can think about is the man who is lying unconscious on an operating table somewhere in this building.

I check the time. He's only been gone fifty-two minutes. Seems like hours.

I tuck my phone facedown beside me and try to focus again, but the lines on the screen blur. My stomach knots with every passing second. I chew on my thumbnail, something I haven't done in years.

Then my email notification dings.

Tyson McRae—bold, unread—sitting there like it belongs in my life.

I don't open it right away. I just stare. Because I've been more than clear about my feelings. About my boundaries. About the fact that I want nothing more to do with him.

So what does he want now?

I open it. Not because I want to. But because I don't trust him not to try something shady—legal threats, emotional manipulation, a guilt trip disguised as sincerity. I've figured out how he works. He's shown me who he is.

Our contract is airtight, something I made damn sure of it before I ever signed my name beside his. I had to protect myself—my business, my future—in the event of a fallout. I may have been naïve about him and his motive, but I was never naïve when it came to protecting myself and my business.

Protecting myself—that's one thing I'm very good at.

The email is long. Too long. Desperate in the way only guilt can be.

Subject: Please Read This

Magnolia,

I know I'm the last person you want to hear from right now. And I don't deserve your time—not even a second of it—but I'm asking anyway. Please.

I miss you so much. More than I thought was even possible.

I've spent every day since you left trying to figure out how I let this happen. How I lost you. And how I ruined it. I know I did. I took your trust and smashed it to pieces. And now I'm the guy waking up every morning filled with nothing but regret.

I don't sleep. I don't eat. I don't even know who I am anymore.

Please don't throw us away. Please don't let this be the end.

I'll do whatever it takes. Just tell me there's still a chance.

You're the best thing that ever happened to me.

—Ty

I close the email and stare at the screen, jaw tight, breath shallow.

Tyson McRae is a lot of things. A liar, manipulator, master of twisting truth. But one thing he is not—a man who gets a second chance. Not with me.

He shattered my trust. He is the source of me being wrecked from the inside out. Destroyed for months.

And now he wants a chance to do it all over again? Hell no.

I don't hesitate. My fingers move fast, fueled by disgust, as I block his email address without blinking.

He doesn't get to speak to me again. Not now. Not ever.

I close the laptop, set it beside me, and stare straight ahead. The waiting room is too cold, too quiet, and I can't sit still.

I glance at the time again. Only ninety minutes have passed. It feels like five hours.

I shift in the chair. Cross and uncross my legs. Run my hand down my jeans and then across the armrest, like movement might keep the fear from settling.

Panic is whispering to me.

What if something went wrong?

What if they opened him up, and it was worse than they thought?

What if he doesn't wake up?

I close my eyes, press my fingers to the center of my chest. There's no reason to spiral. No logical reason to fall apart. But love doesn't care about logic. And fear doesn't need facts to make itself at home.

Time stretches, and I pace the hallway, my sneakers whispering over polished tile. I try sitting again, but the seat's too stiff, the silence too loud. I grab a coffee from the vending machine in the corner just to have something to do with my hands. It tastes like burnt water, but I drink it anyway.

Because anything is better than feeling this helpless.

And then—finally—

"Mrs. Sebring?"

I turn on instinct. Hearing myself called that... God, it does something to me. Lodges something soft and warm right beneath my ribs.

The nurse smiles and gestures for me to follow her. "This way."

She leads me down a short corridor and into a small consultation room. Neutral walls. Soft lighting. A table with tissues in the center, just in case.

The door opens again a minute later, and in walks the doctor— still in scrubs, surgical cap on his head. He offers me a warm smile as he sinks into the chair across from mine.

"Alex is out of surgery. He's in recovery now."

I'm able to breathe again.

"He did great. The damage was a little more extensive than what we saw on the scans, which is why it took longer than expected. But I was able to repair the ligaments and reinforce the joint."

"That's great."

"He'll have some pain, of course. The next few weeks won't be easy—but with the right rehab protocol, he should make a full recovery."

I close my eyes for a second, press my palms together like a silent prayer answered. Relief floods me, leaving warmth in its wake. "Thank you so much."

He stands to leave, reaching out to shake my hand. "He's tough. You'll see. He'll be back on the rugby field next season, better than ever."

The words land like a stone in my stomach.

I blink. But by the time I look up, the doctor's already gone, door closing behind him.

And I'm left sitting there. Stunned. Silent.

Back on the rugby field?

I don't go back to the waiting room. Instead, I wander the hallway on autopilot until I find an alcove—just a narrow bench beneath a window that faces a blank brick wall. I sit—slowly—like my body weighs twice as much now.

He didn't tell me.

My eyes burn, but I don't cry. Not yet. I'm still too caught by surprise.

He's going back to rugby?

Was this always the plan? The surgery, the rehab, the clean return to the sport that almost destroyed him?

My heart beats faster, the panic catching up to my lungs.

Despite all the opportunities, he didn't say a word. And that's what hurts the most.

Did he not trust me with the truth? Or was he trying to protect me from it? I don't know which answer feels worse.

I would walk through anything with him. Even watching the man I love push his body to the edge for a game that's already taken so much from him.

Did he not think he could tell me?

I came here to help him heal. But now I don't know what that healing means.

Not for him. Not for me. And definitely not for us.

Chapter 33

Magnolia Steel

ALEX PROPS ON A SEA OF PILLOWS, HIS LEG ELEVATED. THE pain's not gone, but it's easing. He hasn't gritted his teeth once tonight. That has to be a win.

I help him with the last of his meds, brushing my fingers against his when I hand him the water glass, and something about that small touch makes my chest tighten. These past two weeks have been tender. Healing. Familiar in a way that both comforts and wrecks me. It's about more than recovery.

It's been about us.

This isn't the kind of intimacy you plan for—helping him to and from the bathroom, guiding him in and out of the shower, making sure he's hydrated and fed.

Real life, unvarnished. No filters.

And it's been good. So good.

But something's shifted.

Now I'm lying next to him in the dim bedroom after his pain medicine has kicked in, and my heart won't stop beating like it knows something I don't. I should be asleep. But I'm staring up at the ceiling, replaying a hundred tiny moments in my head, trying to make sense of what's missing.

He hasn't brought up rugby. Not once.

It's not only the silence. It's the weight of it—like he's carrying something he can't bring himself to tell me yet. And the longer it goes unsaid, the more convinced I become that whatever he's planning may not include me.

I turn on my side, studying the sharp line of his jaw in the low light, the way his lashes fan out against his cheeks. His hair's still damp from the shower, a little unruly at the crown. One hand rests on his stomach, the other rests between us.

I love him so much.

I love him in a way that terrifies me, in a way that is uncertain if I think too far ahead. Because what if this ends again? What if we fall apart not because of anger or betrayal... but because of distance? Or bad timing?

What if we want different things?

His fingers flex, like he's feeling for me, and I lace my fingers through his.

"You're quiet," he says, voice low and rough with sleep.

"Just thinking."

"About what?"

I stare up at the ceiling, where the shadows stretch long. "Tomorrow. Leaving."

His grip tightens. "Yeah, me too."

His thumb caresses the top of my hand. "You okay?"

"No." How could I be when I'm getting on a plane in the morning and leaving half of my heart behind in this bed?

I roll onto my side, letting my hand drift across the warm expanse of his chest, the steady rise and fall beneath my palm.

His eyes find mine in the dim room like he senses it too—this hunger. This unspoken thing pulling tight between us.

"Are you in pain?"

His eyes don't leave mine. "Not pain. Just aching for you."

I don't need him to explain. I feel it too. This desire, this need, that lives somewhere deeper than skin.

My lips curve as I slide my hand farther down, fingers brushing the waistband of his briefs. "Lucky for you, I have the cure for that particular ache."

His brow lifts, and he watches me like I'm something to behold.

I sit up and tug the blanket down, careful of his leg. He shifts for me, wincing as I push his waistband down. When he's bare, I press a kiss just below his navel, and he breathes out my name—low and wrecked.

I kiss lower. Then lower still.

I smile against his skin, teasing the edge of his hipbone with my tongue, dragging it slow. Deliberate. He sucks in a breath, hips twitching beneath my touch.

"Fuck... babe."

I trace the defined cut of his abdomen, fingers trailing light as a whisper, making him shiver beneath me. My nails scrape along the inside of his thigh, and he groans.

"Open up that pretty little mouth for me. Show me how much you want to taste my cock."

I flatten my tongue and lick a slow, lazy path from base to tip, taking my time, my gaze locked on his face.

His jaw clenches, and he fists the sheet.

"Babe, you're fucking killing me."

I hum, letting the vibration tease against him. Because I know he loves it.

My hand grips the base of his cock, stroking slow and steady while my touch traces the crown of its head. When I take him into my mouth—inch by inch, warm and wet and deliberate—it's not a physical act. It's connection. Pure and consuming.

It's about us. The trust. The want. The need to give this to him— this pleasure, this devotion—because there's no one else I've ever wanted like this.

He groans, deep and guttural, hips bucking before he steadies himself with a rough exhale.

"Fuck, Magnolia... you feel so good. So damn perfect."

His hand tangles in my hair. I hollow my cheeks and take him deeper, letting my tongue swirl and drag as I move, slow and steady. His thighs tense. His breath stutters.

"Don't stop... please don't stop." And I don't. Because I want this—every sound, every twitch of his body, every broken word that falls from his lips like prayer.

Because I want him undone by me.

And he is.

His fingers twist in my hair, and his hips twitch, breath going ragged as I work him slow, steady, deep. Every flick of my tongue, every soft moan that spills from his mouth, roots itself inside me.

His fingers tighten in my hair, and his voice breaks into a groan. "God, I love your mouth. But I want to finish inside you. You know that's where I want to be."

I kiss his stomach, slow and deliberate. He's shaking by the time I crawl up his body and straddle his hips. My fingers wrap around him, guiding him inside me inch by inch.

A shared breath—and soft gasp—when I sink down all the way, careful not to put any pressure on his leg.

His hands grip my thighs, his eyes locked on mine. "Fuck."

"You okay, big guy?"

His hands move up to my hips. "Never been better."

I rock against him, slow and deep, and he lets out a strangled sound, head falling back into the pillows. "Yeah, ride me just like that. I want to feel all of you."

His hand slides between us, finding my clit with the ease that comes from knowing a body by heart.

"Does that feel good?"

"Mm-hmm."

I ride him, rolling my hips. His fingers work in tandem with my rhythm until I'm spiraling, clenching around him, crying out as I fall apart.

He follows with a low, broken groan, his body arching, burying himself deeper as he lets go. His arms wrap around me, pulling me against him as we both come.

Neither of us says it—but we're both thinking it. How are we going to make this work?

I rest my head against his shoulder, letting the steady thump of his heart anchor me.

His lips brush my temple. "Don't move yet. I want to stay inside you like this for a while."

His arms wrap tighter around me. "I've been thinking about what comes next for us."

My breath catches.

His hand traces a slow line up and down my spine. "You're building something incredible in Charleston. I see how much it means to you. How much you love it."

I lift my head, searching his eyes in the low light. I see the question there. And the truth is I've already asked myself that same question.

"I'm going to say what neither of us wants to bring up: one of us must relocate, which means one of us is going to give up life as we know it."

My chest tightens. Because he's right. Someone is going to let go of something big. And the thought of it guts me.

Alex has such a wonderful life in Sydney. A tight-knit family, not only in Australia but also in Samoa. So many people who love him, who've raised him. A family business built on legacy. Lifelong friends. And possibly a career in rugby again. Even if he's not saying it yet, I can sense it. The door that was once closed is now open again.

What do I have in Charleston?

Violet. A business in its infancy. A tiny studio and a hopeful blueprint for a future I've only just started building. But there's no blood there. No unshakable roots. No one waiting on me but the version of myself I'm still trying to become.

How can I ask him to give up everything he has when I have so little?

He brushes a strand of hair from my face. "I know what you're thinking, but this isn't about who has more to give up."

I pull back and meet his gaze. "But it matters, doesn't it? You have so much there. And I love that for you. I could never ask you to walk away from it all. It wouldn't be fair."

He holds my stare for a long beat. "You're not asking me for anything. We're trying to figure this out—together. And we don't have to have it all figured out tonight. We just need to agree that this is worth figuring out."

I press a kiss to his chest, right over his heart. "It's worth it. You're everything to me."

His hand curls around the back of my head as he holds me close. "We'll figure it out."

And we will.

Even if it remakes us in the process—we'll find our way through. Because I love him too much to not try.

He exhales like he's been holding the breath in for weeks. "Let's get through the recovery first. Then we'll revisit this."

I kiss the corner of his mouth, letting the promise settle between us. "It's you and me. Forever."

His arms tighten around me again, and for the first time in days, the ache in my chest dulls.

We may not know where we're going yet—but we're going together.

Chapter 34

Magnolia Steel

IT'S EDGING PAST OFFICE HOURS—THE TIME WHEN MOST PEOPLE have shut their laptops and gone home. But not me. I'm still here, because building a business doesn't happen on a nine-to-five schedule.

Swatches sprawl across the design table, a few notes jotted in the margin of an open sketchpad. One more thing to finish before I can call it a day.

The bell over the front door jingles.

I glance up, not alarmed. The woman from the bakery next door often brings me an end-of-the-day treat after closing time. I hope it's a cupcake today. Red velvet with cream-cheese icing would be great. Hers are the best.

"Back here," I call out.

No reply.

I glance up—and freeze.

He's standing inside the doorway, the light casting his features in shadow. The broad frame, the dark, tousled hair, the sheer size of him —too big to be anyone else.

My heart stutters in my chest, and I take a step back. "What are you doing here?"

He lifts his hands in a slow, disarming gesture. "I just want to talk. That's all."

"No, Tyson. You shouldn't be here. You need to leave."

His smile is tight. Wrong. "I'm not here to argue. I just... I miss you. I've been going crazy, Mags. You haven't replied to my emails, my texts, or calls. I didn't know what else to do."

How about leave me alone?

"I don't want to talk to you. This isn't okay. You showing up here *is not okay.*"

He flinches but only for a second. Then his expression hardens. "So that's it? You're just done? After everything?"

"Everything?" I say, a brittle sound. "You mean the lies? The manipulation? The way you wrecked my life?"

His jaw clenches. "Sebring would've come sooner if he loved you. It took months."

I move around the desk, putting the wide table between us. "I'm not doing this with you."

"You were falling for me before he showed up."

I stare at him, stunned for half a second before my voice finds its edge. "No. I opened myself up to the person I thought you were. But that version of you was a lie."

His jaw tics. "Something was happening between us. Don't pretend our relationship wasn't real."

"My perception of you was based on lies. You manipulated me, Tyson. You made me believe in something that never existed."

"It wasn't like that."

"It was *exactly* like that. You lied... used me. And now you're standing here trying to rewrite history like I didn't learn the truth of who you are."

He shakes his head, stepping toward me.

"Don't come any closer." My voice is firm despite the fear curling tight in my stomach.

"You can't believe that I would hurt you."

I square my shoulders, voice like ice. "I'm not sure what you will or won't do because I don't trust you."

"Magnolia—"

"Leave!" My voice breaks on the word.

He takes another step forward, something in his posture shifting. The mood changes. Heavy. Off. Threat laced in silence.

He continues to ignore my warnings, something sharp clicking in my head.

He's not backing off. And that alone is enough to set every instinct I have on high alert.

My eyes land on the decorative glass bottle sitting on the display table—sea-glass green, smooth and coastal, part of the spa project I've been finalizing. I grip it by the neck and slam the base against the edge of the table.

The break echoes, sharp and final. Shards fall. What's left is jagged and ugly—the weapon I need. I lift it between us, somehow steady and unshaking, the broken glass glinting under the warm light.

"Fuck around and find out how fast I'll cut you."

Something flickers in his expression and his mouth presses into a tight line. "I just wanted to talk and remind you of what we had."

"You aren't taking no for an answer, and that's a problem."

He looks at me for a moment, then turns and leaves without another word.

By the time I get home, the sun has dipped low behind the city skyline, throwing long shadows across the floor of my apartment. I drop my bag on the table, kick off my shoes, and sink onto the couch.

I'm okay. Nothing happened—technically—but the remaining tremble in my hands says otherwise. The way my chest still rises too fast, as if my body hasn't realized the danger has passed.

Or has it?

I press the heels of my palms to my eyes and sit there, breathing slow and deep, trying to steady myself. To not let his voice echo in my head. But it's there anyway.

I want to scream. Or cry. Or both.

Instead, I reach for my phone. Alex called while I was driving home, but I couldn't answer. I wasn't ready to talk, too afraid he'd hear it—the fear I couldn't hide in my voice.

I could tell him what happened, let the anger in his voice wrap around me like armor. Let him rage for me. Worry for me.

But I don't. Because I know what this would do to him.

He's still healing, still in pain, even if he won't admit it. If I tell him Tyson showed up at my office and crossed a line, I know what will happen.

Alex won't just be angry. He'll be consumed. And right now, he needs peace, rest, time to recover without this polluting his mind.

So I swallow it.

THE FLOWERS ARRIVE MID-MORNING.

I'm in the middle of reviewing fabric samples when the delivery driver walks in, holding a tall glass vase overflowing with red roses.

Beautiful. Thoughtful. Deliberate.

But Alex knows I prefer white hydrangeas and pale pink roses. That's what he always sends me.

Alex didn't send these.

My stomach turns as I reach for the envelope, fingers stiff, breath held.

Magnolia,

I'm sorry. For everything. I'll make it right.

—T

I walk the vase to the back of the studio and toss the entire thing in the dumpster, water and all. I don't care how beautiful they are. They reek of manipulation.

THERE'S A CAR PARKED ACROSS THE STREET FROM MY OFFICE, blacked out from top to tires. Matte finish. No chrome. No shine. The windows are tinted too dark to be legal.

It's there when I arrive in the morning. Still there after lunch. Gone by early afternoon... but back again before I shut down for the day.

I try not to let it get to me, but my skin is tight with awareness, my every move more careful. I find myself repeatedly glancing over my shoulder without meaning to. Listening for footsteps I don't hear.

It might be nothing. A coincidence. But deep down, I know it's something.

I try to shake it off. Charleston isn't that big. People park in weird places all the time. But it sticks with me—that tight feeling at the base of my spine. The itch of being watched. Of knowing I'm not alone even when I am.

My nerves are frayed by the time I leave work and go to Violet's. I'm two steps in before she picks up on my vibe. "What's he done now?"

God, how does she do that?

"Vi, I'm okay. It'll——"

"Nope." She cuts me off with a glare that could peel paint. "You don't get to minimize what's happening just because you're used to carrying everything alone. Not this time."

I open my mouth, searching for something to say—some defense, some excuse—but nothing comes out. Because she's right. I've been rationalizing, trying to make it feel less serious than it is. But it's not nothing.

It's Tyson. At my office. Uninvited. Unhinged.

It's the flowers I never wanted.

It's the car with black windows and timing too perfect to be coincidence.

"You have to report this."

"He lied, showed up uninvited, sent flowers, parked on public property. I'm not sure there's anything to report."

"Maybe not but doing nothing isn't an option. This isn't the type of man you ignore and hope he gets bored. You go to the police, and if they won't do anything, you at least make them aware."

And when I close my eyes, he's there again—Tyson. That wild, unhinged look in his eyes. The sharp, dangerous edge in his voice. It takes a lot to shake me. But that? That got under my skin.

I nod. "Okay."

I sit in the police station giving my statement, filing a formal report, requesting a restraining order. The officer is nice, professional. Seems to take my concern seriously.

But when I walk out of the building, the weight doesn't lift. If anything... it's heavier. A piece of paper will not stop a man like Tyson McRae. Not when he wants something. And for whatever reason—he thinks that something is me.

Chapter 35

Magnolia Steel

ALEX'S NAME STARES AT ME FROM MY FAVORITES LIST, GLOWING at me like it knows I'm hesitating. I should've called hours ago, right after I left the police station. But the words are too big. The fear, too heavy. And I didn't want to be the reason his healing is delayed.

But now I'm sitting on the edge of my bed wearing one of Alex's T-shirts, a towel wrapped around my damp hair, fresh from a shower I barely remember taking.

My thumb hovers, then taps. It rings twice before his handsome face fills the frame.

He's reclining against a mountain of pillows in his bed, shirtless, jaw rough with days-old stubble. Hair a little wild. He looks tired. But when he sees me, he smiles, slow and soft.

"There's my girl. Hey, favorite."

The knot in my chest loosens a fraction. "Hey you."

"Been waiting to see your face all day. You okay?"

"Yeah. I... needed a minute after work to take care of something."

"Fair." His smile tugs crooked. "I left you a voicemail about how it's way too quiet here without you stealing all the covers."

A laugh slips out. "Puh-lease. You're the cover hog and we both know it."

He smirks. "Evidence or it didn't happen."

But the teasing fades when I don't keep it going. His eyes sharpen. Hone in.

"Hey... what's wrong, babe?"

My chest caves a little. I look down, swallowing. "I need to tell you something."

The smile on his face disappears and his voice becomes steel. "That motherfucker. Tell me what he's done now."

I take a breath.

"He came to my office two days ago and said he wanted to talk. He was... so *intense*. I told him to leave multiple times, which he didn't like at all. He kept inching closer, and that made me feel threatened, so I picked up a glass bottle and broke the bottom off to use as a weapon if he came at me. He left after that."

"Jesus, Magnolia."

"He sent me flowers yesterday with an apology. And today, there was a blacked-out car parked across the street from my office. I'm not certain it was him, but it seemed off. So I filed a police report and got a restraining order."

His jaw tics, rage simmering. "This isn't something you casually tell me about two days after it happens."

"I know, I'm sorry, but I didn't want to stress you out. You're still recovering, and I had hoped it would stop after I threatened to slice him open."

He mutters a string of obscenities beneath his breath. "I'm not mad at you. I'm pissed off about this whole situation—that he can get near you and I'm not there to keep him away."

I love that Alex wants to protect me, but I'm not helpless. "I've been protecting myself since I was a little girl. I'm very good at it."

"Don't care. Pack a bag. I'm chartering a plane for you tonight. You're coming to Dallas."

I love the lengths he's willing to go for me. It's overwhelming sometimes—this fierce, unapologetic way he shows up. "I can't. I have a site walk-through on Friday. Violet's staying with me—we're doing a sleepover with wine. I'll be okay."

His eyes are hard. Unyielding. "I'm not comfortable with this. Not when he's showing up where you work. Not when we don't know what he's capable of."

I shift the phone, curling tighter into myself. "If anything else happens, I'll come. I promise."

He stares at me for a long beat, like he's trying to hold himself together. "I need you to take this seriously now. Not after something happens."

"I can't drop everything and leave when I have a business to manage. My client is depending on me."

His voice softens. "I don't like this. Not one fucking bit."

"I know, but I can't allow him to control my life."

"If anything else happens, you promise me you'll come to Dallas."

"I promise."

"Send me your location when you go somewhere, even if it's just to the grocery store."

I nod. "I will."

"Promise me, Magnolia."

"I promise."

And that's one promise I'll keep. Because I'm afraid of Tyson now. Not in the abstract. Not in the maybe. In the real, bone-deep way that changes how you move through the world. That makes you look over your shoulder twice.

I DIDN'T GO INTO THE OFFICE TODAY. I TOLD MYSELF I COULD BE more productive from home. But the truth? I couldn't stomach the idea of unlocking that front door and spending all day wondering if I was being watched. Wondering if that car would show up again across the street.

So I stayed home. Locked every door. Double-checked every window. Made a second pot of coffee I didn't drink.

I've been camped at the kitchen table for hours—laptop open, fingers hovering, pretending to work. But I'm not seeing the screen.

I keep glancing at the front door, flinching at every sound—every creak, every voice in the hallway, every buzz of a neighbor's phone vibrating through these paper-thin walls.

To say I'm on edge doesn't even come close.

Violet offered to bring lunch and keep me company—and I didn't say no.

A knock sounds—sharp and urgent—and I almost jump out of my skin.

"Be right there, Vi," I say, already pushing away from the table, assuming she's juggling too many takeout bags to use her key. But when I open the door, it's not Violet.

My stomach drops so fast I become dizzy.

He looks more put-together today—dark jeans, a fitted tee, clean-shaven. But the intensity in his eyes is the same. Off.

"What are you doing here?" I try to keep my voice calm, but my fingers tighten around the edge of the door.

He steps forward, pushes past me like he has every right to. "We need to finish our conversation."

I whirl around, my heart hammering. "No, we don't. You need to leave."

He doesn't budge.

"This is your fault. You shut me out. You dropped everything we had as though it meant nothing. You want to play the victim now, but you lied too. You made me believe you wanted this."

Something snaps inside me. The fear coiled in my chest unravels —not into panic, but into fury. Red-hot and righteous. Because how fucking dare he.

"You want to talk about lies?" I laugh, but there's no humor in it. Just venom. "You are the reason Alex and I broke up. Then you pursued me just to get back at Alex. How fucked up is that? And now you want to rewrite the story like I asked for it? Don't you fucking dare twist this around on me after everything you did."

He scoffs, eyes flashing. "Yeah, I pursued you because it would destroy Sebring. But then you let me in. You made me believe we could become something. You said yes to dinner, yes to that gallery opening. You gave me permission to touch you. I finger fucked you until you came all over my hand. You led me to believe there was something real growing between us. And I fucking fell in love with you. Hard. And then you flipped the script and made me the villain."

There's a wild look in his eyes now—unhinged and glassy. Like a man coming undone in real time, right in front of me. It's not just anger—it's desperation. Entitlement. A spiral that comes when someone realizes they've lost control, and they'll claw at anything to get it back.

Gaslighting at its finest.

He wants me to question everything. To rewrite the truth into something more convenient for him. But I'm not confused about what happened.

My pulse roars in my ears, my whole body shaking.

And then I hear it—Violet's voice. "What kind of fresh hell is this?"

She steps into the apartment like a bullet, keys still in one hand, takeout bags swinging from the other.

She sees him. Sees me. And without a second of hesitation, she plants herself right between us like she's been waiting her whole life for this fight.

"Ten out of ten don't recommend you being here. You need to turn the fuck around and walk out that door and never come back."

I'm glad Violet's my best friend because, fuck, she can be a little scary when she's mad.

"This is between Magnolia and me. It has nothing to do with you, so fuck off."

Oh shit.

His jaw tightens, hands flexing at his sides. But Violet doesn't flinch.

"Everything that happens to her is my business. I'm more than her best friend—I'm the motherfucking fire-breathing dragon at the gate."

I grab my phone, heart slamming in my chest, and dial 911.

Violet crosses her arms, lips curling like she's just getting warmed up. "You ever come near her again, and the police will declare it *a case of fucked around and found out.*"

Tyson's eyes flick to the phone in my hand. He hears me give the dispatcher our address and turns, leaving without another word.

Violet races to the door and locks it, deadbolt and chain. "Holy shit, Mags. That dude is enormous. I'm a chihuahua who chased away an Irish wolfhound."

I slide down the wall, legs folding underneath me, hands trembling.

She crouches beside me. "Are you okay?"

I nod, but I'm lying. I've never been less okay in my life.

"That's it. You're not staying here with Hulkenstein on the loose."

I nod, this time meaning it. "It's time to call Alex."

My hands tremble as I scroll to his contact. The moment he picks up and sees my face, his expression shifts from happy to terrified.

"Babe, what happened?"

"He showed up at my apartment again. This time, he forced his way in. If Violet hadn't shown up when she did... I don't know what would've happened."

"That motherfucker!" he yells. "Call the police."

"I already have."

"Pack a bag. Now. No arguing this time. I'm chartering a plane. I'll text you the details. Violet, don't leave her side until she's in the air."

Vi doesn't miss a beat. She never does. "Copy that. I'll get her on that jet like precious cargo. And if Tyson shows his face, we're gonna have ourselves a come-to-Jesus meeting with claws and consequences."

I don't argue with their plan to pack me up and send me off. Because they're right. And I'm done pretending this isn't serious.

Violet helps me pack while I tremble and fight tears. She moves through my apartment with a quiet, steady rage—folding clothes, zipping suitcases, muttering under her breath about men who can't take no for an answer.

"This shit starts the second a girl grows anything resembling a breast." She shoves a toiletry bag into my suitcase. "We're fair game to anyone with a dick, like existing in a female body means we owe them. I'm so fucking sick of it. I wish I was into women... but, dammit, I like dick too much. I just don't like the jerks they're attached to."

She doesn't stop moving or muttering, rage vibrating off her.

By the time we're in the car, she's still mad as hell—hands tight on the steering wheel, eyes blazing as she tears down the road toward the airstrip.

"It's always the same damn story. A man gets told no, and it becomes a vendetta. You pull away, set a boundary, and they act like you've just dismantled their whole damn identity. Like we were put on this earth to stroke their egos and hand them our peace of mind on a silver platter."

She blares the horn at someone driving too slowly.

"Fucking patriarchy!" she screams.

I don't say anything. I just sit there, clutching the handle on my bag like it's the only thing keeping me tethered. But every word she spits lands because she's not wrong.

When we pull up beside the hangar, the plane already waiting, she throws the car into park and turns toward me.

"You know I like him, right?" Her voice is softer now. "Alex, I mean."

I nod. "I know."

She smiles. "He takes care of you, and you deserve that. He's one of the good ones, Mags. Don't let him get away."

Not a chance in hell. "I won't."

Dallas is waiting.

Alex is waiting.

And this time, I'm running toward something good.

———

By the time the car pulls up in front of the hotel, it's late and I'm exhausted. I use my keycard and ride the elevator to the penthouse. It's quiet. Dim. Just the low mechanical hum of gears turning, the soft whir of the elevator rising floor by floor, and the distant pulse of city noise beyond the glass.

When the doors slide open, I step inside and pause.

Alex is there. Waiting.

He's sitting in the chair near the windows, one leg propped up on an ottoman, crutches leaning beside him. He looks pale and tense, like he hasn't slept in days. His eyes snap to mine the second I step inside, and he starts to stand—but he doesn't get far before I drop my bag and rush to him across the room.

I'm on him in seconds, careful of his leg, climbing into his lap like gravity's been pulling me there all along. His arms lock around my waist, his face burying in my neck as I curl against him.

We don't speak. We don't have to.

His chest rises and falls against mine, erratic, like the weight of seeing me knocked something loose in him. My fingers sink into his hair, anchoring myself to the man who is my home.

"Babe, I've been losing my mind."

I press my lips to his temple. "I'm sorry."

We stay like that for a long while. Just breathing. Holding. Letting the world fall away.

My heart calms, and he pulls back just enough to look at me. His hands tighten at my waist. "Tell me everything."

So I do.

I can feel it—Alex's anger. The way his jaw locks. The way his hands flex beneath mine like they're dying to be fists.

When I finish, his voice is low and wrecked. "I should've been there."

"No," I say, brushing his hair back. "You don't get to do that. This isn't your fault."

His eyes flash with fury. "He's obsessed with you because of me."

I sigh. "Maybe it started that way. But it's become something different now."

"What do you mean?"

The words are heavy, but I owe him the truth. "He believes he loves me. Like, truly. In that twisted way that some people perceive love."

Alex looks like he might break something.

"You're staying here until we figure this out."

I pause. Not because I'm resisting—but because I'm not used to being the one who surrenders.

"Okay."

His brows lift, surprised.

"I've never been afraid like that of someone before."

He squeezes me to him.

"Right now, I need to feel safe."

He presses a kiss to my temple, fierce and full of everything he hasn't said yet. "You are always safe with me, favorite."

"I have a walk-through later this week. My only client. I'll have to go back, at least for that."

"Don't worry. We'll figure it out."

"I'm so tired. Can we go to bed?"

"Yeah, sure."

He shifts, adjusting his leg, and I help him to the bedroom. We don't bother undressing. We just climb under the sheets, limbs tangling, breath syncing. His arms wrap around me like armor, and I melt into him like I've been needing to all along.

It's late. It's quiet. For the first time in days... I feel safe. And for now, that's everything.

Chapter 36

Magnolia Steel

I WAKE, BLINKING AGAINST THE SOFT LIGHT SPILLING THROUGH the curtains. For a moment, there's nothing but warmth—the heavy weight of Alex's arm slung across my waist, the press of his chest against my back, the deep, steady cadence of his breathing.

I stay still, because I know the second I move—the second I let the real world in—it'll all come rushing back.

And it does. The anxiety settles in my gut like a stone, heavy and cold.

My business.

My clients. *Client.*

The life I've worked so hard to build in Charleston now seems a million miles and a lifetime away. All because of him.

Tyson-fucking-McRae.

A man who wouldn't take no for an answer. A man who made me afraid in my own city, who pushed me to a point where the only place I feel safe now is tucked beneath the arm of this man lying next to me.

I hate the loss of control, the way fear has rooted itself in my bones like it has any right to be there. And most of all, I hate that

Alex has to bear the weight of this too. No matter how many times he tells me I'm not a burden, some dark, bitter part of me still wonders if I am.

I shift, not wanting to wake him. But the second I move, his hold tightens. His hand slides from my waist to my belly, pulling me back against him like he can sense me slipping away even in sleep.

I close my eyes and let myself sink into the moment for just a second longer—into the safety of him. Because today, I have to figure out how to take back the pieces of my life without falling apart.

A low, sleepy rumble vibrates against my back.

"Morning, favorite." His voice is gravel-rough, still thick with sleep. His arm curls tighter around me, pressing me closer to the hard wall of his chest.

I bite back a laugh, the sound escaping anyway. "Don't squeeze me too hard. I gotta pee."

He lets out a reluctant groan but loosens his grip. His hand lingers for a second longer than necessary, brushing along my ribs before he releases me.

I slip out of bed, the cool air whispering over my skin. Padding toward the bathroom, I sense his eyes on me—his gaze almost as tangible as his touch.

When I emerge a few minutes later, the room's energy is different. Empty. Because I don't find Alex waiting for me.

I find Alex in the kitchen, leaning against the counter, one crutch tucked under his arm, the hotel phone pressed to his ear. He's shirtless, wearing only a pair of black athletic shorts that hang low on his hips, the sharp cut of his abs catching my attention.

His black hair is a little wild, like he's been running his hand through it, unruly and beautiful without even trying. There's something about the sight of him, casual and rumpled and real, that sends a soft ache through my chest.

Home.

That's what he looks like to me now.

He catches sight of me—barefoot, hair twisted into a messy bun on top of my head, drowning in one of his T-shirts—and his entire face softens.

He covers the receiver with his hand and tips his chin toward me. "What do you want for breakfast?"

My stomach knots. Food sounds like the last thing I could handle. "Just coffee."

His eyes narrow a little. Not angry—more like disapproving. Protective in that quiet, stubborn way that's become second nature between us.

"You need food. No negotiation."

I roll my eyes, but it's useless. Alex Sebring doesn't bluff. Not in taking care of me.

And not when it comes to breakfast.

"Fine," I say, padding toward him. "An omelet."

"Everything but tomatoes?"

He knows me so well. "That sounds good."

He smirks, victorious, and speaks into the phone again, rattling off the order—the very long order—and I shake my head, smiling.

God, this man can eat.

Breakfast ordered, he pops my favorite coffee pod into the maker. He doesn't even have to ask anyone how I take it. He knows.

"Thank you."

"Welcome, babe."

I wrap my hands around the cup, letting the heat sink into my skin. Reminding me that no matter how messy things are, no matter how much fear tries to root itself inside me, I'm not alone. Not anymore. Not since I met Alexander Björn "The Iron Wall" Sebring III.

I slide onto a stool, tucking my bare feet on the rung beneath it, sipping my coffee. All the while trying to quiet the voice in my head that won't stop whispering about everything in Charleston.

Breakfast arrives and the scent of bacon and fresh bread fills the space. I lift the lids, surveying the spread, and I can't help but smile.

Someone went overboard.

"How hungry are you?" I ask over my shoulder, grabbing two plates.

Alex leans on his crutch, watching me with an expression that's half amused, half fond. "Are you kidding me?"

I laugh, a real one this time, not the kind dragged out by nerves. "Right. Silly question."

I busy myself plating the food, sliding very generous portions onto his plate. It's easier to focus on the tangible small tasks—setting forks beside napkins, pouring coffee—than the messier bigger thoughts crowding my mind.

By the time we sit down at the dining table, the mood has shifted. Some of the tightness in Alex's shoulders has eased, replaced by the slow, familiar rhythm of him eating with single-minded focus.

Food always puts him in a better mood.

"I talked to my family last night while you were sleeping."

I blink, surprised.

"You did?" I wipe my mouth with the napkin. "I didn't hear you get up."

"You were out cold. Your body needed the rest."

"Is everything all right?"

"Nothing has happened. I spoke with Elias and asked if he could come to the States for a little while."

I sit up straighter, confused, the words taking a second to sink in. "To be with you while you're recovering?"

"No, to be with you in Charleston."

Alex shrugs, like it's no big deal. Like he didn't just drop a bomb on me about my life over breakfast.

"Elias said yes. He's always looking for an excuse to visit. Loves the U.S., and he's never spent time on the East Coast. He's excited about it."

Guilt rises fast and hot, clawing its way up my throat.

"I'm so sorry, Alex. I hate that your brother will have to rearrange his life because of me."

Alex leans back and pins me with a look that's equal parts gentle and fierce. "You're not causing a thing, Magnolia."

I open my mouth to argue, but he cuts me off. "Elias offered. You're one of us now, and that's how we roll in the Sebring family. When someone needs backup, we show up. No questions. No guilt trips. Only love."

The words hit me harder than they should.

I swallow against the lump rising in my throat, trying to process the simple, staggering truth of what he's saying. I've never known loyalty like that. Never known what it is to be someone's priority without having to earn it or beg for it.

Robin and Charlene can't be bothered to return a text or call, much less book a plane ticket.

The raw, aching difference between duty and devotion settles in my chest, stealing my breath for a moment. I don't argue. I don't downplay it or brush it off.

Instead, I meet his gaze and say the only thing big enough for the moment. "Thank you for looking out for me."

He studies me for a beat, something dark and tender flickering in his eyes. "I wish it could be me with you. If I were in Charleston and Tyson showed up at your apartment while I was there—"

He trails off, but I see it in his eyes. The promise. The violence he would unleash without hesitation.

"It's better you're not there." I couldn't stand it if he injured himself fighting Tyson and ruined the reconstruction on his ankle.

His mouth curves into a slow, almost dangerous smile.

"You're probably right." There's no mistaking the fierce protectiveness in his voice—the raw, unflinching need to shield me, to fight for me.

The fear in my chest loosens its grip just a little because I know, no matter what's coming, I won't be facing it alone.

We finish breakfast and I push away from the table. Alex follows my lead, rising, balancing his weight on his good leg as he grabs his crutch.

I hover like a mother bird, and he shakes his head, not wanting me to fuss over him. So I trail him to the sofa instead.

"I have to get back to Charleston. The client walk-through is tomorrow afternoon." I know that isn't what he wants to hear.

Alex nods, slow and measured. "You know I don't want to see you go, but I get it. Elias's flight lands tonight. He'll go straight to your place and stay with you for however long you need him."

I nod, trying to process it all—relieved because I won't be alone, that someone will be there, ready, if Tyson tries anything.

"I'll have Violet meet him at my apartment. She has a spare key. She can let him in, show him around. Make sure he's comfortable until I get there."

We sip the last of our coffee, the day stretching out ahead of us, neither of us moving to fill it.

Not yet.

Alex shifts beside me, setting his mug on the coffee table with a soft thud. "Come on. Let's get some fresh air."

The balcony door slides open, letting in a breeze laced with the warmth of the morning sun. We step outside together, the city stretching wide and endless in front of us, bathed in the soft burn of sunrise.

I move to the railing, wrapping my fingers around the cool metal, letting the first of the day's heat soak into my skin.

A moment later, his arms come around my waist, strong and sure, pulling me back against the solidness of his body.

He rests his chin on my shoulder, his breath warm against my skin.

I lean into him, closing my eyes for a moment, memorizing the way this feels. Like being found. Like being home. And maybe... I am. Because this instinct to protect, to show up, to be each other's safe place is what a real partnership looks like.

Not polished, not perfect. Messy. Inconvenient. Raw and real in the ways that matter.

But I'm not running from it now. I'm running toward it. Toward him.

Chapter 37

Magnolia Steel

THE WHEELS BUMP AGAINST THE TARMAC, AND I EXHALE.

Charleston.

Home.

But is it really?

I pull out my phone, thumbs flying across the screen as I shoot a quick text to Violet.

> Just landed. 😊

She takes all of two seconds to respond.

> We're here! Can't miss us. I'm the one waving like a crazy person.

She better not be wearing that ridiculous inflatable dinosaur suit again—or waving some embarrassing giant sign like last time.

Love the girl, I do, but if she pulls that stunt today—especially with Alex's brother there—I might just pretend I don't know her.

I tap Alex's name, bringing the phone to my ear. It rings once before he picks up.

"You made it, babe?" His voice wraps around me like a second skin.

"Just touched down," I say, looking out the window for Violet's SUV.

"Always relieved to hear that."

"It was a pleasant flight. Smooth. Quiet. I slept a little."

"I'm glad. You need your rest."

"Thank you again for the plane. For...everything."

"You don't have to thank me." His voice deepens, drops into that soft, serious place that always makes my heart ache. "I'm happy to do it. Anytime. But only if you keep using it to come back to me in Dallas."

My breath catches, a stupid, giddy smile tugging at my mouth. "Missing me already, huh?"

"Yeah, well, I'm kind of stuck on you," he says, rough affection bleeding into his voice.

The words land somewhere soft and tender inside me, cracking something open in my chest.

"I'm kind of stuck on you too."

The plane slows, the engines shifting to an idle hum, and the seat belt sign dings off overhead.

Time to move.

I adjust my grip on my carry-on and lean against the armrest for just a second longer.

"Vi and Elias are here to pick me up, but I'll call you later, okay?"

"I'll be waiting."

"I love you." Those three words have become more natural to me than breathing.

"Love you more." I can imagine the grin tugging at his mouth.

I step down onto the tarmac, the thick Charleston heat washing over me like a wave.

I spot them, Violet waving like she's trying to flag down a plane. Beside her stands a man I haven't seen in months—not since Samoa.

Elias spots me, his face lighting up.

"There's my favorite teine!" he says, his voice full of laughter and affection.

Teine. I remember the word from my time in Samoa. Girl, friend, someone you claim as your own. It's what all of Alex's brothers called me. It made me feel special, like I was one of them.

He crosses the distance between us in long strides with those legs that go on forever and wraps me up in a bear hug so big and warm it almost knocks the air out of me.

I laugh, squeezing him back just as hard.

When he lets me go, I blink fast against the sudden sting behind my eyes.

Elias grins down at me, all mischief and sunshine.

"Still so little." He ruffles my hair like I'm his kid sister.

"*Still* not funny," I shoot back, swatting his hand away, but grinning.

He laughs and grabs my bag without being asked, slinging it into the trunk of Violet's car.

The second we pull out of the parking lot, Elias rolls down the window, sticking his arm out and grinning like a kid tasting freedom for the first time. "Man, it's like a sauna here. Everything smells green and salty and... old."

"That's Charleston for you. Historic and humid. We aim to please," I say.

Violet shoots Elias a mischievous smile in the rearview mirror. "Wait until the mosquitoes introduce themselves. You'll really get the full-on Southern experience then."

He laughs, tossing his head back, and it's such a good, easy sound that I find myself smiling too.

I settle back against the seat, watching them trade quips. Violet's even more charming and quick-witted than usual—her grin brighter, her laugh a little softer—and Elias is eating it up like she's the best thing he's seen all day.

It's sweet. And a little funny. But mostly ridiculously obvious.

There's a current running between them—bright and electric—

and even though I'm bone-tired and still carrying a heavy pit of anxiety in my gut, I'm glad to see it.

The conversation drifts for a few minutes—favorite foods, worst travel stories. But eventually, it shifts. And I sense it before he even says a word.

Elias leans forward between the seats, his tone changing, a new seriousness threading through it. "I hate to bring it up, teine, but we gotta talk about McRae."

I nod, already expecting it. "Of course."

He glances at Violet—like he's weighing whether to say what he needs to say in front of her.

"It's fine. She knows everything. My little chihuahua went head-to-head during the last incident with him and scared him away."

"Impressive." Elias settles back in the seat. "You don't have to be afraid of him. I'm here on behalf of my brother. He was very clear about what he expects from me. McRae tries anything, and he's going to regret it."

The certainty in his voice—the quiet, unflinching promise—hugs me like a shield. I am safe with Elias here.

"Thank you for coming." It means more to me than he will ever know.

Elias smiles, easy and sure. "Don't mention it, teine."

We pull into the lot outside my building, the bright heat of the afternoon beating down on the asphalt. I don't have time to protest before Elias is shouldering my bags and tossing me a grin over his shoulder.

"Lead the way, boss."

Elias carries everything in, stacking my bags by the couch like it's nothing. He straightens up, glancing around—and his gaze catches on the corner of the living room.

He whistles low under his breath, stepping toward the basket filled with rolled-up Samoan mats, the shelf stacked high with books about Samoa and its culture, and the framed map of the islands hanging on the wall, surrounded by a handful of small

Samoan artifacts I'd picked up when Alex took me to meet his family.

"Wow," he says, grinning. "Tinā thinks she loves you now? She'd straight-up lose her mind if she saw this."

"I love Samoan culture. It's beautiful. The people. The history and tradition. The heart behind everything."

Elias nods, warmth in his eyes. "Trust me, we know." He taps his chest over his heart with his fist. "The whole family knows. We saw it in Samoa—how you didn't just visit. You soaked it in. And cared. You loved it like it was already part of you."

The words hit hard, a bittersweet ache blooming behind my ribs. Because even when I wasn't trying to belong to anyone, they claimed me.

Elias lingers by the basket of mats, his hand brushing over the rough weave of one of them before he glances back at me. "I'm glad you're back in the family. It was a rough time for Alex."

My heart squeezes, the ache still sharp. "I didn't handle being apart from him very well either."

Violet sucks air between her teeth. "Magnolia did not thrive during her sad-girl era. It was bad."

Before the moment becomes too serious, Violet claps her hands together. "You know what we should do?"

"I'm sure you're going to tell us."

"Let's take Elias out. Show him a real Lowcountry welcome his first night here. Shrimp and grits, fried green tomatoes, the whole shebang."

Her grin is pure mischief.

What are you up to, Vi?

"Elias just got off a transpacific flight. He deserves something way better than sad airplane food."

I bite back a smile. Because let's be real—Elias flew business class. He wasn't choking down some sad, plastic-wrapped sandwich and lukewarm coffee at thirty thousand feet.

Still, the way Violet's looking at me—vibrating with excitement—I can see she's not about to let this go.

The weight of exhaustion presses into my bones. "I don't know. I'm pretty wiped. And I'm sure Elias is tired after his long flight."

Out of the corner of my eye, I catch Violet behind Elias's back.

She widens her eyes, mouthing. *"pleeeeease,"* and pressing her palms together.

Sleep can wait, I guess. "You know what? It's still early. I could eat."

Violet's face lights up like she just won a lottery scratcher.

"If Elias is up for it."

He nods. "Always starving."

I shake my head, laughing. "A family trait, no doubt."

Elias flashes a grin that's pure trouble. "Let's do it. Feed me all the Lowcountry, teine. I'm ready."

We end up at one of my favorite spots tucked away near the Battery—a worn brick building with creaky floors, mismatched chairs, and food that tastes like home.

The second we step inside, the scent of butter and spices and something rich and fried wraps around us. Elias breathes in deep, his whole face lighting up.

"I think I'm gonna like it here," he says.

Violet slides into the booth next to me, bumping my shoulder with hers as she grins across the table at Elias.

"You're about to be ruined forever." Her voice drips with flirtation.

I don't need to turn my head to know she's turning on the sparkle. She's so obvious, she's leaving a trail of glitter across the table.

Vi rattles off a list of appetizers and entrees to the server. I order some of my favorites, and Elias grins like he's ready to eat whatever we throw at him.

The table fills up, one plate after another. A heavy cast-iron skillet lands in front of us, steaming with creamy shrimp and grits, the buttery sauce pooling around the edges.

Next comes a wide bowl of she-crab soup, the smell so rich it makes my stomach growl out loud.

A basket of hush puppies follows, golden and hot, a tiny pot of honey butter melting faster than we can slather it on.

By the time the last plate drops, every inch of the table is covered with bowls, skillets, and baskets balanced on top of each other like a game of edible Tetris.

Elias digs in like he hasn't eaten in a week, groaning around every bite.

"Zero regrets," he says, grabbing a hush puppy and taking a huge bite, eyes closing like he's having a religious experience.

Violet laughs, resting her chin in her hand as she watches him eat.

"So... you like Lowcountry food, huh?"

Elias waves a forkful of grits in the air like he's delivering a sermon. "This is the best thing that's ever happened to me. No offense to the rest of my life."

I lean back, sipping my drink, watching them banter across the table. Violet is shining in a way I haven't seen in a long, long time.

It's subtle—the way she leans in just a little closer when Elias talks, the way her smile lingers a beat longer than usual—but it's there.

That spark. That bright, ridiculous, hopeful thing that's been missing from her for too long.

And Elias...he's eating it up. Every glance, every grin. Like he already knows he's in trouble and he's not even trying to fight it.

It's sweet. It's fast. And it feels good.

After everything Violet's been through—all the heartbreaks and dead ends—watching her light up like this makes something inside me ache in the best way.

Elias glances around. "Excuse me for a moment, ladies. Be right back."

He slides out of the booth, tossing his napkin in his seat before heading toward the back of the restaurant.

The second he's out of earshot, Violet leans into me, grabbing my wrist like she's about to deliver a life-or-death confession.

"Mags! My ovaries went into overdrive the second I saw him." She is wide-eyed, dead-ass serious.

I choke on my sweet tea, coughing as I laugh.

"Violet!"

"I'm so fucking serious," she says, flailing a hand. "I think I got pregnant with his little Samoan baby just by standing next to him. And I'm not even mad about it."

I laugh harder, doubling over a little in the booth. God, it's good to laugh like this. To be like this.

But honestly? I get it. Alex and Elias come from the same mold. I remember how my heart sped up when I first saw my big guy.

Violet leans closer, lowering her voice to a whisper even though Elias is nowhere near.

"Will you be mad at me if I fuck him?" She looks so serious that she might as well be asking for a kidney. "Mags, I really want to fuck him."

I laugh so hard my ribs hurt. "I don't care. Just... don't do it on my couch please."

Violet grins, the kind that says she's already planning trouble.

"Don't worry. I have plans. Filthy plans. Plans that are not couch-appropriate. I'll take him to my apartment."

"He's my bodyguard right now. You can't just whisk him off for mattress wrestling with optional choking. I need him in one piece."

Violet waves a hand, unbothered. "You'll be flying back to Dallas to be with your man soon enough, leaving his brother here. Which means—" She grins even wider. "He's all mine."

I'm still laughing when Elias returns, sliding back into the booth with that charming Sebring grin.

Violet and I exchange a look—loaded with mischief and a thousand unspoken things—and burst out laughing all over again.

I'm hopeful for Vi.

Maybe things are falling into place for both of us.

Chapter 38

Alex Sebring

MY SURGERY WAS WEEKS AGO. IT'S BEEN LONG DAYS OF ICE packs, stiff muscles, and slow, stubborn steps. Weeks of staring down the ugly reality that my body isn't invincible—and maybe never was.

The boot is gone. The crutches are leaning useless in a corner. I'm walking again, careful and measured like some old man trying not to snap in half. Every step is a reminder: don't screw this up. Don't rush. I pushed too hard last time, chasing something that slipped through my fingers anyway. I'm not making that mistake again.

Magnolia's soft humming drifts from the kitchen, pulling me out of my head. The scent of chicken and a buttery decadence wafts through the penthouse as I sit on the couch, an ice pack battling the swelling in my ankle.

I watch her move—barefoot, hair piled up in a messy bun, humming along to the song playing over the speakers. God, I love seeing her like this. Not dressed up, not guarded—simply Magnolia.

My American beauty knocks the breath right out of my lungs. Need hits me low and hard, the way it always does when I least expect it. Not just for her body pressed against mine, not only for the high I get when she smiles at me like I'm her favorite thing. But for this.

My phone buzzes against the cushion beside me. I pick it up, thumb sliding across the screen to find a text from Elias: a selfie of him and Violet on a rooftop bar somewhere, sunglasses on, toasting each other with cocktails.

I chuckle. "Looks like Violet's giving Elias the full Charleston experience."

"Oh, I'm certain he's getting the full experience all right. But it's not the Charleston experience he's getting. It's the full *Violet experience.*"

Magnolia reaches for a bowl in an upper cabinet, the stretch of her body doing things to me that I don't need right now.

I don't know Violet well, but Magnolia has told me plenty about her best friend. And if even half of it's true, Elias doesn't know what he's gotten himself into. "Should I be worried?"

She flashes me a wicked grin, all sin and sass. "Only if he can't keep up."

I raise a brow, playing along. "Yeah? What does that involve?"

Magnolia pauses, spoon still in her hand, and turns toward me, her mouth curved in a slow, wicked smile. "If he's lucky? A lot of stamina. Possibly a little property damage. A few things that would make Malie blush."

Yeah. I bet Violet's giving him an experience. And judging by the stupid expression on Elias's face in this picture, he's enjoying the hell out of whatever's happening.

"What's she looking for in life? A good time? Or someone to share a future with?"

Magnolia shrugs one shoulder, checking the oven before glancing over at me. "Violet loves a good time, sure. But she's thirty now. She's ready to find someone who wants the same things she does."

"Which is what?"

"She's ready to settle down. Marry. Start a family."

I nod, letting that sink in.

Violet's ready to settle down. Ready to build something real. But what about her best friend?

Magnolia wasn't ready for that months ago. Hell, not even close. She'd made that much clear. She wanted freedom, not chains. And I respected her feelings. I still do.

She has said some things since that make me wonder where her head is now.

But being parted from her changed me. I realized there isn't a single version of my future that doesn't have her in it. I want her in my life. Always. Every single day.

I want to marry her even more now than I did when we were tangled up together in Australia. Putting a ring on her finger is the only way to quiet this fire in my chest—to let the whole damn world see that she's mine. The need to call her my wife hums beneath my skin, constant and aching, like a second heartbeat I can't shut off.

The smell of dinner pulls me back to the moment, and I let myself get lost in watching her move around the kitchen. If this is what married life looks like—Magnolia making dinner while I stare at her like a lovesick idiot—I want it.

All of it.

I'd be in there with her if my ankle wasn't wrecked—stealing bites, wrapping my arms around her from behind, making a mess of whatever perfect plan she had for dinner. But for now, I settle for sitting here on this sofa watching, feeling the want for her deep in my bones.

Magnolia plates everything, sliding a big helping of fried chicken, mashed potatoes, green beans, and a buttery biscuit on one plate like she's feeding an army.

She glances over her shoulder, catching me staring.

"What is it?" she asks, one brow lifted.

I grin, pushing up from the couch and hobbling my way over to the kitchen table.

"You're good at this."

"At what? Feeding you?" she says, laughing as she sets the plates down. "I know how much you love food."

"I meant you're good at making me want to never live without you," I say, pulling out a chair and lowering myself into it with a groan. "At this rate, I'm gonna end up proposing over a plate of mashed potatoes."

Magnolia freezes for half a second—long enough that my heart stutters—before she smiles, soft and a little shy, like she's trying to hide it but can't.

She didn't perceive it as a joke. Or maybe she did—but part of her liked it anyway.

I tuck that thought away to ponder on later and tear into the Southern heaven she has served to me on a dinner plate. "Damn, woman... you can cook. Who taught you this kind of sorcery? Because no way it was Robin or Charlene."

Magnolia shakes her head. "Definitely not. I learned after I moved away to college. I realized there were other ways of living. Better ways." She shrugs like it's no big deal. "I taught myself how to cook by watching the Food Network. Took notes. Burned a lot of things. Ate a lot of pasta before I figured out how to season chicken."

She says it like it's just a thing she did, not the true accomplishment that it is.

I sit there for a second, staring at her—this woman who had no one to teach her how to love, how to nourish, how to nurture, and she still did it all. For herself.

Life handed her lemons, and she made limoncello with her bare damn hands.

That's Magnolia for you.

I'm halfway through my second biscuit when Magnolia glances up, resting her chin in her hand.

"So, big guy... now that you're on the mend, what's next?"

I set my fork down and lean back in my chair, letting out a breath. God, I hate this question. Mostly because I don't have an answer. Or I do—and I don't like it.

"Taking over my dad's position and working for Sebring Hotels has always been my family's expectation, but, babe... it feels so hollow to me. Like I'm just taking up space because my last name's on the building."

Magnolia doesn't interrupt. Doesn't rush to fill the silence. She just waits, her eyes steady on mine, like she's giving me all the room I need to say the hard things.

"Even if I wanted it—which I don't—it's not a job for someone like me. My dyslexia makes the task of filling my father's shoes completely out of reach. I've always been able to fake it when I had to, but not in that world. Contracts. Spreadsheets. Legal documents. Meetings where everyone expects you to catch the fine print in real time. It's exhausting and humiliating. Half the time, I'm drowning and too damn proud to admit it."

Magnolia's expression softens, her hand reaching across the table, brushing the back of mine with her fingertips. "You don't have to force yourself into a life you don't want. But if it's not Sebring Hotels, what is it? What's your passion?"

I smile—small but real—and squeeze her fingers. "You mean besides you?"

Oh fuck, that wicked little grin of hers could set me on fire. "Yes, I mean besides me."

"Rugby. It's always been rugby—the only thing that's ever made sense to me, made me feel like I was where I was supposed to be."

I shake my head, the ache for the sport curling in my chest.

"Bloody hell, babe, I miss it." The words scrape something raw inside me. "It feels like there's a hole in my chest some days. I didn't know how to move on from it three years ago, and I still don't."

Magnolia reaches across the table without hesitation, her fingers curling around mine. Her touch is soft, steady—a touch that anchors you when you're close to breaking apart.

And the expression on her face... Christ, it guts me. It's like she's hurting because I'm hurting, like she feels it all right along with me.

She always has. She's always been in sync with me, without even trying.

And that is what I want in my wife. Not just someone who stands beside me when things are easy, but someone who leans in when it's hard, when it's messy, when it would be easier to walk away.

I squeeze her hand, needing the connection more than I want to admit.

"But when you came into my life, I could breathe again. And something other than rugby could make me happy."

Magnolia's thumb brushes over the top of my hand. "You don't know how special that makes me feel." She gives me this look—half awe, half ache. "I don't think anyone's ever said anything like that to me before."

She looks at me like she's trying to hold it together.

"I fell apart when I thought we were over. Nothing was helping. Not time, not therapy, not anything. Nothing could get me back to how I felt when I was with you."

She says nothing, just listens. God, she's always been so good at that. Not trying to fix anything. Not rushing in with hollow reassurances. Just sitting with me, holding the weight without flinching.

"It's easier—so much easier—with you in my life. When you're here, the noise in my head shuts the hell up. You make it better. All of it."

Her fingers tighten around mine.

I sit back in my chair and stare down at my plate, no longer hungry. There's something else I've been carrying, something heavier. And if I'm ever going to ask her for forever, she needs to know the whole truth.

"I never told you why I picked this surgeon in Dallas."

Magnolia looks up, brows pinching together. Waiting. "I assumed it was because he was the best."

"I've been struggling more and more to walk. It wasn't just an occasional limp anymore. The surgery was inevitable. And my agent recommended this doctor because he specializes in getting athletes back on the field. The plan was to do the surgery, recover, rehab, and then go back to playing rugby for as long as I could. But that plan was before you came back into my life."

She doesn't react. Doesn't blink. Doesn't flinch. And that's when I realize. "You already knew, didn't you?"

She swallows and nods. "The doctor came out to update me about how the surgery went. He mentioned it."

I stare at her, stunned. "You knew all this time and said nothing?"

Magnolia nibbles her bottom lip. "I wasn't sure what it meant. I didn't know if it was still your plan, or things had changed, or you were just waiting for the right time to tell me."

"You should have said something."

"I didn't want to ask because I was afraid you might be going back to your old life without me. I didn't want to hear you say you were leaving without asking me to come with you."

It knocks the breath out of me.

Because I've been so wrapped in my fears, I didn't stop to think about hers.

"I would not leave you. I can never be parted from you again. You get that, right?"

Her eyes shine, but she doesn't look away. "I didn't. But I do now that you've told me."

It guts me—knowing she's been walking around with that weight in her chest, wondering if I'd disappear again. Wondering if she was temporary.

It makes me realize I've been too quiet. Too careful. Too damn slow.

So I push forward, needing her to hear the truth—all of it.

"I need to make something clear." My eyes lock with hers. "I will not let you go again, Magnolia. Ever. I don't care where we are or what happens. We will never part ways again."

She stares at me, that hopeful wariness flickering in her eyes again—the kind you get when you want to believe something so badly that it hurts.

"What does that mean to you? Never parting from me again?"

It means everything to me. But I have to know where she is before I lay it all out.

I hesitate, just for a breath. "Can I ask you something?"

She nods. "Sure."

"Have your feelings changed about marriage? About having kids?"

Magnolia draws in a shaky breath. "Being apart from you has changed everything for me."

I don't breathe. I don't blink.

She hesitates for a moment and swallows. "I want it all, and I want it with you."

I swear, my world tilts.

"Say it again."

She smiles—full, sure, radiant. "I want to build a life with you—marriage, our little Samoan babies, all of it. Everything you told me about when you described what marriage means to you... that's what I want too."

Something inside me lets go. A rope pulled tight for too long, finally easing. And in its place, that wild, consuming hope I've been trying to keep at bay comes rushing in.

For a second, I can't even speak. I just sit there, stunned, flooded with something so big it almost knocks me over. Joy. Relief. Love. All of it.

"Okay," I manage.

She tilts her head, blinking. "Just... *okay?*"

"I'm absorbing," I say, trying to rein in the dumb grin taking over my face. "This is a big shift from our last marriage conversation. You've surprised me. I wasn't prepared for that kind of shift."

Magnolia narrows her eyes at me, playful and confused all at once. "I just told you I want to be your wife and the mother of your children. This isn't exactly the reaction I was expecting."

I reach out, tugging on her hand. "Come here, babe."

She stands, her eyes avoiding mine as she rounds the table. When she reaches me, she climbs onto my lap, straddling me, her legs sliding around my waist the way she's done it hundreds of times before.

Her hands settle around my shoulders, but her brow is tight, confused, a little hurt. I hate that look on her face. I hate I put it there.

My hands grip her waist. She leans in, forehead pressed to mine, like she's searching for the truth in my silence.

"It makes me so damn happy that you want to be my wife."

"Does it?"

"Hell yes. Of course."

Her body relaxes. "Then why not ask me?"

I close my eyes, breathing her in. "Because when I do, I want the proposal to be perfect. I only get one chance to ask you to be my wife. And I want it to be unforgettable."

She exhales, and her lips curve into a half-smile against mine. "Whatever the moment looks like, it'll be perfect because it's you."

She pulls back just enough to meet my gaze, her fingers gripping my shoulders. "And in the meantime?"

I rub my hands over her hips. "*In the meantime,* we love each other. And I remind you every day that you're mine—until I get to call you my wife."

Her throat works as she swallows, and the shine in her eyes isn't confusion anymore—it's hope. Peace. Love so big it doesn't need to be said to be felt.

She leans in, brushing her lips against mine in a kiss that's slow and deep and final in all the right ways.

I didn't ask her to marry me tonight—but somehow, it still feels like she said yes.

Chapter 39

Magnolia Steel

ALEX STEPS OFF THE PLANE. NO CRUTCHES. NO LIMP. ONLY that easy, confident walk I haven't seen in in a long time.

He's wearing jeans, a fitted black T-shirt that hugs the muscles he's fought like hell to build, and a soft grin that hits me dead center. My heart does this slow, twisting ache thing in my chest as I watch him close the distance. Because I know what it took to get here. Every painful stretch. Every night icing down his ankle, frustrated and quiet.

When he reaches me, he doesn't say a word. Just pulls me into his arms like he can't help it. One hand curves around the back of my neck. The other fists in the fabric at my waist. And he kisses me— slow, deep, and purposeful. Like we're not in a public place with people milling around us. Like it's just us.

I melt into it.

When we pull apart, I whisper against his mouth, "Well, look at you. Graduated and everything."

"Top of my class. Straight A's in range-of-motion exercise."

I laugh, my hands still resting on his chest. "I'm proud of you, big guy."

His mouth curves. "Yeah, well... you're my reward."

Alex tosses his suitcase into the back of my car and slides into the passenger seat like he's been doing it forever. The sight of it—the casualness, the comfort—makes me smile.

I slide into the driver's seat and glance over at him. "So. What's the plan, graduate? You want to eat in or grab some pizza or go out?"

He leans his head back against the seat, eyes closed for a second like he's soaking it all in. Then he turns his head toward me, grin lazy and a little too charming.

"Let's go out and celebrate the end of PT. Get back to normal. Move on with our lives."

My heart tugs a little, but I keep it light. "Okay. Where do you want to go?"

He lifts a brow. "What about that French place you love—the one with the champagne risotto and the waitlist from hell?"

"Le Rue?" I laugh. "Alex, I don't think we can walk in. It takes weeks to get a reservation there."

He smirks and shrugs. "Leave it to me. I'll take care of it."

That wink he throws in shouldn't work—but on him, it does.

I shake my head as I pull out of the airport lot. "What are you gonna do? Slip the host some money?"

"Maybe," he says, grinning.

There's something simmering beneath his surface. Something electric. And though he has said nothing, a question rises in the back of my mind, unshakable and quiet: What are you up to, Sebring?

His phone buzzes twice. He checks it both times. Thumbs out a reply.

"Everything okay?" I ask, keeping my eyes on the road.

"Yeah. Elias is checking in."

I nod, trying not to overthink it. But my brain, being my brain, runs with it anyway—because I know this man. And something is off. Not bad, but different. And I can't help but wonder what the hell he's not telling me.

Dinner at Le Rue is perfect in every kind of way. The food is rich and ridiculous and full of things I can't pronounce, let alone order with confidence. I fumble with the food on the menu and Alex leans over, taps the corner of the page. "You'll love this one—trust me."

I do. And of course he's right. Somehow, he orders all my favorites. He's good like that—quietly observant, always three steps ahead, a man who listens.

He pours the wine, calm and unhurried. At one point, he slides a fork across the table, offering me a bite of something from his plate. I don't even ask what it is—I open my mouth and let him feed it to me, slow and deliberate, his eyes locked on mine.

I swallow, arch a brow, and murmur, "Careful, Sebring. Keep this up and I'm gonna think you're trying to seduce me over duck confit."

He grins like he is. "Is it working?"

His thumb brushes over the back of my hand, soft and possessive, like he can't help reaching for me. And all of it is making me crazy.

But I want more. And lately, I've been waiting for the big question. Hoping for it. Craving it.

I want to bring it up—our future, what we said we wanted, what we promised each other that night in Dallas. But I can't quite find the nerve.

Not here. Not now. Not when I've told myself he'll ask when he's ready.

Alex watches me for a beat. "You're quiet tonight. Is everything okay? You feeling all right?"

I smile, probably a little too quickly. "Yeah. I'm good."

He doesn't push. Just gives my hand a light squeeze and flags down the check with a nod.

A few minutes later, we're stepping out into the golden spill of early evening. The air is thick with the scent of salt and honeysuckle, and Alex slips his hand into mine again.

"Take a walk with me? I enjoy using my new ankle every chance I get since it doesn't hurt anymore."

"A walk sounds perfect."

It's warm as we stroll through Waterfront Park, the breeze

carrying salt and laughter and something else I can't name. Golden light spills across the harbor, soft and honeyed, wrapping the world in that kind of glow that makes everything look like it has a filter on it—too perfect to be real, too beautiful to capture in a photo.

We walk in silence for a bit, the good kind that only happens with people who know you to your bones. As we near the Pineapple Fountain, it glistens in the day's last light, water spilling in soft, steady arcs that catch the fading sun like strands of gold.

A street musician nearby starts playing something familiar and low—a string cover of "Can't Help Falling in Love."

I pause, eyes drifting toward the sound. "God," I whisper, the notes tugging at something deep in my chest. "That's beautiful."

Alex squeezes my hand and slows.

Right there in front of the Pineapple Fountain, he stops walking altogether. The music floats around us—haunting, gentle, familiar—but everything else falls quiet.

Alex turns to face me, still holding my hand, and something in his eyes makes my breath catch.

He stops in front of the fountain and turns to face me, both of my hands held in his like they're something sacred.

"Two strangers. A wall between us. No names. No faces. Only voices. A connection that made no sense while making complete sense at the same time."

My lips curve, even as my heart thuds harder in my chest.

He lifts my other hand, holding both of mine in his, his thumbs brushing over my skin.

"We spent three months chasing something neither of us could say out loud. And when you left, it felt like someone cracked my ribs open. Every version of life without you felt hollow—off, like the world was tilted sideways. But as awful as it was... I think we needed that time apart. Because it gave you the space to see what you wanted."

He draws in a breath, eyes locked on mine like I'm the only thing that exists in this entire city.

"I'll never part from you again. No walls. No distance. No maybes. I don't know where life will take us, where we'll end up, but I know one thing without a doubt..." He lets go of one hand and lowers himself to one knee, pulling a ring from his jacket pocket. I gasp—quiet, breathless. "...wherever it is, we'll be there together. Always."

"Magnolia Elizabeth Steel. Favorite." He looks up at me, eyes shining. "Will you marry me?"

For a second, the world blurs. The fountain, the music, the golden light—it all sways around me like a dream I don't want to wake up from. One hand flies to my mouth, covering the tremble in my lips. My heart is thudding so loudly I can barely think.

Tears fill my eyes, and my voice shakes.

"Yes," I whisper, then louder. "Yes. Yes, Alex. I want to be your wife more than anything."

He exhales, a shaky breath that sounds like relief and joy all at once. He slides the ring onto my finger, and when he stands, I throw my arms around him like I'll never let go again.

And then—I hear it. Applause.

I pull back, blinking, and turn to find people clapping. And not just people. Alex's parents and all of his siblings.

And then my person. Violet.

They step out from the edges of the park where they'd been hiding in plain sight, beaming.

Violet rushes in, laughing, teary-eyed, and wraps me in a hug. "My bestie is getting married."

I glance to the side and spot a man holding a video camera, a woman snapping photos—and it hits me. A videographer. A photographer.

I look back at Alex, shaking my head in disbelief. "I cannot believe you pulled this off."

He smiles, that lazy, pleased-with-himself grin that always wrecks me. His arms slide around my waist again, pulling me in.

"Well, I had help from Violet."

I laugh through the lingering tears. "Of course you did."

He leans back enough to look me in the eye, his tone gentling. "I wasn't sure how you'd feel about who was here tonight. Things with Robin and Charlene are... complicated. But I didn't want you to have my whole family here and none of yours. I invited them. They said they had other plans."

"Story of my life. So yeah. That sounds about right."

"I'm sorry, babe."

"I'm not." I reach up, brushing my fingers along his jaw. "It's okay because your family is now my family."

As if on cue, the Sebrings make their way over—Elias leading the charge with that big, goofy grin of his. Malie crying, arms already open for a hug. His father gives me a smile that makes me feel safe. Like I belong.

And maybe for the first time in my life... I do.

They surround me in a bubble of laughter, warmth, and welcome —no performance, no show. Just love. The kind that doesn't ask for anything in return.

I look over at Alex—my fiancé—and something in my chest settles. This isn't just a special moment.

This is our beginning.

———

Alex and Magnolia's story continues in
Beloved Beauty
Alex and Magnolia Book 3
(The Beauty Series Book 6)

About the Author

Georgia Cates is a New York Times, USA Today, and Wall Street Journal bestselling author—and a former labor and delivery nurse who now delivers swoony love stories instead of babies. A lifelong reader and proud cat wrangler of three, she writes romance with heart, heat, and a dash of Southern charm. Originally from rural Mississippi, she's married to her best friend and is the proud mom of two amazing daughters.

Sign-up for Georgia's newsletter at
www.georgiacates.com.
Get the latest news, first look at teasers,
and giveaways just for subscribers.

Stay connected with Georgia at:
Facebook, Instagram, Amazon and Goodreads

www.ingramcontent.com/pod-product-compliance
Lightning Source LLC
Chambersburg PA
CBHW070846260626
47170CB00007B/2519